P9-DDZ-778

The Family Fortune

The Family Fortune

LAURIE HOROWITZ

WM

WILLIAM MORROW
An Imprint of HarperCollins*Publishers*

This book is a work of fiction. The characters, incidents, and dialogue are drawn from the author's imagination and are not to be construed as real. Any resemblance to actual events or persons, living or dead, is entirely coincidental.

HarperCollins books may be purchased for educational, business, or sales promotional use. For information please write: Special Markets Department, HarperCollins Publishers, 10 East 53rd Street, New York, NY 10022.

FIRST EDITION

Designed by Sarah Maya Gubkin

Printed on acid-free paper

Library of Congress Cataloging-in-Publication Data

Horowitz, Laurie, 1960–
    The family fortune / Laurie Horowitz.— 1st ed.
      p. cm.
ISBN-13: 978-0-06-087526-8 (acid-free paper)
ISBN-10: 0-06-087526-7
    1. Boston (Mass.)—Fiction. I. Title.

PS3608.O768F36 2006
813'.6—dc22   2005054492

06 07 08 09 10 JTC/RRD 10 9 8 7 6 5 4 3 2 1

For my father, Benedict Horowitz,
who would have been so proud

All the privilege, I claim for my own
sex . . . is that of loving longest, when
existence or when hope is gone.

      —Jane Austen, *Persuasion*

. . . and their prejudices reminded him of
sign-posts warning off trespassers who
have long since ceased to intrude.

   —Edith Wharton, *The Custom of the Country*

Acknowledgments

I am extremely lucky in both friends and professionals, many of whom I am fortunate enough to claim as both. I am deeply grateful to my literary agent, Gail Hochman, for the innumerable ways in which she has supported me in both my life and my work. Thank you to my film agent, Amy Schiffman, who was there from the very beginning. Thanks to David Fox, a lawyer with unfailing good sense. Many thanks to everyone at William Morrow/HarperCollins: specifically, Carolyn Marino, my editor, who made this experience so painless and positive, and Jennifer Civiletto, whose attention to the brass tacks of the process was invaluable.

To those who were willing to read early drafts and give emotional support, I give thanks: Jeff Steinberg, Jonathan Bates, and Carole Merritt. Thanks to Myra Morris for listening to me kvetch. I also want to thank my writers' group: Buffy Shutt, Susan Cartsonis, B. J. Robbins, and Denise Stewart.

I am very grateful to Elinor Lipman for her generosity of spirit and for both emotional and technical support. And thanks to Sally Brady, mentor and teacher. Also to Laura Rappaport, who got me to finish.

And to my family, who are nothing like the Fortunes—thank God. My mother, Barbara Horowitz, my sister, Wendy Ribeiro, and her family, Jeff, Kimberly, and Ricky.

Lastly, I'd like to thank Leo Kelley, who has changed my life and makes sure I enjoy it.

The Family Fortune

Chapter 1

In which we are introduced to Miss Fortune

I once knew a girl named Hope Bliss. How her parents didn't realize that they were putting a curse on her, I'll never know. I myself am a Fortune, from a long line of Fortunes, and though I am simply Jane, I live under the cloud of being Miss Fortune, though I prefer Ms.

At thirty-eight I still lived at home. I told myself I had good reasons for that, or at least excuses. My sister Miranda lived there, too, and she was almost forty, even older than I was. Ours was not an ordinary house. It was a stately town house in Louisburg Square, a prestigious and historic location on Beacon Hill. The only people who could afford to live there were the nouveaux riches and people like us.

Who were we, the Fortunes of Louisburg Square? We were the old-money aristocracy. During the time of the robber barons, the Fortune family was in textiles, but most of our money came later, from an array of fancy mustards. We had been, you could say, the condiment kings of the East. We had, however, sold the company to Basic Foods before I was born.

I had known boys who came out of the womb in dinner jackets and girls who could preside over high tea before they could speak in full sentences, but really, what was the relevance of that in the new millennium?

We old-money Bostonians were an anachronism, the Lost Tribe of the Wealthy, wandering through the desert of modern life, cut off from the world, never realizing that our days were numbered. We were a generation of dilettantes, trying our hands at cooking, weaving, pottery, always with a dwindling trust fund to back us up. Our creativity, our determination, and our will to succeed had been diluted by comfort. We existed on the complacent understanding that we never had to strive for anything. Our ancestors had been captains of industry, but some of us had never even held a job. Deep down, we knew we were becoming obsolete. Maybe that's why we, the old guard, kept such a tenacious grip on our way of life.

Louisburg Square is one of the stops on the many walking tours of Boston. The town houses in the square encircle a shared and gated park. The park is charming in all seasons—snow-laden or bright with blossoms. Our square is, in its way, quintessential Boston with its bricks, bay windows, and cobblestones.

Though our house could have accommodated the entire string section of the Boston Symphony Orchestra, the only people, besides my sister and I, who lived there were my father, Theodore Henry Adams Fortune III, whom everyone called Teddy, and Astrid Fonseca, our housekeeper and cook.

My younger sister, Winnie, was married and lived in a neighboring town with her husband, Charlie, and their two boys, but Miranda and I had never left. We were modern spinsters, remaining at home long after any self-respecting woman would have moved out.

Our mother died right after I graduated from college, and that's the time you are supposed to make plans for the next stage of your life. Whether it's graduate school, work, or simply a studio apartment in a questionable part of town, the big choices are upon you.

Somehow I never got around to making them.

Not long after my mother died, I fell in love with a man named Max Wellman. He asked me to move to California with him, but my mother's best friend, Priscilla, talked me out of it. She said that I'd ruin his life, which, looking back, doesn't say too much about what she thought of me at the time. Maybe she just wanted to keep me at home. Priscilla doesn't like change and I'm sure my mother's death was all the change she could tolerate.

After my mother died, Priscilla swept in to help our family get back on its feet. Who knows, maybe Priscilla was trying to cushion her own loss when she bought that apartment right around the corner on Mount Vernon Street. She and my mother had been best friends since they were children. Priscilla, who had been divorced for many years, made our family her own.

My father's most endearing quality is his awareness of his own limitations, so without my mother to guide him, he relied on Priscilla for all sorts of things—mainly her judgment. Many people in our set thought Priscilla would marry my father after a respectable time. I knew better. Pris thought Teddy vain and foolish, though when my mother was alive, Pris put a good face on it. Later, she told me that my mother had been able to disguise many of my father's failings. That's what marriages are for, Priscilla said, to shield your partner from the world's bad opinion. I hoped that marriage was more than that. Priscilla said that if she had to listen to Teddy crack his knuckles—one of his few unattractive habits—for the rest of her life, she'd find a way to jump from the Hancock Tower.

"I swear to you," Priscilla said, "your mother died of boredom." No,

I thought. It was definitely the cancer. "They looked like a perfect match, your mother and father. They each came from old Boston families. There was absolutely no opposition to their marriage even though, by today's standards, they were young. And your father was even more handsome then than he is now. And he was so charming. How could she know that the charm was the sum and total of it? Jane, I would never want that to happen to you."

I don't blame Priscilla, not really. I was twenty-three and could have made my own decision. I just wasn't strong enough to fight the opposition, which included not only Teddy but also Max's grandmother in Boca Raton.

So I lost my first love and first love never comes again. That's what *they* say, the *they* of stories and fairy tales. Second love didn't come, either, which, I suppose, precluded third and fourth.

It wasn't so bad. I filled a niche in my family. I was the sensible one, the ponderous one, the one who did the extra laundry our housekeeper, Astrid, couldn't keep up with. I was the one who cooked on Astrid's day off.

And though I wasn't crazy about it—neither the niche nor the family—I was comfortable with it, and there's something to be said for that.

Sometimes I looked out my third-floor window and saw the tourists there—in their sneakers and sweat suits holding guidebooks and cameras and staring up into our windows.

What were they thinking when they peered up at us like that? Maybe they thought that behind our bay windows we lived charmed lives. And depending on your idea of what a charmed life is, maybe we did.

Chapter 2

Jane stays home on a Saturday night

It was a Saturday night in August and it was not unusual for me to be sitting at home with a book on my lap. At some point in the evening I had fallen asleep in front of the empty fireplace.

I woke to the sound of my sister Miranda dropping her keys in the front hall.

"I'm exhausted and drunk," she said.

"You were the life of the party," Teddy said.

"It was the dress. It was expensive, even for me—but worth every penny." When she left the house that evening she was wearing a midnight blue sheath that accentuated her narrow hips. The color would have made her look cadaverous had she not drenched her porcelain skin with expensive self-tanners. She used makeup liberally and was no stranger to artifice. Miranda, though she was flat as a pancake, always allowed her nonexistent breasts to precede her into a room. She had such a regal way of walking that she could actually convince you that her figure was something more than that of a prepubescent boy.

Teddy and Miranda wouldn't be caught dead at home on a Saturday night. Through the Fortune Family Foundation, I wrote the checks that sent them to charity balls and parties, but I rarely went myself. These charitable contributions were expected of us. Not only that, we were, as part of the Boston establishment, expected to make an appearance. I didn't have much interest in going to parties, not that Teddy and Miranda ever invited me. We usually bought only two tickets. Before my mother died, she had accompanied Teddy to these events, but Miranda took my mother's place when it came to her public duties.

Maybe an outsider would think it strange that Miranda and Teddy did everything together, but it wasn't really. These events were often attended not just by couples but by family groups—Mr. Endicott and his two daughters, Bill Cushing and his sister Alice. It wasn't so unusual for a father and daughter to go together, especially if the wife was gone. Teddy and Miranda liked going to parties together because it gave them a freedom they wouldn't have if they took actual dates. A woman was perfectly respectable, yet at the same time unfettered, when escorted by her father. And Miranda was a convenient shield for Teddy. Since my mother died, he'd been pursued by most of the single women in the *Social Register*. Both Miranda and Teddy wanted to play, but neither of them wanted to be forced to commit to a relationship that would last longer than two hours.

I stayed in my seat by the empty fireplace and listened to them talk about the party.

"I couldn't believe that bitch Veronica Buffington snubbed you like that, Daddy," Miranda said.

"Well, I did forget to send a note when her husband died."

"Michael died five years ago," Miranda said.

"Terrible breach of etiquette. I can hardly forgive myself. Though I was so busy at the time. And people do make mistakes. I tried to apologize, but I guess it was too little, too late. Your mother usually took care of those things. But it really is no excuse. I should have come home from St. Barths for the funeral. That's what I should have done. Michael being my distant cousin and all, and we were close when we were children, but, well . . . " He trailed off. Teddy understood that he had breached a convention, but it never occurred to him that he might have hurt the Buffingtons' feelings. He was much better at dealing with social laws than human emotion.

"For God's sake. They don't have to hold a grudge. You were on vacation and then you forgot. Things happen—not that I mind not having to talk to Glenda-the-Good-Witch. Mother and daughter, always together— a little odd, don't you think? And Glenda always doing good works. I hate people who are always doing good works. I don't trust them."

"Some of them are sincere, I think," Teddy said.

"Oh, Daddy, you always have such a good opinion of people. You make me feel so jaded."

I listened from the other room. If Teddy, who had all the depth of a drop of rain, could make Miranda feel jaded, there was really no hope for her, maybe no hope for any of us.

"Well, tonight you lit up the room," Teddy said to her. He believed that looking good could make up for any number of other insufficiencies.

"Did I?"

"Of course. James Putnam couldn't keep his eyes off of you."

"His *googly-googly* eyes." Miranda sang these words off-key.

"I think he's a good-looking boy, and they say he's going to run for state senate."

"Let me know when he's president." Miranda giggled.

I went out to the foyer. I was still holding the book I had been reading.

"How was the function?" I asked. I didn't know what to call a formal dance that benefited battered women.

"It was a party, Jane," Miranda said. She leaned in close to me and said, "Can you say 'party,' Jane? Try it." Each time she pronounced the *p* in "party," a jet of spittle landed on my cheek.

I wiped it off with the back of my hand.

"If you can't keep your thoughts to yourself, can you at least contain your own saliva?" I asked.

She stared at me. I was so used to this kind of behavior from Miranda that I usually let it go, but I had been having a pleasant evening. I was reading Maugham again, and I always enjoyed Maugham. I didn't appreciate this barrage of abuse. I hadn't done anything to deserve it.

"You spend the whole night reading again, Jane?" Teddy asked. He treated my passion for reading as if it were a sick compulsion, much like a mild case of kleptomania.

"You and your stories—they aren't real, you know," Miranda said as she swayed toward me. I put my hand out to steady her. "It's downright antisocial. That's what it is."

"You look washed out, Jane," Teddy said. I could always count on my father to comment on the lackluster quality of my looks. It wasn't that I was unattractive. All the Fortunes were as attractive as money and good genes could make them, but of all of us, I took the least care with what had been naturally bestowed, and Teddy considered my attitude a personal affront.

"At your age," Miranda said, "you should wear a little makeup. It would be a service to society."

It was typical of Miranda to focus on something like my bare face at midnight. Though she sometimes picked at me when she was sober, she couldn't help herself when she was drunk.

"I haven't been out in society," I said.

"More's the pity," Miranda said. Miranda sometimes talked as if she'd just walked out of a nineteenth-century novel, though, to my knowledge, she had never read one.

Both Miranda and Teddy were handsome in a well-kept sort of way. They shared the belief that appearance should be a priority and that great amounts of time and money should be expended to attain a polish so pure that only the sharpest critic could discern that its artificial glow wasn't absolutely natural.

Teddy and Miranda shared many beliefs that the rest of the world didn't, and that's probably why they were such perfect companions for each other. Of course, it was inevitable that someday someone would come along to break up the happy duo. I hoped so, especially for Miranda's sake. Teddy had been married once already and perhaps he was in no hurry to do it again, but a father is a poor substitute for a husband, no matter how well you get along.

As for me, I was coming to terms with the fact that I was going to be left on the shelf to sour like cream. I didn't like it, but I was coming to accept it.

"Anyway, tomorrow's a big day," Teddy said.

"What's so big about it?" Miranda asked. She tripped on her gown but managed to remain upright.

"Littleton's coming for brunch." Teddy called Littleton our "counselor," but he was really just a lawyer and not a very good one. He took care of our personal finances. Though my father might have found someone more adept than Littleton, Littleton, or a member of his family, had been with us for decades, and that counted for something in our family.

"So Littleton's coming for brunch. He comes every third Sunday. What's the big deal?" Miranda asked.

"Tomorrow is not a third Sunday," I said.

"Technicality, technicality," Miranda slurred. She disappeared up the stairs, pulling herself up by the oak banister.

My father usually looked at least a decade younger than his sixty-two years, but tonight the only people he could have fooled were the visually impaired—and, perhaps, Miranda. I put my hand on his arm.

"Everything okay?" I asked.

He nodded but looked distracted. He often looked distracted, but not this distracted. He touched my cheek.

"Your skin is so dry, Jane." He turned to go up the stairs. "Don't stay up too late. If you don't get a good night's sleep, you'll age much faster than necessary. They don't call it 'beauty sleep' for nothing. You can borrow some of my Crème de la Mer. It's on the top shelf of my medicine cabinet."

I thanked him, even though I had no intention of borrowing one of the panoply of beauty products he kept in his bathroom. I just couldn't bring myself to borrow emollients from my father. I didn't even like to go into his bathroom, because it retained the fruity scent of a person too well preserved.

Before I went to bed, I took a look at myself in my bedroom mirror. I had to admit that though the mirror was beautiful, an antique from the nineteenth century, the picture it reflected back was not inspiring. I was hardly a woman in full flower. I took out my ponytail and shook my head. My hair was long and thick, but I had recently sprouted two gray hairs. I'd been wondering what I should do about them. I didn't like the idea of going gray. I felt old, but not that old. I took hold of the grays and tweaked them out.

I could make a trip to the salon, but I refused to waste my time on what I believed to be inherently trivial. This gave me a feeling of moral superiority which was, I suppose, its own form of vanity.

I turned toward my desk. There was an invitation from Wellesley College, my alma mater, tucked into the blotter. The desk was a Shaker table with clean lines that didn't go with the rest of the furniture. The other furniture was older, more ornate, darker. I had chosen this desk myself on a trip to Pennsylvania with my mother. She told me the desk wouldn't match my furniture, but I didn't care. I wanted something in my room that I had chosen myself.

Dean Lydia McKay wanted me to give a talk about my work with the Fortune Family Foundation. I had been running the foundation for a little more than fifteen years. Before she died, my mother had called me into her room one afternoon and pointed to an ugly wooden chest in the corner.

"I want you to have that," she said.

"Thanks," I said. Why was she giving me an ugly chest? It wasn't as if I'd ever admired it.

"That box contains all your great-grandmother's papers. I want you to take over the foundation. I didn't do as much as I might have done," my mother admitted, "but you, Jane, can return the foundation to its former glory."

I dug into that box after my mother died and read every paper in it. My great-grandmother Euphemia wrote copious journals. I followed some of Euphemia's advice and came up with a few ideas of my own. If I had my way, the Fortune Family Foundation would someday have the same prestige as the MacArthur.

I fingered the invitation. Despite my debut as valedictorian at Wellesley, I hated speaking in public and refused invitations or handed them off to Evan Bentley, the coeditor of the *Euphemia Review,* but Wellesley was my own college. I'd have to consider it. Still, I was never sure why anyone would want me to speak. My claim to fame was having established a literary magazine. All I did was read stories: I didn't write them. Who was I compared with all the literary luminaries that were available in Boston?

I marked my calendar and leaned the invitation against a lamp so I wouldn't forget to respond. I didn't feel much more accomplished now than I did when I was a student. I knew there was physical evidence of achievement. I had published thirteen issues of the *Euphemia Review* and was just about to publish the fourteenth. I had discovered several writers and at least one of those, Max Wellman, my first love, had gone on to be a huge commercial and critical success. In my heart, though, I was a background person. I wasn't the type of *success* people should be asking to speak at a college, even if I went there myself.

One of the Red Sox shirts I usually slept in was hanging over a chair and I slipped into it, then pulled down the silk duvet on my bed and crawled in. I looked up into the white canopy as I had done since I was a child. Not much had changed since then, or so I had led myself to believe. Even Mathilda, my one-eyed doll, still lolled on the bed, long after she should have taken her rightful place with the other toys in the attic.

Chapter 3

A change in the family's fortunes

The next morning Priscilla was the first to arrive for brunch. She arrived at ten o'clock on the dot. She was always on time and always brought her knitting with her. If there were an Olympic event for nonstop knitting, Priscilla would definitely place. She sat in her favorite camelback chair and pulled out her current project.

When Dolores trailed her father into the sitting room before breakfast, Priscilla started to steam like a teapot. Dolores Mudd was Littleton's errant daughter who had recently returned to Boston after an unsuccessful adventure in Hollywood. Miranda found something riveting about Dolores, and that summer Miranda had anointed Dolores her new best friend. It felt like Dolores spent more time at our house than at her own. Dolores served as Miranda's lady-in-waiting and peppered her with compliments. "You look just like Grace Kelly," she said. Miranda does not look like Grace Kelly. Okay, maybe she does—a very skinny one.

Dolores was a worn twenty-seven and her hair had been bleached so many times it looked like it might crack off her head. She had a crooked front tooth that was more endearing than unattractive. It made her look vulnerable, and a little softness was just what she needed. She wore black jeans and spiked heels. The heels were unnecessary for a casual family brunch. Who on earth was she hoping to impress? And what would those shoes do to our hardwoods? I'm sure they weren't friends of Chinese carpets either.

I thought Miranda's fascination with Dolores was peculiar. Miranda herself had a fine-wine kind of beauty, while Dolores was more like Boone's Farm fermented apple beverage. Maybe Miranda was fascinated by Dolores's presumed unconventionality. Dolores had followed her dream to California, even if it only resulted in a messy divorce and a small part in a sitcom called *Life Itself*, which was canceled after six episodes. Neither Miranda nor I had had the gumption to follow our dreams. As far as I knew, Miranda didn't even have a dream, unless it was marrying a suitable CEO.

Dolores was wearing a pink mohair sweater. It showcased her artificially enhanced breasts. She wasn't shy about her implants. The first time I met her, she took my hand, placed it on her right breast, and said, "Feel this. It's hard as a rock."

"I'd rather not," I said. I pulled my hand away, but not before noticing that Dolores's breast was indeed as dense as petrified wood.

"Jane is not very experimental," Miranda apologized for me. Perhaps not, but I wasn't interested in touching another woman's breast, even in the interest of science.

"And they'll never sag, not even when I'm a hundred," Dolores said.

"That's lucky," I said, but I couldn't really see how a shriveled old woman sporting the sprightly breasts of a sixteen-year-old cheerleader was a good thing. It seemed to me that all the parts of your body should age together as some kind of unified whole.

On the way into the dining room, Priscilla pulled me into an alcove in the hallway near the front door. She kept her voice low, more of a hiss than a whisper.

"I don't understand the attraction Miranda has for that girl," Priscilla said.

"Dolores glitters, I guess," I said. It was the best explanation I could come up with. And it was true in its way. At the very least, Dolores sparkled, whether it was her hair clips, her bracelets, her dangling rhinestone earrings, or a combination of these that rendered the effect, I don't know, but something about her was arresting.

"Like costume jewelry," Pris said. "She doesn't fool me with that bottled tan and bleached hair. Dolores Mudd is completely ordinary, if you ask me." No one did ask her, but that never stopped Priscilla from offering an opinion.

"And it's so inappropriate," she said, "her being here, today of all days." I still didn't know what Pris meant by that, since Dolores had joined her father for every monthly brunch since she'd returned home in May. "She was definitely not invited, I can assure you."

Dolores had made a lame excuse when she arrived—something about needing to catch a ride with her father into the city because she was going to a concert on the Esplanade that afternoon—but I didn't believe her. She was as fascinated with us as Miranda was with her. I feared that it might also have something to do with Teddy, a good catch for someone like Dolores, despite the difference in age. My father is almost irresistible to women, and that's hard to admit, especially when I haven't made a dent in the social landscape for years.

"Remember Guy Callow?" Pris asked. She was still holding me in the alcove with a hand hooked into my elbow.

"You can't blame Miranda for that. It was so long ago."

"Just an example of Miranda's bad judgment when it comes to

friends." Priscilla didn't want to miss yet one more opportunity to offer a negative opinion.

Guy Callow was a short-lived boyfriend of Miranda's, the son of some of Teddy's out-of-town friends. The summer Guy took the Massachusetts bar exam, Teddy offered our house as a base of operations. I met Guy briefly but went out to the Vineyard to open our summer house. Teddy and Miranda waited a couple of weeks to make sure Guy had everything necessary to fortify him for the exam—which, apparently, included Miranda. After Teddy left for the Vineyard, Miranda stayed behind. Guy was supposed to come out to the island with her, but a month later she came out alone. She was not happy. She spent hours sitting in the sunroom staring at nothing in particular.

"You want to talk about it?" I asked once.

"Nothing really to say," she said. "He thinks I'm spoiled, and if he thinks that, then he doesn't know me at all. I'm hardly spoiled." She fingered her three tennis bracelets. They sparkled in the sun.

"Do you think I'm spoiled, Jane?"

She had never asked me a question like that before. A better sister would have given a more honest answer.

"He shouldn't have said it," I said. "We were all very kind to him, very hospitable. Whatever he thought, he would have been better off keeping it to himself."

Miranda stared at me and tapped her fingers on the arm of the chair. Perhaps she realized I had given no answer, but she was as morose as I'd ever seen her and I couldn't hurt her more. I lived by that old rule, "First, do no harm." Miranda's malaise lasted five days, but after that, she went back to her tennis games and parties.

Three years later, we heard from Guy's parents that he had married a Dutch supermodel named Ooh-Lala. When Miranda heard about this she walked down to Saks and bought a Louis Vuitton train case. When she came back from the store, her mood was much improved. The purchase of an expensive piece of luggage, apparently, cured her of any residual feelings she had for Guy Callow. I couldn't understand how a designer bag could so easily repair a broken heart. I was a different animal. I could remain inconsolable for years.

I finally extricated myself from Priscilla and went into the kitchen, where our housekeeper, Astrid, was cutting mushrooms for a frittata. Her black hair was wrapped around a serving spoon. Tendrils fell forward and she periodically wiped at them with the back of her wrist. Astrid was around my age, but she always acted like an older sister. She must have thought I needed one, despite the obvious fact of Miranda.

"The king is ready," I said.

"Well, I'm not," she said. She chopped with ferocity. Astrid joined our family on the heels of my mother's death. We always had cooks and housekeepers, but compared with Astrid they had all the emotional depth of a kitchen appliance. Astrid floated up our walk one winter, swinging her hips like a Brazilian Mary Poppins, and I don't know what I would have done without her.

I picked a mushroom from the cutting board, slipping my fingers around her moving knife.

"I cut your fingers off," she warned.

"Not on purpose, I hope." I popped the mushroom into my mouth. "Need help?"

"You take the coffee out." She nodded toward the Limoges coffee service.

"Astrid?"

"Yes?"

"Do you know what's going on here today? What this brunch is all about?" She looked at me. She knew. "Tell me," I said.

"Ouch," she said. I looked at her hand. She had sliced into her finger. The cut was bleeding into the mushrooms. "Damn," she said. "Toss those, will you, Jane? The ones with the blood." She went over to the sink to run some cold water over her hand, then wrapped her finger in a paper towel.

"Are you all right?" I asked.

"Take the coffee out," she said.

"Astrid?"

"Please, Jane, take the coffee out."

I lifted the heavy coffee urn, balancing it with one hand on its base, and carried it into the dining room, where the entire party was now seated.

"About time," Teddy said. "Where on earth is Astrid?"

"She cut her finger."

"That was clumsy of her."

My father liked to think that one person—Astrid—could handle every chore in our house. It was as if he never noticed me picking up after him, folding his clothes, putting Miranda's shoes away, throwing in a load of laundry, dusting a room. The illusion of "help" was especially important to him when we had company. We were a family with a full-time servant, and for Teddy, the show was more important than the service itself.

"She's finishing the frittata," I added. This was his favorite of all Astrid's dishes and I knew that this would appease him.

"I *do* love Astrid's frittatas," he said.

I poured coffee for Dolores. Although she hadn't been invited, she was still a guest. Priscilla, who sat across from her, was a guest also, and older, so proper etiquette would indicate that she should be served first, but Priscilla was as good as family.

Whatever was going to happen that morning, I wanted them to get it over with. Maybe Teddy was sick. Whatever it was, I wanted to know. If something had happened to my sister Winnie or to one of her boys, someone would have told me before this. There would be no need for Littleton, no buildup.

Astrid came in with the frittata. She had a bandage on her finger. I followed her back into the kitchen to help her with the biscuits, bacon, and fruit.

"You're not going to tell me anything, are you?" I asked.

She gave me a bowl of berries.

"Not my place," she said. Astrid, who came to us speaking very little English, was now fluent, but she still retained a mild accent. She shouldered me gently to let me know I should head back into the dining room.

"That never stopped you before," I said.

"Well, it's stopping me now."

Between us, we put everything on the table. Astrid didn't stay to serve. That was my job. Or, if Miranda was so inclined, she could play lady of the house.

When I sat down, Dolores was talking.

"I was in Starbucks," she said, "in West Hollywood." She talked as if we should all have a clear picture of the West Hollywood Starbucks. Our picture had only as much clarity as it could get from all Starbucks being just alike. "And you would not believe who I saw." She paused. When no one responded, she continued. "It was none other than Tootie from *The Facts of Life*." She ended with a flourish.

"That's nice," Teddy said. He gave her a twisted smile. I knew that he had no idea that *The Facts of Life* was a dead sitcom from the 1980s. Even if he knew, he wouldn't have cared. He was not impressed by celebrity. He was much more interested in having an old Boston name and the old Boston money that went with it.

"Oh," Miranda said with feigned interest and less enthusiasm. We were not a television-watching family. My mother had seen to that. When we were children, she had orchestrated our spare time like a symphony. Miranda had been a tennis champion. Winnie had won ribbons for dressage, and I was told I could have been an Olympic skater if I had given the time to it. My mother thought it unnatural for a child to focus too much on one thing, so I became a very good skater, but nothing more.

Miranda made up for her childhood television deficiency by becoming addicted in college to a soap opera called *All My Children*. My assistant, Tad, was named after a character in *All My Children*, and though I'd never seen it, I thought the idea of naming your child after a soap opera character delightfully silly. My little sister Winnie, a housewife in the suburbs, has also made up for the dearth of television, and now she compares almost everything in life to an episode of *Seinfeld*.

"And I saw, if you can believe it, Sally Struthers in Ralph's. That's a supermarket," Dolores said. She was trying for more traction, but the ground she was treading was just too slippery.

"Who?" Priscilla said.

"You know. From *All in the Family*."

"I don't know," Pris said, "and I'd rather not know. Dolores dear, whatever happened to your husband, Mr. Mudd?"

The silence in the room took on a shape of its own. Dolores tucked a fugitive hair behind her left ear and summoned all her dignity.

"We had a falling-out," she said.

"So I assumed," Priscilla said. She took a sip of coffee. Priscilla had the posture of someone who never dropped fine china.

"They just didn't get along." Littleton stepped into the ring to defend his daughter, but compared with Pris, he was a mere featherweight.

"If you must know," Dolores said, "my husband, Howard Mudd, was gay." She sank her chin toward her pert breasts in a gesture that was calculated to inspire pity.

"Before or after you married him, dear?" Priscilla lowered her voice and made it soft and inviting.

My father shot Pris a glance meant to let her know that she'd gone far enough. No one was allowed to be rude to guests at his table.

After the meal, we took our remaining coffee back into the sitting room.

Dolores sat down on the edge of a settee and took a sip of coffee. Littleton stared at her until she looked up.

"Oh yes, right. I must be going or I'll miss the concert," Dolores said.

I still believed that the concert was a complete fabrication.

"Thank God," Priscilla said.

"Pris." Teddy and I spoke at the same time. If we didn't watch out, Priscilla would soon be shooing Dolores out of the house on the end of a broom. I wasn't entirely sure this would be a bad thing, but it wouldn't be polite, and the Fortunes were nothing if not polite.

"She shouldn't be here. It's as simple as that," Priscilla said.

Dolores put her cup down on an inlaid table and stood up.

"I'll be heading out, then," she said.

"I wish you didn't have to leave," Miranda said. "The afternoon will be so boring without you."

Dolores looked at her father.

"I have to," she said. "We can do something later."

"I'm shopping this afternoon. You'll miss the shopping," Miranda complained.

At the mention of shopping, Teddy looked at his feet. Finally, Dolores trotted out of the room on her impractical heels. If she was really going to the Esplanade, those heels would be a hindrance. She'd sink right into the grass.

After she was gone, Littleton put his cup on our elaborately carved mantelpiece. He stood at the fireplace with his back toward us, his arms outstretched in an odd, theatrical pose.

He spun around so quickly his body made a swishing sound.

"I've been going over your finances, and we need to take drastic measures," he said.

Astrid, who had just come in with some mini-biscotti and more coffee, put the tray down on an ottoman and backed quickly out of the room. I tried to catch her eye, but she wouldn't look at me.

Drastic measures?

What was he talking about and why didn't Teddy look surprised—or Priscilla? The words *drastic measures* yanked Miranda from her natural lethargy.

"Whatever this is," Miranda snapped, examining a pearl-toned fingernail, "can we get it over with? I dislike histrionics of all sorts. *Drastic.* Please. What on earth are you talking about? There's a special sale at Louis today and I'd like to get there before everything is gone." Though Miranda is always happy to pay full price, she can never resist a really good sale.

"Louis will have to wait," Littleton said. "I want you to sit and listen very carefully. This is the bottom line." I hated the term *bottom line*.

It always struck me that the people who used it didn't really know what it meant. It was something a slick financial adviser would say, and Littleton was hardly one of those. "You have overspent and invested unwisely."

The room, though large, felt like the inside of a cigar box. I wanted to pull back the velvet drapes and open some windows. Didn't anyone else notice how hot it was?

"I don't understand," Miranda said. She was looking at Littleton as if he held the key to the vault at Shreve, Crump & Lowe.

"The Fortune family is experiencing an insufficiency of funds."

"Go on," Miranda said.

Littleton was sweating at his hairline.

"Economies must be taken," he said, "compromises made. Your fortunes, excuse the pun, have diminished."

Miranda continued to stare blankly at him as if he were speaking in tongues.

"We're broke," I said.

Miranda turned on me.

"Jane, must you be so dramatic? Must you always be so dramatic?" Miranda must have been very upset, because as everyone knows, I am not in the least dramatic. "We couldn't be broke. We're not broke, are we, Daddy? Broke—it's such a shoddy word. We may be experiencing a financial shortfall, but people like us—we don't just go broke." She spat out the last word as if it were made of broken glass. "What does it all mean?" Her words were drawn out and her voice was as nasal as Gwyneth Paltrow's when she played English. Miranda slumped onto her chair. Teddy walked over to her and put his hand on her shoulder, but he couldn't look at her. He ran his fingers through his thick blond hair. Teddy's hair, like Dolores's, was a deception, but he had a good colorist and his looked completely natural.

Miranda peered up at him and touched his hand. Her look was pleading, the same look she gave him as a child when she wanted a new toy.

"Littleton discussed it with me and I discussed it with Priscilla last week," Teddy said. "She and I thought it best that Littleton explain it to you, but the fact is—Jane's right." There had been many times when I had wanted to hear those two words, but this was not one of them. "We're broke."

And in Teddy's mouth, the words sounded oddly like a curse.

Chapter 4

Jane makes a discovery

There was a pile of manuscripts on my nightstand and I wasn't really in the mood to read them, but I picked one up and started to give it the quick once-over. By now I was usually able to spot a story's potential within the first paragraph, certainly within the first page.

My hand tightened on the pages I was reading and I began to salivate. That was the sign for me. One writer I knew could tell if he had a good story because the hair on his arms stood on end. With me, finding a good story elicited the same reaction as good food.

I scrambled out of bed, sat at my desk, and finished reading. The story jumped off the page. It was full of characters who would remain with me long after I'd slipped the pages under my blotter. The story was called "Boston Tech," after one of Boston's tougher high schools, and was a version of *Romeo and Juliet* set in the time of busing and racial desegregation in Boston. A white family. A black family. Love. Violence. It was electrifying. My heart beat fast. The idea was simple, but brilliant in its simplicity. It was the type of story that could change a life. I flipped to the last page where all the writers who submitted to the Fortune Family Fellowship were asked to provide their basic information. The author's name was Jack Reilly. Jack Reilly. He lived in Lynn, a rough working-class city north of Boston. There's a rhyme about Lynn: Lynn, Lynn, the city of sin, you never come out the way you went in.

Lynn, the city of sin. Back in bed, I tried to picture Jack Reilly. Someone who could write like this would have to be remarkable. Lynn. Jack Reilly would frequent neighborhood bars. He would wear a black leather jacket and smoke nonfiltered cigarettes. His hair would be thick and slicked back from his forehead. His jeans would have a hole near the right rear pocket. He'd work in a factory and write with a pencil in a crumpled spiral notebook during his breaks. He'd be the guy other guys looked to for advice. He'd be a man who inspired love in women. He'd be dangerous. Maybe on parole. Jack Reilly. Lynn. Lynn.

Of course, he could be nothing like that. Max, the first winner of the fellowship, wasn't the man I expected him to be. I expected a four-eyed geek with a leatherette folder, but the man who walked into Maison Robert to meet me and my coeditor, Evan Bentley, had an unusual beauty. His good looks should have made me dislike him. I was suspicious of beauty. Teddy and Miranda had taught me, by example, that some beauty was only skin deep, and I had come to believe that all beauty was only skin deep—that behind every handsome face lurked a shallow man.

None of that mattered when Max Wellman walked into the restaurant. I was immediately tongue-tied and I was afraid he would think me a dimwitted dilettante. I wasn't much more than that at the time, but at least I'd thought to recruit Bentley to give the contest credibility. Bentley had been one of my literature professors at Wellesley. He had written one novel to critical acclaim but had been unable to repeat the performance. Since he was the only writer I knew at the time, I asked him to help me. The credibility of the whole enterprise was severely threatened that evening when Bentley got drunk and vomited on Max's shoes in the men's room. Max was wonderful. He insisted on going all the way out to Newton Highlands with me to take Bentley home.

We dragged Bentley up three flights of stairs. Max fished around in Bentley's pockets for keys, found them, and let us into his apartment. Max turned on the hall light. We found Bentley's bedroom and put him to bed. I wanted to leave him there, just tossed on the bed with all his clothes on, but Max removed Bentley's jacket and shoes, and loosened his collar. He covered him up with a blanket from the foot of the bed.

There is an intimacy to putting a drunk to bed, like putting a child to sleep. Max and I stood across from each other. Bentley started to snore. I looked down at Bentley's shoes. Max had lined them up next to the bed.

"You should take those," I said. "To replace yours."

"I could never take a drunk man's shoes," Max said. His voice was low and serious, but it made me want to laugh. He smiled up at me and we slipped out of the apartment.

In the cab, I apologized again for Bentley.

"I like a good fallen icon," he said.

I didn't know exactly what he meant, but I suspected that he had more compassion for Bentley than I did.

I could hardly wait to call this Jack Reilly and tell him he'd won the fellowship. I'd have to talk to my intern, Tad, and then to Bentley. We'd arrange to meet Mr. Reilly. What kind of restaurant would he like? Maybe something down on the waterfront.

Of course, I should read the other stories, if only in the interest of fairness, but I already knew "Boston Tech" would be the winner. I'd learned a little something in fifteen years and stories like "Boston Tech" didn't come along every day.

Chapter 5

Euphemia vs. Isabella

The fact that I administer a trust based on one woman's desire to outshine another doesn't bother me in the least. My great-grandmother Euphemia Fortune was a contemporary of Isabella Stewart Gardner. Isabella left, as her legacy, the Gardner Museum, a Venetian palace on the Fenway. Had Isabella known that the Fens would suffer decades of high crime, she might have chosen another location for her museum, but when she chose that location, the worst that could be said of it was that it wasn't central to the other cultural highlights of Boston.

On the surface, Isabella and Euphemia had everything in common. Neither was especially attractive, but Isabella was one of those women who knew how to transform limited physical gifts into an overall magnetism. You can see it in Sargent's famous portrait of her. Both women were rich, but Euphemia took one look at Isabella over tea on the lawn of the Gardners' Brookline farm and decided she had to have some of what Isabella had—whatever it was. A certain glamour. A savoir faire.

I read all about this in Euphemia's journals. She was not a public person, but she was not shy about pouring out her ambitions on the page. I would have liked to follow in Isabella's footsteps—joyful, and heedless of certain conventions—but instead I am more like Euphemia. She feared the limelight, but her great tragedy was that she also craved it. I often wonder if I'm more like my great-grandmother than I'd like to admit.

When I took over the foundation I used Euphemia's journals as instruction manuals on how to run it. Like her, I offered a place for a writer to work for three months and a stipend. Euphemia bought a house for the fellowship in a town called Hull, only about forty minutes from Boston.

In her day, Hull was a convenient seaside town, close to Boston, and the home of some of Boston's brighter lights. Even the Kennedys owned a gabled house in the hills there once, but the town had since fallen on hard times from which it had never completely recovered.

One day I drove down to find the cottage Euphemia bought to house the first recipient of the fellowship. It was high on a hill overlooking the ocean. In her day, it stood alone, but now it was surrounded by suburban-style homes. Children's toys littered the yard, but I could still imagine the first recipient of the fellowship walking up the front steps.

I might have chosen another town, since Hull was no longer fashionable and we no longer owned that house, but I went back to Hull, choosing a cottage that was for rent on a street called Ocean Avenue, a street that ran from the ocean side to the bay side of the peninsula. From the cottage's upper window, on the ocean side, you could see the Boston skyline.

That is where Max and I fell in love. I drove down there with a pair of shoes from Brooks Brothers. That was my excuse. I needed to replace the shoes Bentley had ruined. The shoes were the most expensive pair in the store. I told myself that it was the least I could do after Bentley and the vomiting incident, but really I wanted to impress Max with my generosity. He said I shouldn't have done it, that the ruined shoes weren't nearly as nice as the new ones. (I didn't doubt it.) He seemed to like them, though I never saw him wear them that summer. That was a summer of flip-flops and shorts.

Max said that I had arrived just in time, because he was going crazy.

"Solitude is great," he said, "in theory, but I've never been so alone in my life."

"I thought writers like to be alone," I said.

"They need to be alone. It's different."

We walked down to the pier for fried clams. He already knew the woman who served the food from behind a screened-in window and called her by name—Jo, short for Josephine. I was impressed by anyone who made friends that easily, and Max was one of those people. He brought the world in around him so that wherever he was, he was inside a circle.

I hardly left the beach that summer. Max said that it was much easier to work when I was there.

"Isn't it your responsibility to make sure this thing is a success?" he asked. I was too happy to care about responsibility. A responsible person wouldn't have slept with the first person to whom they gave a grant. It could come back to haunt me.

Max worked all day, except for the few afternoons we took off to play. I learned to cook and each night served something new and interesting, though not always good. After I worked on it half the day, I was always disappointed when the results didn't live up to my expectations, but Max didn't seem to mind. I could have served him macaroni and cheese every night and he would have been just as happy as with my Stroganoffs, bouil-labaisses, and risottos.

After that summer, the foundation continued to rent the house for three years, then we bought it. I replaced the old dusty furniture, had the house painted, and put a deck on the roof. From there you could see both the ocean and the bay.

Though it's been years since I delved into the competition between Euphemia and Isabella, I still like to go and sit on a particular stone bench at the Gardner Museum. Except for the ring of the occasional cell phone, I can imagine myself back in time and hear the crinolines rustling. Euphemia would be happy to know that for all of Isabella's grand pretensions, the museum is a somber place despite the airy atrium and fresh flowers. It feels as if the color gray has descended on it like dusk. Euphemia would have been even more delighted to know that these days the museum's collection is sometimes considered second rate.

Upstairs on the third floor, in a corner, is a picture of several women standing together. Euphemia is in the picture, off to the side. The catalogue names her. She has a full chest, a huge bustle, and a receding chin. If anyone resembles her, it is my sister Winnie, who often wears that same air of perpetual dissatisfaction. The painting is known as a lesser work, and that's where Euphemia is memorialized forever. If she knew of our financial troubles, she'd be so mortified she would probably remove herself from the painting entirely. The next time I climbed the stairs to see her, she'd be gone, hiding in some other picture where no one would be likely to find her.

The morning after the "big announcement" I walked to my office in Kenmore Square. It's a good walk from Beacon Hill, but on a beautiful day— and it was a beautiful day—I preferred it to climbing down into the subway and rushing around underground like a mole.

Like Isabella, I hadn't chosen prime Boston real estate for my enterprise. Kenmore Square, near Fenway Park, is an unglamorous part of the city, catering to students and baseball fans. In fact, it is not too far from the Gardner Museum.

I rented the office shortly after taking over the foundation. My mother thought that an office would give the foundation more legitimacy.

A tasteful plaque on the door says "The Fortune Family Foundation," but I never did much in the way of decorating. The inside of the office looks like it belongs to a low-rent detective in a Raymond Chandler novel.

I opened the door. My intern, Tad, was stacking manuscripts on my desk. He separated the stories into several piles, depending on how much he thought I'd like them. I gave him the coffee I'd picked up at the shop on the ground floor, the shop that had the real teapot spouting steam out front. I'd loved that enormous teapot since I was a child, and maybe that was why I took this office just above it.

I pulled "Boston Tech" out of my tattered L. L. Bean tote and slapped it onto the desk.

"You have to look at this," I said. Each time I touched the story, I felt a low jolt of excitement.

"Lunchtime soon enough?" Tad asked. He was very serious about keeping the office organized and usually read on his own time.

"Can't wait," I said.

"Is this Jane Fortune that I see before me? I think you are—dare I say it—ebullient?"

"Shut up." I blushed.

"You can only speak to me like that because you don't pay me," he said, smiling.

"Just read it," I said.

He was embarrassing me. I hated to see myself as he must see me, a desiccated old maid with a lonely passion for literature.

He sat at his desk, a big oak block I had acquired when my old school was auctioning off some of its ancient furniture. While he read the story, I looked through the mail. There was a packet of clippings about Max Wellman. I used to pull the clippings myself, but eventually I hired a service. Since Max was the first winner of the Fortune Family Fellowship, I had a responsibility to keep up with him, didn't I? I had been in love with him—maybe I still was—so I used the clipping service to stalk him, in a genteel way, of course.

The article that arrived that day was a profile of "the author at home" in *Vanity Fair*. It showed him in his Tribeca loft. He was, if possible, even more handsome than he was when I first met him. I read the article, not just for what was in it, but also for what I could find between the lines.

"So," the interviewer, a woman, asked, "you've been connected with all sorts of women. Do you have anything to say about that?"

"What would you like me to say?"

"Do you have anyone serious in your life?"

"Isn't everyone in your life serious?"

"You are teasing me."

"I'm not," he said.

"Let's face it, Mr. Wellman, you are known as the Literary Lothario, New York's bad boy. Casanova with a pen. Do you care to comment on that?"

"No, I don't."

"Okay, then. Your first big success. *Duet for One*. It's been said that it was based on a true story, that you could never have written it with such truth, such feeling, if there wasn't something personal in it."

"I write fiction. It was a story."

This interviewer wasn't having much luck with Max. I knew that *Duet for One*, at least the first part, was about me. I knew it, but since I had been so closemouthed about my relationship with Max, no one else did. Max had re-created the scene in the restaurant with Bentley, the scene in the bathroom when Bentley vomited on his shoes (a scene Max managed to make laugh-out-loud funny), and the trip back to Bentley's apartment. He had written about my arrival at the beach cottage with a new pair of shoes. In *Duet for One*, the couple's relationship hinges on that pair of shoes.

Tad finished reading "Boston Tech" and looked up with the glazed expression of someone who's been far away.

"It's awesome," he said. That was high praise for Tad, though it was a word I would have liked to cure him of. So few things in life were really awesome, and it was such a wonderful word when used sparingly. But maybe, this time, he was right. Maybe "Boston Tech" was awesome.

"Should I call Bentley?" I asked.

Tad brandished a pile of stories.

"I haven't found anything as good as this," he said. "I don't think you'll find another one as good."

"I know."

With Tad listening on the other line, we called Bentley.

"I want to call this Jack Reilly right away," I said.

"I'd like to read the story first," he said.

"Then meet me. Meet me now, and I'll give it to you."

"I can't meet you until later," he said. "I have a class to teach."

"Six o'clock at Finn's, then?"

"Okay."

Bentley now lived on the other side of the Charles River. He moved there after he married Melody James, who inherited a two-family clapboard house in Somerville. It was convenient, since Harvard had snatched him away from Wellesley. His work with the foundation had given him a reputation for literary discrimination and taken his career to a new level.

I didn't know what to do with myself for the rest of the afternoon. I was too excited to sit in the office, so I packed all the stories into my tote.

"How old is that bag?" Tad asked. He seemed to have a new haircut every week, and this week's caused him to keep pushing his bangs out of his eyes.

"Older than you are," I said, "and your point?"

"It's ancient, stained, and ugly. You could use something new. Ever think of getting rid of that Talbots look and going for something a little more hip?"

"I don't shop at Talbots and this bag is fine. The best thing about it is it will last forever."

"No, Jane, that's the worst thing about it."

"I'll take that under advisement," I said.

I decided to kill some of the time before meeting Bentley by walking over to the Gardner Museum. I could have some lunch, then wander upstairs to see if Euphemia was still there. She would be, of course. She was in a painting and therefore trapped. Besides, even if she could walk away from her spot in that second-rate painting on the third floor, I didn't think she'd have the nerve.

Chapter 6

Jane Fortune and Evan Bentley confer

Finn's was a small restaurant-bar on Beacon Street on the Brookline-Boston border. From Kenmore Square to Finn's you pass several neighborhoods and you can easily slip from a safe one to an unsafe one just by taking a few steps in the wrong direction.

Finn's is on the safe side of the line, a neighborhood full of brick town houses that have been converted into apartments and student housing.

The first time I ever went to Finn's, I was meeting Bentley to convince him to come help me with the fellowship and the *Review*. I had recently graduated from Wellesley College. Wellesley

College was argyle kneesocks and wool skirts. It was field hockey and long afternoons staring at the ducks in the pond while doodling poetry on thick white tablets. They say that going to a women's college is good for a girl's self-esteem. I think it would have worked for me if I hadn't been derailed by my mother's illness. I couldn't locate my self-esteem for a while after that.

Since Bentley was a "blocked" writer, he spent his days advancing the crushes his students had on him. I hadn't been one of those students. His bad-boy tweed and air of dissipation hadn't impressed me. Still, he was the only published author I knew, so I called him to ask if he would help me with my project.

"Which one were you?" he asked on the phone.

"Jane Fortune." I had already given my name. I gave it again while I tried to think of something about me he might remember, but I couldn't think of anything that made me stand out from the other girls.

While I was still thinking he said, "I remember you. I remember the journal you wrote in my class." Evan Bentley had his students keep a journal about the books he assigned us. We were supposed to write as we went along, but I ended up pulling an all-nighter and writing the journal in a frantic rush. He gave it back to me with an "A++" written at the top. Thanks to Bentley, I still keep a journal.

Bentley agreed to meet me at Finn's that long-ago afternoon. When I arrived, I opened the door to a windowless calm. Everything about the place was muted. It was four o'clock and the bar was empty except for two barflies, an ancient waitress, a boy bartender with braces on his teeth, and Bentley, who stood when he saw me and pointed to the stool beside him.

I hoisted myself up and tried to find a place for my pocketbook. It was a green leather Kelly bag that had belonged to my mother and I wore it like courage. I held it in front of me, then put it on the bar, but it looked awkward there, so I dropped it to the floor and worried about what detritus was going to end up stuck to its bottom.

"Thank you so much for meeting with me, Professor Bentley," I said. I was attempting to play the role of confident patroness of the arts.

"It is my pleasure, Miss Fortune, but call me Bentley. I find the 'Professor' highly superfluous."

I didn't know if I could lose the "Professor." I was brought up in a formal household.

Bentley was attractive enough for an older man, if you liked his type. Floppy brown hair, a five o'clock shadow, and baggy khakis falling over a pair of loafers.

"I'd like to buy you a martini," he said. "Do you drink martinis?"

"I've never had one," I said.

"Then it would be my pleasure to buy you your first." He waved at the elderly waitress and called her Mary. She got up from where she was chain-smoking at a back table and left her cigarette burning in the ashtray.

I wasn't sure I wanted a martini but I didn't want to appear unsophisticated, so when it came with its three gigantic olives on a toothpick, I sipped it and wondered why anyone would voluntarily drink something so vile. I have since acquired a taste for martinis. Bentley had a scotch. He drank the amber liquid with gusto, licked his lips when he was finished, and immediately ordered another.

I told Bentley how much I had liked his book. I took it out of my bag so he could sign it. I checked the bottom of my bag with a surreptitious swipe of my hand.

"You're a very pretty girl," Bentley said after his third scotch.

"Thank you," I said.

"And rich," he said.

I shrugged and blushed. I didn't like talking about money. We didn't talk about money in my family. (To our detriment, as it turned out.) Besides, I had yet to come into my trust, and even that wouldn't make me what we'd call rich.

"Rich is rich," he said. "I grew up poor. Very poor. You know what my first job was?"

"No," I said. Of course I didn't.

"I sold Bibles door-to-door."

I had never met a Bible salesman before. It sounded so fictional, so *Paper Moon*.

"Well, you've written a wonderful book," I said.

"It *ain't* the Bible." He smiled. "And wonderful books don't always translate into money." Fourth scotch. "So how much would I make?" he asked.

"For what?"

"For helping you with your little project?"

I hadn't even thought of that. How naïve could I be? My mother had arranged for a stipend for me, but I didn't even think about paying Bentley.

"It would be prestigious. You could be the next George Plimpton," I offered. I had been poring over the *Paris Review* in an attempt to understand what the *Euphemia Review* should be like. At the time, Mr. Plimpton was very much alive, well respected, and invited everywhere, whether it had to do with film, theater, or literature. You could do far worse than becoming George Plimpton.

"Ha. You don't know that, Miss Fortune," he said.

"Call me Jane, please," I said.

"Yes." He gave a thoughtful nod and bit his bottom lip. He considered me. "Would you like to hear the story of my life?"

"Not really."

"No?" He stared at me as if he found my answer unbelievable. Then he laughed. "But I've had an interesting life."

"Still," I said, "it's not really relevant to me, is it?"

"Relevant? What's that got to do with anything? How do you know you want to work with me if you don't know anything about me? Bartender, another scotch, please."

"I don't know if I want to work with you," I said. I turned to the bartender. "Could I have a glass of water, please? And a cup of coffee?"

"Coming right up." When the bartender smiled at me his braces sparkled.

Bentley, despite the fact that I told him I wasn't interested, relayed a story about his work as a traveling Bible salesman in West Virginia. It was a cheap, shoddy, bawdy story, and certainly a fabrication. When he was finished he turned to me.

"So do you believe it?" he asked.

"Not really," I said.

"Does literal truth matter?"

"If you just told me a lie about yourself, then I don't know any more about you than I did before."

He smiled a subtle smile and lowered his eyes.

"Maybe you know more," he said. He looked up. "Jane," he said, "do me a favor, will you?"

"Okay." There was doubt in my voice.

"Try not to be so literal."

I still don't know if Bentley was ever a Bible salesman, or if he ever slept with a woman who told him stories in a room festooned with paper roses, but I came to believe that he was right. Literal truth doesn't always matter. What he told me became a part of his history because, somewhere inside, he was able to make me believe it on a level that didn't have anything to do with intellect. I didn't want to believe it, but he painted it so vividly that it was now a part of him, and whether that West Virginia woman could walk right up to us and lay a sloppy kiss on Bentley's cheek didn't matter a bit. It was Bentley who convinced me that how we remember things is more important than how they actually happened.

"Memory is long," he said, "and the present is only a moment and the future does not exist. So it's what we carry with us into the present that's important."

Bentley had been resting one of his arms on a green paper place mat. When he picked up his drink, he noticed that the ink from the place mat had stained his white cuffs. His shirt had been the only noncrumpled thing about him, but now his cuffs were stained green.

"Goddammit," he said.

I turned the place mat over so that only the white side showed. He looked at me and nodded.

"You're a very practical girl, I see," he said. I cringed. I had been praised for my common sense too often for me to enjoy it as a compliment. Besides, I don't think Bentley meant it as a compliment, and being a compliment was all that redeemed it.

"Whatever stories we choose," I explained, "will be published in the *Euphemia Review*. The best one will win the author a place to work for ninety days—and a stipend."

"Terrible name. The *Euphemia Review*. Where did you come up with that?"

"Euphemia was my great-grandmother's name and it's nonnegotiable."

Poor Euphemia. I could do this much for her. Even if she had created her trust in an effort to vanquish Isabella, Euphemia still deserved some glory. So what if her efforts had not been terribly successful, nor her motives exactly pure.

"It's quite an undertaking," Bentley said when I explained the whole project to him.

"But will you help me?" I asked.

"I'd still like to know what I get out of it," Bentley said.

Most of the people I had grown up with had plenty of time to volunteer for things. They'd think it inelegant to ask for compensation. I sipped my martini and wondered why I was trying to finish something I found so odious.

Bentley looked up when the door opened and a shadow stood in the door.

"Hey, Finn," Bentley called out, "I have a bone to pick with you."

"Ah, fuck off," the man said.

Bentley turned to me. "Protect your virgin ears."

"My ears are not virgins," I said.

"Finn, your goddamned place mats stained my new Brooks Brothers shirt."

"What do you want me to do about it?" Finn asked. He walked behind the bar, took a box of place mats, and deposited them in the trash. "Satisfied?"

"You could pay my cleaning bill," Bentley said.

"Fuck off," Finn said.

"There's a lady present," Bentley said.

"Fuck off."

Bentley turned to me.

"So, Miss Fortune, what do I get?"

I maneuvered myself off the barstool. I had chosen the wrong man, not that I had so many choices. Still, I could find someone else. Boston was full of colleges and universities, full of writers of Bentley's limited success.

"I suppose I could come up with an honorarium," I said. I stood straight as a lamppost and held my Kelly bag in a knotted fist.

"I've upset you," he said.

"I just have places to be."

"I take it you don't spend most of your afternoons drinking in bars."

"I do not," I said. I was so prim. Looking back, I am surprised he could tolerate me.

"Sit back down. I never said I wouldn't do it."

"I'm not sure I want you to do it," I said, but I hoisted myself back onto the barstool.

"That's it, Jane. Get in touch with your inner fire. If you could do that, you might be writing yourself."

"Not everyone has to be some kind of artist. I am a sensible person who knows what I am trying to do here. I didn't come here to be psychoanalyzed or second-guessed." I felt a film of sweat on my forehead.

"But shouldn't we all take the risk to find out if we have what it takes to be a real artist?"

"No," I said, and took a large sip from my glass.

"If, like me, you eventually find out that you're not the artist you thought you were, you can play disappointed genius like I do. I've made that into its own art form." He finished the rest of his scotch.

"You can make feeling sorry for yourself into an art form if you want to, but I think you're a coward."

It was unlike me to be so confrontational, especially with a relative stranger, and someone so much older than I was.

He looked down at the bar, examined his stained shirt cuffs, then looked up at me.

"I always wanted to be George Plimpton," he said.

I paid for the drinks. We slipped from our stools and walked out of the dark bar and into the dimming light of a late April afternoon. Bentley shook hands with me, and with that handshake, Evan Bentley and I became the team that would discover some of the best writers of the next decade.

Before I turned toward the trolley, he asked, "Did I tell you how pretty you are, Jane?"

"You mentioned it."

"Well, you are," he said. "You are very pretty, Miss Fortune."

Finn's hadn't changed much in fifteen years. Its busiest nights were when the Red Sox played. This was not one of those nights and the place was empty.

Bentley and I arrived at the same time. We walked in and sat at a table.

"Hey, Finn," Bentley called.

"Fuck you," Finn said.

We ordered two steaks. The only thing missing from Finn's was Mary. Fifteen years ago, she was seventy-two, so she had retired or died—or both. It took two waitresses to fill Mary's shoes.

I passed "Boston Tech" over to Bentley. He and I had gotten into the habit of meeting whenever we had something important to discuss, even though most of our business could be done by mail, e-mail, or over the phone. We called each other the Luddites, because any time we could do something the old-fashioned way, we did. Bentley still wrote his novels (his writer's block had finally ended) with a favorite fountain pen on expensive Italian paper.

I had bought Bentley countless drinks and meals on the foundation. Then, five years ago, Bentley stopped drinking. I didn't begrudge him one meal or even a drink. His company, when he wasn't plastered, was well worth the time and money I'd spent on him. And tonight I was happy to spring for a New York sirloin if Bentley would read "Boston Tech" before he ate his salad.

"Read it now," I said.

"Right here?"

"Yes. I'll just sit here."

"And stare at me?"

"Not that I don't find you fascinating, but I'll do some work." I pulled a sheaf of stories out of my bag.

I snatched glimpses of Bentley as he read, but he didn't notice me. He was absorbed. He was always absorbed when he read.

When he looked up, he immediately ordered a cup of coffee.

"You liked it?" I asked. Bentley's taste had always been important to me. Even though I trusted myself more than when we began, I still needed to know what he thought just to be sure. Our food had come and it sat uneaten in front of us. Bentley put down the story and picked up his knife and fork.

"It's okay," he said.

"Just okay?" Was I going insane? Had I lost my judgment? Did I want to discover a new writer so badly that I couldn't see straight?

"It's better than okay," Bentley said, and smiled crookedly. He finished his salad and started in on his steak. I stared at him. "Call him." He smiled.

"Bastard," I said.

He continued to chew without paying much attention to me.

"You think I have to read the rest of the stories?" I asked.

"That's up to you, Jane. I'm not your father or your guru. You're almost forty years old."

"I'm only thirty-eight."

He shrugged and took another bite of his steak. His bites were huge and he chewed each piece for a long time.

"You know what it reminds me of," he said. I knew. I took a bite of my own steak. "It reminds me of that first time, the time with Max Wellman. I mean, we've seen other good stories since, but this is better than most. You know, when I read Max's story all those years ago—'Hook, Line, and Stinker'—I was so envious, I could have spit."

I swallowed.

"What about this one?" I asked.

"I'd like to find this Jack Reilly and beat the hell out of him."

"Excellent," I said.

$\mathscr{C}$ h a p t e r 7

$\mathscr{L}$ynn, $\mathscr{L}$ynn, the city of sin

I sat up most of the night reading the rest of the stories. By morning I was sure that I could call Jack Reilly and tell him that he'd won this year's fellowship.

I waited until I got into the office. Tad wasn't there. He had an early class. I took a sip of my coffee and picked up the phone. This was my favorite part of running the foundation. I loved calling people with good news. I dialed the number on the last page of the story only to receive the message that the number had been disconnected. No forwarding number was given. I held the phone to my ear and listened to the electronic message over and over again.

I knew I was more disappointed than I should have been. It was only a story, but I couldn't lose Jack Reilly, not after he'd entered my fantasy life, which at the time was none too rich. The rational thing to do would have been to go to the next story, but I wasn't interested in the next best.

Maybe this time, with the discovery of Jack, I'd even let myself be interviewed. The two of us would be interviewed together from the house where he would be working, the house with a view of the ocean and the bay. Maybe Max Wellman would be flipping through *Poets & Writers* and read about us. Even though I hadn't seen Max in years, I'm ashamed to say that sometimes I compared my life with his. And when I did, it left me feeling even more stunted than usual.

I had to find Jack Reilly. Maybe he was my second chance. For all I knew, he was twenty years old, gay, or married. Still, when my imagination took hold of something, it wasn't likely to let go until the fantasy had played itself out.

Tad came in while I was still staring at the phone.

"Jane?"

"His phone's been disconnected," I said.

"Whose?"

"Jack Reilly's."

"On to the next."

"I don't want the next person. I want Jack Reilly."

"Jane, you look feverish."

"I'm going to find him. You want to come?"

"Cool—an adventure." He grabbed his jacket.

My car was garaged at a place on Beacon Hill, about three blocks from our house. I didn't use the car often. There wasn't much need for it in Boston and parking was always a problem. Our house didn't have much garage space. When it was built, cars weren't an issue.

I took the story and put it in my bag. I was now seeing everything through the eyes of Jack Reilly, a man I didn't even know. The bag looked dingy.

"I'm going to have to change my clothes," I said. I was wearing one of my usual outfits, black wool pants, a gray turtleneck, and black sneakers. It wasn't that I had no fashion sense exactly, it was just that I didn't care.

I remembered once going into the old Ritz with Priscilla before it was renovated. We had tea and I noticed that the arms of the chairs in the lounge were worn. The furniture was good and expensive, but shabby.

"Old Bostonians like that," Priscilla had said. "It makes them feel comfortable. The Ritz has a tattered grace."

I was like the old Ritz. I had a tattered grace. I was indifferent to what was modern and fashionable. I liked fine things, but I was happy to keep them until they crumbled in my hands.

"We can shop on the way," Tad said.

"I can go home and take something out of my closet."

"No you can't," he said. "Let's shop on the way. We'll take a cab to Newbury Street and walk from there."

"You don't think I have anything appropriate?"

"Jane, I've known you for six months and I've never seen you wear something that would be appropriate for anything other than a funeral."

What I was wearing was not appropriate for a funeral. I'd never wear trousers to a funeral. I was embarrassed to think that I was so somberly and carelessly dressed that a young man would notice it. Still, I figured he was doing me a favor. We stopped at Alan Bilzerian's, a boutique on Newbury Street, where I picked up a forest green suit with a crisp white shirt. In the back of the store there was an array of expensive shoes and bags. I checked over the shoes and chose a brown pair of flats that were made in Italy. The price of the shoes could have been used to take a chunk out of the national debt, but I bought them anyway. I had the money because I rarely spent any. My own trust had barely been used and I had never touched the principal. I also got a stipend from the foundation, enough to support the average schoolteacher. I lived at home and had few expenses, so I could splurge occasionally.

Since I don't like to shop, my excursions are over quickly. We were out of there in half an hour. I wore the suit out of the store and carried the clothes I'd been wearing in the Bilzerian bag.

"Major improvement," Tad said.

I looked down at the green suit.

"Feels good," I said.

"Still pretty conservative," Tad said.

"It's simple and elegant."

We picked up my car from the garage. I had the Mercedes 460SL that had belonged to my mother. It was ages old and Miranda hadn't wanted it for that reason, but I liked it. The car was barely used and still reliable.

Tad was impressed by the car. "This is awesome," he said. There was that word again—awesome. Yes, it was a lovely car, but *awesome?*

We drove north toward Lynn. Tad navigated. I knew how to get to Lynn, but we needed a map to find the exact address. Lynn is a run-down city that is always preparing for a renaissance that never arrives. We followed the map to 61 Kennedy Ave. I found a parking spot on the street. Tad looked around when we got out.

"You want me to stay and watch the car?" he asked.

"It'll be okay," I said. I was none too sure about that, but I was willing to risk it. In minutes, we'd be ringing the doorbell and Jack Reilly would come to the door. He might slouch a little, have heavy brows, and a sexy smile. He'd be thrilled when I told him he'd won the fellowship, just as every winner had been thrilled. He'd be grateful and an instant connection would be made.

Jack Reilly's apartment was on the third floor. Tad and I walked up the stairs. Someone had clipped their toenails onto the carpet and the hall smelled like fried fish.

We reached the door and I rang the bell. Nothing. We looked at each other and waited. Tad hit the bell again. There was movement inside.

The door was opened by a woman. She had one sponge curler in her hair and an unlit cigarette dangling from between her lips. She was thin and wore gray sweatpants and a pink T-shirt with no bra underneath. Tad stared at her as if he'd never seen a woman before.

"Yes?" she asked.

"We're looking for Jack Reilly," I said.

"You the police?"

"No." In my suit, I guess I might have been mistaken for a very well-dressed detective, but Tad was every inch the college kid. "Jack Reilly has won an award," I said.

"Are you Publishers Clearing House? Where's Ed McMahon?" She poked her head into the hallway and looked around.

"I am Jane Fortune of the Fortune Family Foundation. Jack applied for our fellowship."

"Fellowship?"

"Isn't he a writer?" I was beginning to think something was terribly wrong. Maybe we had the wrong address.

"I guess you could say that. He scribbles. Won't even get a decent job." The woman's voice was nasal, not too different from my sister Miranda's.

"Is he here?" I asked.

"He took off. I don't know where he is," she said.

"Do you have his phone number?"

"I doubt he even has a phone. I had to beg him to get his own phone when he lived here. He likes to live off the grid."

"Off the grid?"

"No phone, no address. He wouldn't want the IRS to be able to find him, not after all the years he's forgotten to pay his taxes." She hadn't invited us in and it didn't look like she was going to.

"Isn't there any way we can reach him?" I asked.

"I think I have his sister's address around here somewhere," she said. "But how do I know you are who you say you are?"

"You don't, really," I said. "I do have a card somewhere, but that doesn't mean much." I dug into my bag—the old canvas one—and fished a card out of my wallet. I handed it over.

She shrugged. "You know, I don't even know why I asked. I guess it just seemed like the right thing to do, not that Jack would ever do the right thing. To tell you the truth, I wouldn't care if you were the Mafia. If you find him, can you remind him that he owes me two hundred bucks? I'll go find the address. I'll be right back." She retreated into the apartment, leaving the door open a crack.

Tad looked at me. "That's that, then," he said.

"What do you mean?"

"We looked for him. We can't find him. He seems like a loser anyway," he said.

"We don't know that," I said. "Look at her. She isn't exactly an arbiter of good taste. For all we know, he could just be some kind of iconoclast, which would be appropriate for a really great artist."

"I thought you didn't believe that artists had a license to misbehave. That's what you always say."

"Well, that's true." He was making me a little uncertain. I did have a long-held belief that the true artist spent more time on his art than on creating an artistic persona.

"He owes her two hundred and fifty dollars," Tad said.

"Two hundred," I said.

"Two hundred, then. He still sounds like a loser."

"She probably doesn't understand him," I said.

Tad looked at me as if I'd gone mad.

"You sound like *the other woman*," Tad said.

He was right. I had all the symptoms of infatuation for a man I hadn't even met. Maybe you become susceptible to that sort of thing when you've been alone too long.

The woman came back with a slip of paper that had been ripped from a notepad. She was also carrying a spiral notebook and two books, *Jitterbug Perfume* and *Duet for One*. "This is his sister's address. She lives in Vermont. I'm sorry, but I don't even know her name. I know it isn't Reilly."

I took the paper and pulled out my wallet. I slipped the paper in and took out a hundred-dollar bill. "Here," I said. "Some money came with the fellowship. Here's a down payment on his debt."

"Thanks," she said. She smiled. "That's white of you. Look," she said, "if you find him, can you give him these?" She handed over the notebook and the books. "He left them here and frankly you have a better chance of seeing him than I do. I hate when men abandon stuff after they leave. So if you take it—whatever you do with it—it would be a favor to me."

I slipped the things into my bag. Of course I'd find Jack Reilly. I might as well take them.

We walked back down the hall, then down the fish-stinking stairwell and out onto the street. The car was still there, and untouched.

"That's that, then," Tad said after we got inside.

"Why do you keep saying that?"

"There's no point in looking for him. I don't know why you took that stuff. I think we should just dump it right here into the sewer."

"I disagree," I said.

Tad frowned. "Come on. Let's get out of here," he said.

I pulled from the curb and we drove away from *Lynn, Lynn, the city of sin—you never come out the way you went in.*

Chapter 8

In which the finer points are discussed

We reconvened Tuesday evening to discuss the finer points of our financial collapse.

After dinner we went into the sitting room. I sat on the brocade sofa in one of what Priscilla called the "conversation areas." I didn't want to take a seat in the corner. My days of sitting in the corner like a china figurine were over—at least for the moment.

Littleton perched on a Chippendale chair near me. Miranda sat on a settee. Dolores had stayed at home for once. I glanced at Pris, who was knitting with a fluffy green wool. Teddy was slumped in a wingback chair by the fireplace. He sat just apart from our little group, as if he couldn't bear to join us.

"You'll have to cut out the Christmas party," Littleton said.

"You've got to be kidding," Miranda said. Miranda was a renowned Boston party-giver. People jockeyed all year to get onto her Christmas party list. She had three-by-five cards on her dressing table with people's names on them and she moved them from one pile to another depending on how well disposed she was toward the person on that particular day.

Though I wasn't much of a party person, even I enjoyed Miranda's Christmas parties. They were always done in a Roaring Twenties style with a big band and costumes. I liked watching the couples pull up to the valet in their fancy cars. They'd rush into the cold, the women hobbling toward the house in spiked heels, the men secure in their spats, and arrive at the door all flushed and smiling, blowing the frosty air like smoke.

Miranda loved to pull the strings of Boston society. She got invited to all the best parties because people hoped that their invitations would be returned. It was as if after my mother died, Miranda and I split her traits down the middle. Miranda got everything that was outgoing and social and I got all that was thoughtful and sedentary. Miranda flourished and became, in her way, a social luminary. *Town & Country* did a story on her. When Miranda and Teddy went out together, their pictures often appeared in the society pages of the *Boston Globe*.

"To be honest, you can barely afford to run this house, and if you are to continue to do it, you'll have to make some major changes. Perhaps you could take in boarders," Littleton said.

Priscilla's head snapped up. I tried to picture myself as the proprietor of the Fortune Family Bed & Breakfast. We would introduce our guests to the moneyed class of the twenty-first century, the diminishing, foolish, useless moneyed class that didn't even have the sense to hang on to what they had been given.

But, of course, the city would never allow it, nor would our neighbors, nor would our sense of propriety.

"Take in boarders?" Miranda whined. "What can you be thinking, Littleton?"

Littleton was perspiring into the collar of his shirt. He took out a linen handkerchief and wiped it across his neck.

"I don't understand how this happened."

This came from Miranda, whose collection of designer shoes and handbags filled an entire walk-in closet on the second floor. Teddy had some expensive habits also. He collected wines, cigars, antique watches, and first editions of Hemingway and Fitzgerald. He didn't read the books; he just collected them. But all these things were minor indulgences for us. What had really happened was that for two generations we lived extravagantly and made no money. The family had dipped into the principal of its many trusts little by little until they were dangerously depleted.

My father also made some bad investments. He would read something in the paper, get an idea, and call his "broker."

"Couldn't we remortgage the house?" Teddy asked.

"You have two mortgages already," Littleton said.

"We do?" I asked. I thought our house, which my father inherited free and clear, had remained that way.

"Even if you got another mortgage, how would you pay it back?" Priscilla asked. "You could pay it back when you sold the house, I suppose, but are you really planning to sell the Fortune family home?" She continued to knit without looking at her work. She was staring at Teddy. He stroked the arms of his chair as if it were a friend from whom he would soon be parting.

"What choice do we have?" he asked. He was haggard and I had never seen him look that way, except during the few months after my mother died.

I couldn't believe that Teddy would think of selling the house. It had been Euphemia's house. It was a house that gave him status, that defined us as a family. It was the best of what we had.

"You could rent it out," Littleton said.

"Over time, you could rebuild your capital," Priscilla added.

"What would people think?" Teddy asked. He rested his elbows on his knees and his chin on the top of his folded hands.

"No one would have to know that it wasn't your choice. You could make it seem like it was your idea. After all, your girls are grown and this is such a big house. And there's the place on the Vineyard. You could sell that," Littleton said.

"But, Littleton, they always rent the Vineyard house out in the winter," Priscilla said. "It pays for itself. I think they can only gain by keeping the Vineyard house. Besides, they'll need somewhere to live in the summer," Priscilla said.

"What about the charitable trust?" Miranda asked.

"What about it," Priscilla said.

"I don't see how we can keep giving charity when we don't have any money of our own. Can't we break the trust?"

"No, dear." Priscilla bit at the inside of her cheek. "There is no provision in the trust that says 'If my progeny should be such spendthrifts that they run through all the family money in one generation, you can break the charitable trust.'"

"You don't have to be nasty about it. It was just a question," Miranda said. "Still, I don't understand why it isn't possible." She raised her head and stuck out her chin in a combative way.

I shifted in my seat. If the trust were breakable, what would that mean for the work I did? Would we just shut down our office in Kenmore Square and cease to be? Now that we were a known entity, maybe I could raise money. But I had never raised money for anything before, not even for a cup of coffee. Money had never been a problem. The foundation was well endowed and I had used the money carefully, making sure—with the help of the bankers—to continuously grow the capital.

Littleton broke in. "Priscilla's right," he said. "There is no provision for breaking the trust. I checked. Besides, your family name is associated with it. You've done some good in the community through it. You wouldn't want to jeopardize that."

He acted as if the Fortune Family Foundation did the work all by itself, as if the money jumped up and spread itself all over Boston. But there was someone behind it, making the choices and writing the checks, and that someone was me. I couldn't lose the foundation. I had taken it from near obscurity to a position of respect among the other great foundations for the arts.

Miranda stood up. It looked like she was ready to have the kind of tantrum she so often had as a child, but before she could do anything other than stamp a foot, she sat back down. Tantrums don't look good on anyone, and even she knew that they looked ridiculous on a woman who was almost forty.

"No Christmas party. I won't be able to show my face," she said.

"It will be easier if your face isn't here," Pris said.

"What do you mean?"

"Littleton and I think that the best place for the family this winter is Palm Beach. You can get a lovely apartment there with the money you get for renting this house and you'll still have plenty left over."

"The Fortunes are wintering in Palm Beach," Teddy said. "I don't mind the sound of that."

Miranda walked over to the window, tied back the drapes, and gazed out. "No Christmas party." She released a theatrical sigh.

"There are worse things than wintering in Palm Beach," Priscilla said.

I, for one, couldn't think of any. I hated the bright yellows, greens, and pinks of country-club chic. I couldn't see myself walking the streets among the tanned and the leathered. I wasn't big on drinks with little umbrellas in them. And though I could probably run the foundation from anywhere, it helped if I showed up at the office occasionally.

"If we went away for the winter," Teddy said, "no one would have to know the truth." He stood up and looked stronger, less disheartened.

"We could blame it on your health," Miranda said.

"There's nothing wrong with my health."

"I think we should tell people what's easiest for them to hear," Miranda said.

"It might be easier for you to have people think I've lost my health, but it would hardly be easier for me." Teddy was proud of the fitness he achieved at the Boston Athletic Club. Being known for his youthfulness and robust constitution was not one of the things he was willing to sacrifice to maintain any other part of his reputation. The evening wasn't bringing out the best in either Teddy or Miranda. They were usually willing to sacrifice me to any cause, but when they started to sacrifice each other, the situation was grim.

Maybe no one would care that the Fortunes had fallen upon hard times. Perhaps we were foolishly guarding a reputation that wasn't worth a thing to anyone but ourselves.

The meeting was over. Our lives were going to change. What else was there to say?

"Come on, old lady, walk me home," Priscilla said. Her voice had the calm intimacy I had learned to associate with what was maternal in my life. Priscilla had always been there to pull me through the difficult times. Without her, I don't know what I would have done after my mother died.

Priscilla and I walked outside. I was grateful to be in the crisp air. It was sweater weather, and even though we were still in daylight saving time, it was getting dark much earlier. That, to me, always signaled the end of summer.

"They've asked me to come and speak to some of the girls at Wellesley," I told Priscilla.

"Why?" There was an inherent insult in that question—the assumption that I had nothing to offer—but at the time I let it pass.

"To the girls who want to be writers," I said.

"That's nice." She seemed distracted.

"I'm afraid of public speaking."

"You can't be afraid all your life," Pris said.

"Do you think I'm a very fearful person?" I asked.

"I would never call you a risk taker, but then none of you girls is. Your mother wasn't much of one either. That's why she married your father. It was the safe thing to do."

I left Priscilla at her door and walked home. The first fires were being lit in fireplaces and the city was beginning to smell like autumn.

Chapter 9

Eight bedrooms, fully furnished

It isn't easy to find someone to rent a house as big as ours, a situation made more difficult by my father's refusal to have the rental formally put on the market. He wanted to be discreet. To Littleton's credit, he was able to find a tenant even with these limitations.

We were seeing a lot more of Littleton lately. He had shown up several Sundays in a row and he always brought Dolores with him. In between Sundays, Miranda and Dolores went shopping together, even though most of Miranda's credit cards had been shredded in a depressing ceremony at the dining room table. Priscilla had been in charge of cutting up the credit cards. She sent Miranda to get her pocketbook and my unsuspecting sister retrieved it with alacrity, as if Priscilla were about to replace Miranda's current Prada bag with a new one from Gucci. When Miranda returned, Priscilla asked her to drop her credit cards onto the table. Priscilla took out long scissors with an orange handle.

"These are very good scissors," Priscilla said. "They cut right through plastic."

When Miranda realized what was about to happen, she tried to rescue some of the cards, but Priscilla held her lips tightly together and shook her head. In the end many cards were victims of the massacre: Brooks Brothers, Talbots, Victoria's Secret, Louis, three MasterCards, two Visas, Bloomingdale's, Saks, and Neiman Marcus. They littered the table like hard-edged confetti. Miranda was gray. She went up to bed and stayed there for three days.

Finally, in an effort to distract her, Dolores dragged Miranda out to a nightclub where they could look for eligible men, but Miranda preferred the parties of people she knew and she usually attended them alone or with Teddy.

We were drinking coffee in the sitting room three weeks after the initial announcement when Littleton said that he'd found potential tenants.

I had been distracting myself from our change in circumstance by spending the last three weeks absorbed in a less-than-fruitful search for Jack Reilly. Jack Reilly was such a common name, especially in the Boston area, and I was having no luck. I put Tad on the job, too, but neither of us could come up with anything. We didn't even know if Jack was his real name. It could be John. There were plenty of Johns who called themselves Jack.

I couldn't picture myself driving up to Vermont on the off chance of finding Jack Reilly. It seemed like a ridiculous thing to do, and though I knew I should give up on "Boston Tech" and Jack Reilly's potential as a protégé—and who knew what else—he was stuck like gum to my shoe.

Littleton rested his coffee on one knee. The cup looked precarious there. Unlike Priscilla, Littleton did not look comfortable with fine china. I wanted to grab the cup and place it on the tea table where it belonged, but I could hardly lunge at Littleton, so I remained where I was. I had retreated to my usual seat by the window. It seemed clear to me now that whatever happened would do so without any input from me.

Astrid came in with more coffee. She placed it on the low inlaid table in front of me and I smiled up at her. She smiled back and disappeared into the kitchen. I checked the grandfather clock. She should be leaving soon for her afternoon off.

"I hope whoever takes this house has a touch of class," Miranda said.

"I imagine that whoever can afford this house has, at least, a touch of good sense," I said.

Everyone looked at me. It was like watching a painting move. Littleton with his coffee cup balanced on his knee, Teddy in the Windsor chair, Priscilla beside him, Miranda lounging on an Empire-style couch, and Dolores on the ottoman nearby.

"Coffee?" I asked. This was the perfect opportunity to rescue Littleton's cup and saucer. I picked it up with a smile, poured coffee into it, and placed it on the table beside him.

"I'm off coffee this week," Miranda said. I turned from her and poured for the rest of the party.

"I've made some discreet inquiries," Littleton said, "and I have found a producer."

"A what?" Teddy asked. He laced his fingers together and cracked his knuckles. Priscilla looked up.

"A Hollywood producer. Movies, you know. A man and his wife. She grew up in the Boston area and now she wants to come back. I don't know for how long, but they're looking for a furnished place."

"Our furniture?" Miranda asked.

"It would really cost too much to store and insure it, though I'm sure the Museum of Fine Arts would be happy to take a few pieces on loan. There's that Thomas Seymour breakfront."

"I didn't know you knew about furniture, Littleton," Priscilla said.

"It's important to know a little bit about everything," he said. He looked flattered, but I didn't think Priscilla meant to flatter him. He picked up his cup from the table, took a sip, and placed it again on his leg. I could barely stand it.

"Hollywood people," Teddy said. "It's a sure way for obscure people to gain undue distinction. Would I have heard of these people?"

"Joseph Goldman. One of his most famous movies was based on his brother-in-law's book, *Duet for One*."

"I saw that movie," Teddy said. "It wasn't bad. I never read the book. Who wrote it?" If my family could have gotten away with it, they might have remained illiterate.

Priscilla, however, was not so inclined. She had read *Duet for One* and she knew that it was written by Max Wellman. She looked over at me.

I twisted the edge of my cotton jersey until it was wrapped around my finger.

"Max Wellman," I said.

"What? Name sounds familiar," Teddy said. "Don't I know the name for some other reason?"

Priscilla looked over at him. "He was the one," she said, and slid her eyes toward me.

"The one?" Teddy asked.

"You know. The one," Pris said with tight lips.

"Oh, that boy," Teddy said.

I wondered how much he really remembered. He looked over at Dolores and must have decided that it would be indiscreet to say more.

"I hope this producer is not a little balding man with a cigar—someone who will stink up the drapes and the furniture," Miranda said.

"I don't think he smokes," Littleton said. "And they don't have children and you know how children can wreak havoc on furniture. This is really a lucky break. They seem like fine, quiet people."

"That's a new one," Dolores said. "Fine, quiet people from Hollywood."

Littleton shot her a look so incendiary I was afraid she might spontaneously combust and scorch the sofa.

"I'm sure they'll show great appreciation for this house." Dolores tried to save herself.

I doubted she knew as much about "Hollywood people" as she claimed.

"Goldman. That's Jewish, isn't it?" Teddy asked.

"I believe so," Littleton said.

"Well, you can't have everything."

My father didn't have any Jewish friends. You'd think that in this day and age or even fifteen years ago, it wouldn't have mattered—the fact that I was Protestant and Max was Jewish—but it had.

When Max's nana heard about us, she sent him a nasty letter from her condominium in Boca Raton. She didn't want him to run off with a shiksa.

"What's a shiksa?" I asked Max.

"A girl who isn't Jewish."

"Oh," I said. I was surprised there was even a special word for it. It had never occurred to me that anyone could be prejudiced against me. After all, I was a descendant of the Founding Fathers.

"And what about you?" I asked.

"Me, what?" Max sat on the sofa with his legs crossed and lifted a beer to his lips.

"Do you care that I'm not Jewish?"

"Lots of women convert." He said this as easily as he might have said "Lots of women register at Bloomingdale's."

"You never asked me if I would," I said. The whole issue was premature, anyway. We weren't talking about marriage, were we? He had asked me to go to California with him, not to marry him.

It was at this moment that the hot-air balloon in which two new lovers travel hit the ground. It landed gently, not with a thud or a crash, but it landed all the same. Reality was growing through the floorboards like ragweed. Max put his beer bottle down on the wooden table beside him. I slipped a coaster under it. The house was rented. It wasn't our table and the people who owned it wouldn't want to find rings when they came back. It wasn't that Max was careless; it was just that he was more casual than I was, but then I couldn't blame him for that. Almost everyone was more casual than I was.

"How about the rest of your family?" I asked.

"They think we should think about it."

"Maybe we should."

"I don't want to wait," he said. He pulled me toward him and nuzzled my neck.

I didn't want to wait either, but Priscilla managed to convince me that if I ran off with Max, I would ruin both my life and his. I should not impede the progress of a man who could be one of the best writers of a generation. Now, I looked across at Priscilla, who was still knitting.

Miranda said, "You have to admit that glamour emanates from the West."

"I have to admit nothing of the sort," Priscilla said. "Removing the smallest line from your face before it even gains the respectability of a wrinkle is hardly a move forward in civilization."

"Don't knock it, Priscilla, until you've tried it." Teddy smiled.

I hadn't known his vanity extended that far.

"There are more important things than glamour," Pris said.

"Like good taste and good breeding," said Teddy.

"And good values," I said from my place in the corner.

"Did you say something, Jane?" Teddy asked.

"Please. We all know what Miss Holier-Than-Thou thinks," Miranda said.

Priscilla stopped knitting, and I thought, for a moment, that she might stab Miranda in the thigh with a needle.

I excused myself and went into the kitchen.

"You hear that?" I asked Astrid.

"She's a bitch. She's always been a bitch. And your father. He should stand up for you, but no."

I shook my head. "What are you going to do, Astrid? They think you'll go to Florida with them."

"Are you going, Jane?" she asked.

"I don't know. I don't think so."

"Don't go. This is your chance to start your own life." She wiped her hands on her apron and sat across from me at the kitchen island.

"I'm not going," she said. "I have plans." She stood up and walked to the window. "This is a lovely house," she said.

"I know."

"Still, it's only a house. I moved to a different country for a better life. You can move from this house."

"It doesn't look like I have a choice."

"Sometimes that's the best way," she said.

"What are you going to do?" I asked.

"My brother's coming from Brazil and we're going to open a restaurant."

I could see her in her own restaurant, with her music playing, coming to the front to greet the patrons, still in her apron and with a wooden spoon holding up her hair. It was the right setting for her. I had to find the right setting for me. Unfortunately, I had always thought that this was it.

I entered the living room just in time to hear Miranda say, "Okay, then. I guess it's all set. We're off to Palm Beach."

I had to say one thing for Miranda. She might be snippy and she might be rude, but she was suffering this calamity with a good deal more equanimity than I was. The idea of living in an apartment in Palm Beach with Teddy and Miranda was about as appealing to me as a luxury trip to war-torn Afghanistan.

"And I think Dolores should come with us," Miranda said.

"Oh, Miranda, that's too nice of you. I just couldn't impose."

"Of course you could."

Dolores looked up at her father and he smiled back at her in a distracted way. Priscilla stopped knitting and stared at Dolores, then looked at me.

"Daddy, Dolores has to come," Miranda said.

"Certainly, if she wants to." He gave Dolores a benign smile, but the smile Dolores turned on him was anything but benign. Her smile was both ingratiating and insinuating. It was obvious that, despite her Hollywood experience, Dolores was a better actress than anyone gave her credit for.

Chapter 10

Escaping the Goldmans

The day the Goldmans came to see the house, Priscilla and I went to a lecture on Elizabeth Barrett Browning at the Boston Public Library. On any other day I might have been perfectly happy to listen to a bespectacled academic, but on that Saturday morning I couldn't get the Goldmans out of my mind. If they took the house, it was inevitable that soon Max would be standing in the same spot where I had stood just that morning, gazing out of the same window.

By the time the question-and-answer period began, I felt sick.

I looked over at Priscilla. Her attention was concentrated on the librarian type at the podium, as if there had never been a more riveting subject than Browning. The hall felt stuffy, even though the floor-to-ceiling windows were wide open. I was amazed at how many spinsters you could pack into one room. I had attended many lectures with Priscilla and was rarely restless, but after listening to the speaker drone on for over an hour, I had to escape. We were in the middle of a row (Pris always insisted on sitting in the center) so I had to "excuse me" past at least eight frumpy women who were annoyed at being disturbed. Priscilla looked at me with concern, but she didn't follow me out.

In the hall I went to the watercooler, leaned over, and took a long drink.

That summer fifteen years ago, Max and I had been sitting on the seawall in late August and the sun was setting all pink and orange over the Boston skyline. Max handed me a brown paper bag and in the bag was his manuscript. He was finished.

"I'm moving to California and I want you to go with me," he said.

I didn't even have to think about it. It was one of the only times I can remember that I immediately knew what I wanted.

The next morning I took the commuter boat to Boston so I could tell Priscilla. I'd tell my father later, but first I wanted to test the news on Priscilla. Teddy would follow her lead. I found Priscilla in her breakfast nook, nursing a cup of coffee and reading the *Boston Globe*.

"Hello, dear. You've been making yourself scarce. Pour yourself a coffee and sit down so we can have a chat," she said. That summer Priscilla had spent most of her time in Kennebunkport, presumably with some man, and she had just come back so there was no reason I would have seen her.

"How is everything? And why haven't I seen you more? Tell me about your experiment in literature."

I wasn't thrilled by her patronizing tone.

"It's going very well," I said. "The first recipient of the fellowship has finished his book." I tasted my coffee.

"I hope he can find a publisher. That would be a real feather in your cap," Priscilla said.

"And in his."

"It would be good for the foundation."

I paused, not knowing how to approach the subject of Max. I took another sip of coffee and blurted it out.

"Max has asked me to go to California with him," I said.

I wanted Priscilla to act as my mother's emissary, to take all she knew about my mother, put it in a blender, and come out with the essence of what my mother would have said.

"Don't be ridiculous. We don't even know this boy," Priscilla said.

"You can meet him," I said.

"I'm afraid you're escaping your grief," she said.

"You're wrong," I said. I had never told Priscilla she was wrong before, but this was the first time I felt manipulated, as if maybe she didn't have my best interests at heart. The feeling was so deep I could barely reach it, let alone recognize it.

"You'll ruin his career and your life," she said.

"What do you mean?"

"He'll have to spend his time figuring out how to support you both. It will leach his energy away from his writing and he'll resent you for it."

"But I have the trust fund. And I can work."

"The trust doesn't kick in until you're thirty and you've never worked. Besides, do you think any man wants to live off his significant other or partner or whatever you're going to call yourself—even today? You think he'll be proud of himself if his history reads that he married his patroness? Think about the word *patronize,* Jane. Patron and patronize are from the same root."

"He didn't ask me to marry him. He asked me to go to California."

"Worse. At least if he asked you to marry him, you'd have some respectable connection, such as it is. This way, he's free to drop you whenever he wants to. I'm only thinking of you. I'm standing in loco parentis, saying what I think your mother would have said."

"My mother wouldn't have tried to protect me from life."

"You're wrong. She tried to protect you from everything unpleasant in life. Even with her illness. She was sick long before she ever told you. She didn't want you to suffer. She never wanted you to suffer," Priscilla said.

"Well, it didn't work. I suffered all the same. People do, you know."

"I know what she would have wanted. I knew her best. You don't understand anything about men. You never have. I'd be more likely to trust Miranda with something like this." I didn't bring up Guy Callow, but then no one knew what really happened with him—and Miranda hadn't suffered much. "You and Max come from different backgrounds. He's just beginning on what is a very difficult career. Give him a chance. If the love is strong, a few years won't change it."

I didn't believe her. Romantic songs and books prattled on about eternal love, but I knew that if I didn't go with Max now, I'd lose him.

When I called Teddy, who was on the Vineyard, to tell him my news, he told me that he wouldn't give me any money (not that I had asked for any) and that, of course, I'd have to give up the foundation.

"The Fortune girls don't run off to California. Not on my watch," he said. "Besides, you won't like it. It's not your kind of place."

How would he know? He'd never even been there.

Priscilla came out of the lecture and saw me leaning with my forehead against the wall. She put her hand on my back.

"Buck up," she said. "The thing with that writer was so long ago. You really should have forgotten about it by now."

I lifted my head from the wall. Priscilla stood there with her solid stick figure encased in a tweed skirt. Perhaps any normal person would have forgotten, but it wasn't as if so much had happened to me since to make me forget.

"I wasn't thinking about Max," I said.

"I just thought that since we were escaping the house so we wouldn't have to see his sister, he might be on your mind."

"It was hot in there. That's all."

"The windows were wide open. I actually felt a chill."

"I was hot," I said.

"Whatever you say, dear." Priscilla peered over her half-glasses with a look so tolerant I felt like I'd shrunk to the size of the buckle on her shoe.

We walked home from the library and entered the house, where Miranda and my father were having drinks in the sitting room.

"You should have stayed, Jane," Miranda said. "They were really interesting people."

"Nothing like what you'd expect in *show people*," Teddy said. I think Teddy still thought in terms of vaudeville. He didn't equate "show person" with someone like Joseph Goldman, who ran a multimillion-dollar company.

"Emma looks like Lauren Bacall, and you really can't do better than Lauren Bacall," Miranda said.

"And he had presence," Teddy said. "He certainly wasn't what you'd call attractive. He was far too short for that. But he had what it took to command a room."

"So now it's just the brass tacks," Teddy said. His face was ruddy and he wouldn't have liked it if he'd known. The drink in his hand was obviously not his first.

My father, Miranda, Astrid, and Dolores all left on the same day.

Priscilla was furious that Miranda had chosen Dolores as a companion on this sojourn to Palm Beach. She thought Dolores was certainly not in the league of a Fortune, even a Fortune without money. Besides, she thought my claim on my family should be stronger than that of a stranger, and she was far more angry than I was to see me so easily discarded. True, I didn't want to go, but they might have acted, just for a minute, as if I'd be missed. I realized that I had been under the misconception that I performed some important function in my family. But now it looked like my role could easily be assumed by just about anyone.

A black Lincoln Town Car arrived to take Teddy, Miranda, and Dolores to the airport.

"That's the very least we can do," Miranda said. "We can march out of here with style."

"Well, goodbye, dear," Teddy said. He kissed me on the cheek and checked his watch. "Where is Dolores? She's late."

A taxi pulled up and Dolores toppled out. She was lugging an army surplus duffel over one shoulder. With the other hand she pulled a rolling suitcase. She also had a handbag and a carry-on piece. She juggled it all without much grace.

"Come on, then," Miranda called to her from the front steps. "We don't want to miss our plane. We should have ordered a limousine. The Town Car is going to be tight with the three of us," she complained.

"I could keep the cab and meet you at the airport," Dolores said. Miranda paused to consider this. She looked at Dolores and her haphazard luggage.

"Of course not. We'll all fit." Teddy signaled the driver, who took Dolores's bags and shifted them into the Lincoln, then came up the steps and gathered some of Miranda's luggage.

Miranda pecked me on both cheeks, European style, took her Louis Vuitton train case, and trotted out to the car. She was wearing high heels and a Chanel suit—no jeans and T-shirts for her. She would arrive in Florida with all the ostentation of a small-time celebrity.

My father took several bags, and between him and the driver, they eventually filled the car. The trunk wouldn't close, so instead of leaving the neighborhood with the desired aplomb, they looked slapdash and Beverly Hillbillyish. But it didn't matter. There was no one but me and Astrid to watch them go.

After they left, Astrid looked at me. There were tears in her eyes, but she was smiling.

She wrapped me in a strong hug. It made me uncomfortable. I wasn't used to hugging people and I never knew what to do with my hands. I always ended up patting the other person on the back awkwardly.

"You're the only one of them who is worth anything, Jane," she said, "and don't you ever forget it." She handed me a piece of paper with her new address on it. "I want to know how you are, and if you ever need a place to stay, you can always come to me."

Ironically, in the end, it was our maid who thought to offer me a place to stay, but I was going to my sister Winnie's for Thanksgiving. It was a command performance. Winnie's life as a wife and mother wasn't exactly what she had imagined it would be and she had difficulty keeping up with it. She often called to complain that she was sick and needed me "immediately or before."

Priscilla had already left for Canada, where she would spend the holidays with her sister.

I thanked Astrid, thanked her for everything. I could never thank her enough. I watched her walk away toward her friend's car. Several people had come during the past few days to help her move, and it made me wonder about her life outside of our house. It was obviously far more rich than I ever imagined. The end of the Fortune family establishment was the best thing that could have happened to her. She was on the threshold of a new life.

Alone in the house, I spent days wrapping up what Max would have called tchotchkes. The silver service, pewter bowls, snuffboxes, china figurines, the framed letter from President Martin Van Buren. I stored it all in the basement, where at least it would remain insured. I packed the rest of our personal things and moved them to a Public Storage facility on the side of the highway, one of those places with rows and rows of orange doors.

It made me smile to think how horrified Miranda and Teddy would be if they knew that some of their prized possessions would be "wintering" on the edge of Route 128.

Chapter 11

Miss Fortune: the perfect guest

I arrived at my sister Winnie's on a Saturday morning.

"I'm in here," Winnie called from the recesses of her family room. "The door's open." Winnie's voice was weak and complaining, but there was nothing unusual in that. She was out of her depth as a wife and mother and she made up a series of ailments to shield herself from both responsibility and criticism. Complaint had become a habit for Winnie and I think she enjoyed it. It's the prestige of the ill. People can't very well ignore you when you're sick, nor can they expect much from you. I had been humoring Winnie since the day she was born. She had been a fussy child: the first to cry on a long car trip, the first to throw a tantrum if she got bored, cold, or hot. She was just never comfortable, our Winnie.

Winnie was at the back of the house in a large window seat. She had an afghan pulled up to her chest. It was one of Priscilla's signature afghans, made from squares of expensive but leftover yarns. Winnie was staring out toward the enormous field that separated her house from the large farmhouse that belonged to her in-laws.

I went over to her, bent, and kissed her on the cheek. Her cheek was soft and powdery, lacking all resilience, and her smell always reminded me of my mother.

"What took you so long?" Winnie whined. "I thought you'd never come."

"I told you I'd be here today. And here I am."

"It's so dull around here and I've been feeling so sick. Charlie took the boys out and I haven't seen anyone all morning."

"Well, I'm here now," I said. "Can I get you some tea or something?"

"Thank you, Jane. You're a savior. I think if I get up, I'll just fall over, not that anyone cares about that."

On my way to the kitchen, I traversed the carpet, which was littered with toy trucks and action figures that had died on the battlefield.

"I know, it's a mess," Winnie said. She waved her hand toward the room. "It's just all so overwhelming and Jorie already left for Thanksgiving." Jorie was a student from Framingham State College who lived with them and helped out with the boys.

"Charlie's mother said she'd come over to see me," Winnie went on, "but she hasn't come anywhere near me. Typical." Winnie paused and twitched her nose. "Can you smell that? Can you?" Winnie opened the window and cool air rushed in. "It's that damned manure. I think they want to drive me crazy. I really do. They built the house here on purpose just so I'd have to deal with the stink of manure day and night."

Charlie's parents had subdivided their farm and built a house for Charlie and Winnie. It was a five-bedroom Colonial on a rolling piece of land beside some woods. Everything in the house was new and the best that money could buy.

Winnie's house was several acres from the main house, and did indeed exist on the border of a farm that accommodated twenty-four horses, some of which were owned by the Maples, while others were boarded by people from nearby towns. Yes, the constant smell of manure wafted from the barn, but that's how barns smell. I was sure the Maples had not set out to drive my sister crazy.

With horses so easily accessible, I would have thought that Winnie, who had won prizes for dressage when she was young, would take every opportunity to ride, but she never got on a horse anymore.

"I'll get the tea," I said from the far side of the room. I went into the kitchen. The breakfast dishes were piled high beside the sink.

I put the kettle on, filled the sink with hot water, and piled the dishes into it. While I waited for the water on the stove to boil, I went into the laundry room, picked up an empty basket, and carried it to the family room and used it to collect the fallen soldiers.

"You don't have to do that, Jane."

"I don't mind," I said.

"You are so resourceful," Winnie said. "I don't think people give you enough credit."

I wasn't too flattered by Winnie's assumption that I was gifted just because I knew how to pick up a few toys. Still, it's pleasant to receive a compliment no matter how lame or ridiculous.

The teakettle whistled and I went back into the kitchen. Winnie kept a collection of teas in a cabinet over the stove. Black teas—Darjeeling, Earl Grey, English Breakfast—and herb teas—ginseng, Lemon Lift, Passionate Peach. When Winnie put her home together, she relied heavily on *Martha Stewart Living*. Winnie dotted the house with scented candles and dried flowers. Her theme was French country modern. My sister didn't have an original bone in her body, but her talent for mimicry was unsurpassed. Winnie was so good that on some days she was just like Martha

Stewart—all that was missing was the unbridled ambition, the frenetic energy, and the felony conviction.

I chose Darjeeling, and while the tea steeped, I moved the dishes from the sink to the dishwasher. This small domestic task was both simple and satisfying. It made me feel useful and gave me a glimpse into how I might feel if this were my own kitchen and I were part of a young family. I filled a tray with sugar, milk, two hand-painted mugs, and carried the tray in to Winnie. I knew Winnie had painted the mugs at a store in town called Glaze & Amaze. She often went there. I set the tray down on a small table in the corner of the room. The table was covered with a yellow and blue cloth and the bowl in its center held fresh lavender.

"Come on, old girl. Come and sit down," I said. I sounded like Priscilla—stodgy. Winnie tossed the afghan onto the floor (Priscilla wouldn't have liked to see it dropped on the floor like that), came over to the table, and sat in one of the white wicker chairs that flanked it. I poured the tea. Winnie looked up at a wall clock, a wooden reproduction with a yellow face.

Winnie was wearing a velour sweat suit, the type you often see on women as they run around town doing errands in their Suburbans. Winnie's suit was a pale blue that matched her eyes. Her thin blond hair was cut to just below her ears and framed her face with gentle curls.

"I love the mugs," I said.

"Do you? Do you really like them?"

"I do," I said, though the colors were murky.

"I just love doing it. It makes me feel so fulfilled. I asked Charlie to buy me a kiln, but he says my love for ceramics is just a phase and I'll get over it. I think he's wrong. I think I've found my true calling."

It would have been nice if she found that her true calling was motherhood. Winnie had suffered from an intermittent postpartum depression since her younger son was born—and he had just turned five.

"A kiln takes up so much room," I said.

"That's hardly the point, Jane. My creative impulses should be encouraged. You must be careful or you could just die of boredom out here in the burbs."

Winnie didn't exactly live in the suburbs. She lived in a town called Dover—part suburb, part country—and she lived in the more rural section.

"Jane, I feel just awful about the house, don't you?" Winnie said.

I had been working on getting over my feeling of displacement, but yes, I felt just awful about the house.

"It's only a house," I said.

"But it's our house, the Fortune family house. I hate the idea of strangers living in it."

"We still own it."

"For now. If you can trust Dad and Miranda not to drive the family into absolute bankruptcy."

"I think Littleton has a handle on it."

"That buffoon. He has never had a handle on anything in his life. The only reason he's a lawyer is that it runs in his family. He's an idiot. I don't know how he made it through law school."

"Did you ever say anything about this to Dad?"

"Of course not. He thinks I'm thoroughly domestic and lacking all other qualities. He wouldn't listen to anything I said. And if I didn't know that before, I certainly do now. He never even included me in the discussion about the house. He acted as if it would make no difference to me at all."

Winnie was right. We were an out-of-sight, out-of-mind kind of family. It didn't occur to anyone to include Winnie in the discussions about the house. She had her own home and, we assumed, her own life.

"He might have listened to you," I said, but I knew, even as I said it, that this was disingenuous. No one in our family listened to anyone else in our family. I was just trying to make Winnie feel better.

She squinted at me.

"Please, Jane. Sometimes Teddy listens to Priscilla, and that's only because he knows enough not to always trust himself, thank God. But we have to face facts—Teddy and Miranda are two of the most dismissive people on the planet. Look what they did to you."

"What do you mean?" I asked, but I knew what she meant.

"Who is this Dolores character, anyway?"

"She's Littleton's daughter."

"I know that. But why has she wheedled her way into our family and what does she hope to gain?"

"I think she wants Teddy," I said. "He's still a catch, even without as much money. It's hard for us to see it, because we're his daughters, but he's extremely attractive to women."

Winnie made a gagging sound. "You're making me sick."

"It's true," I said. I started to laugh, a little too wildly, and wiped the tears from my eyes.

"Miranda is deaf, dumb, and blind if she lets that social climber maneuver her way into our family," Winnie said.

"You don't even know her."

"I've heard all about her."

"From whom?"

"Priscilla called me."

"Stirring up trouble."

"Isn't that what she does best?" Winnie took a sip of tea. She sighed. "The Wheaton girls will be home for Thanksgiving. I wish I were still in school. It's the only time you get a real vacation."

The Wheaton girls were Winnie's sisters-in-law, Lindsay and Heather. Wheaton had been a small prestigious girls' college until the late eighties, when it had finally gone coed.

When we had almost finished our tea, Winnie's husband, Charlie, came in with the two boys.

"Finally! I thought you'd never come," Winnie said. "Did you get the pies?"

"Apple, pumpkin, and mince. Hello, Jane." I stood up and Charlie scooped me into a hug. His wool sweater was rough against my cheek.

Little Charlie, who was actually Charles Maple III—called Trey— jumped onto my lap.

"Did you bring us a present, Aunt Jane?" he asked.

"Maybe," I said. He kissed me on the cheek and put his chubby arms around my neck. I closed my eyes and took in the little-boy smell of him. He jumped from my lap and Theodore—Theo—named for Teddy, kissed me on the cheek in a formal way. He was already eight and had recently acquired a little man's dignity.

"You want some tea, Charlie?" I asked.

"Still hot?" Charlie put his palm on the teapot.

"It couldn't be," Winnie said.

"I'll heat up some water," I said.

"No. I'll get it," Charlie said. "Besides, you're a guest."

"She's hardly a guest," Winnie said.

"That's right. Jane is family," Charlie said.

"Boys, I picked up some of your toys and put them in a basket in the laundry room. Please take the basket upstairs and put the toys away," I said.

Winnie looked at me as if I might have gone insane, but the boys went off to the laundry room immediately. When they came out, each was holding a side of the basket. Together, they dragged it upstairs. Winnie raised her eyebrows.

"They never do that for me," she said.

"Element of surprise."

Winnie shrugged and sighed. "I wish they'd do that for me."

Charlie came back from the kitchen with a short glass containing an amber liquid.

"That's not tea," Winnie said.

"It's Glenlivet."

"You'd better put the pies in the freezer or they'll never last until Thursday," Winnie said.

"Done," Charlie said. "Can I get you a drink, Jane?"

"It's only two o'clock, Charlie. I don't see why you have to start drinking so early," Winnie said.

Charlie gave me a look that seemed to say that Winnie was the reason, but then he walked over to her and kissed her on the nose. "Thank you for worrying about me, dear. What would I do without you?"

What I didn't know about married people could fill the Boston Public Library. Maybe if I kept my eyes open, I'd learn something, though what good it would do me at this point was an open question.

"You'll never guess who we ran into at lunch," Charlie said to Winnie.

"Who?" she asked, sounding not the slightest bit interested.

"Max Wellman."

"Who?"

"You know, my friend Max Wellman."

Winnie may not have known who Max Wellman was, but I was experiencing hot sweats and heart palpitations, all symptoms of panic. I hoped that's what it was. Weren't those also symptoms of menopause? I was only thirty-eight. It had to be panic.

For fifteen years I had managed to get only as close to Max as his clippings, but now he lurked around every corner.

Winnie poured herself more tea, though it had to be lukewarm.

"You must have heard of Max Wellman, Jane," Charlie said. "He's a famous author."

"I have, but I didn't know you knew him, Charlie." I tried to keep my voice steady.

"From college. Have you read his books?" Charlie asked.

"All except for the last one." Every time one of Max's books came out, I'd run to the bookstore. Then I'd take the book home and devour it. I don't know what I was looking for. Clues about Max? What sort of clues? With this latest book, *Post*, I had decided to hold back. Why should I still be rushing to read Max's books? Maybe I wouldn't even read this one. But, like an addict, I stalked the bookstores and hovered around the shelves. I opened *Post*, looked at the author photo, checked the acknowledgments page, but I always put it down again.

"Well, if Jane's read this Max Wellman's books, why haven't I? You know how much I like to read, Charlie. Why haven't you brought these books home?"

"We have every one of them upstairs in the study," he said.

"The least you could do, then, is point them out if he's someone you know. How do you expect me to better myself out here in the absolute buttocks when you don't share anything with me and when you won't buy me a kiln?"

Charlie slumped. "It's boondocks, not buttocks."

"You don't support me artistically," Winnie complained.

"I support you in every other way." He raised his voice and drained his glass.

"No need to be like that, especially in front of my sister."

"Anyway, Max is here in town. He's staying with his sister in Boston. She and her husband just rented a fantastic house on Beacon Hill for the winter."

"That's our house," I said in a small voice.

"What?" Charlie asked.

"Brainchild, that's our house. The Fortune family house," Winnie said. "You know very well that Father rented it out for the winter."

"I didn't make the connection."

"There's no reason you should," I said.

"I feel stupid. I'm so sorry, Jane."

"What about me?" Winnie asked. "I think I deserve an apology, too. It was my house, too. I have been shamed, by association."

"There is nothing shameful about renting your house out for the winter," Charlie said.

"You'd think that, wouldn't you? It is the way *you'd* think," Winnie said.

"There's nothing wrong with the way I think."

"You just don't know anything about the history of families."

"To tell you the truth, I'm more concerned with my family's present than its history," he said.

"That's because you don't have a history to speak of. Second-generation English is hardly a history."

"And you came over on the *Mayflower*," Charlie said, his voice infused with sarcasm.

We didn't, but we had as many generations behind us in America as you could without coming over on that particular boat. Still, what did it matter in the twenty-first century?

"Anyway, I invited him for Thanksgiving," Charlie said.

"Who?" Winnie asked.

"Max." Charlie seemed exasperated. "Isn't that who we were just talking about?"

"Without asking me?" Winnie said.

"My parents are the ones having it," Charlie said.

"Did you ask them?"

"I don't have to."

There was a small bit of skin hanging from my thumb and I began to chew on it.

"Don't do that, Jane. It will get all bloody," Winnie said. Charlie looked over. I saw myself as he must see me—dour, dry, somber, bookish, and lacking in style.

"Anyway," Charlie said, "Max isn't coming. He's spending Thanksgiving with his sister." Thank God, I thought. "But he might come over for dessert."

Something banged hard on the floor upstairs and one of the boys shouted.

"Oh, Charlie, can you see to that?" Winnie asked. She had that fainting-couch look to her, as if any movement was beyond her strength.

"I will," I said.

"No, Jane, I'll go," Charlie said.

He went upstairs.

"I think my husband is getting bored with me," Winnie said. "I don't know why. It's as if everything I ask him to do is an ordeal. We haven't had sex in a month."

I didn't like this kind of heart-to-heart. I wasn't crazy about heart-to-hearts in general, but I especially hated them when they included the subject of sex. I wasn't a prude, exactly, I just had never been one of those girls who discussed breasts, periods, and boys. My mother said that I had never really been young, but I had been young, only in a different way.

"I'm sure he loves you," I said.

"That's just the easy thing to say. But you've never been in a long relationship, and in a long relationship things fade." She touched her hair. When she was younger it was a more sunny shade of blond. "You know what we need?" she said.

"What?"

"A girls' day out."

I couldn't remember ever having had a girls' day out with Winnie. I had gone shopping occasionally with Miranda, and that was more of a torture than a pleasure. Miranda was so meticulous about her choices: everything had to be by Leonardo da Vinci, look like it had been painted on by a master craftsman, and elegant without being showy. I once shopped with her for five hours and all she bought was a pair of silk socks and a face cream guaranteed to remove every worry line she ever had.

"Now, if they could only make a cream to remove the worry itself," I had said.

Miranda looked at me like I was mentally defective. My family never understood my sense of humor. In fact, if you asked them, they'd say I didn't have one.

"We'll go on the Friday after Thanksgiving. I'm sure Charlie's parents won't mind taking the boys," Winnie said.

"That's the busiest shopping day of the year," I said.

Winnie was undaunted. "Why should I worry about the busiest shopping day of the year? A master shopper never has to worry about the little people."

"Why don't I stay home and take care of the boys," I suggested.

"That wouldn't be any fun."

I was flattered that Winnie thought I might be good company on a shopping trip. I'd never given her any reason to think so.

Charlie came downstairs. "The boys are fine," he said. "Barely. Theo was close to popping Trey's eye out with one of those plastic mega-monster things, but he'll survive. I have to go out to the office for the rest of the afternoon. Max is thinking of moving back to this area and I told him I'd pull some listings. He says he's ready to settle down in a rambling farmhouse. That's what he said, 'a rambling farmhouse with a stone wall and a brook and maybe a swing hanging from a tree.' He thinks he's ordering from a catalogue. Who knows? Maybe I can pull it off."

"What will we do for dinner?" Winnie asked.

Charlie looked at Winnie as if she might manage to get off her ever-increasing behind and arrange dinner, but he said, "We'll figure it out when I get home."

Charlie put on his coat, pecked Winnie on the cheek, and went out to the car.

"I noticed some laundry when I was in the laundry room. I think I'll just throw it in so it can be going while we're sitting here," I said.

"Thank you, Jane. You're an angel. That's such a good idea." One she might have had herself. "I wonder why Marion hasn't come over this morning." Marion Maple was Winnie's mother-in-law. "I thought she'd at least invite us over for dinner on Wednesday night when the girls get home."

"I thought we were going there Thursday for Thanksgiving," I said.

"We are."

"That means two big meals in a row."

"No difference to her. We're family," Winnie said. "Besides, she has help."

Chapter 12

Charlie has complaints

Charlie got home at about five, and before he had even taken off his coat, Winnie called out to suggest that we have Chinese take-out for dinner.

Out in the hall, Charlie mumbled something I couldn't catch. Then I heard, "Chinese food it is. I'll go out and get it. Jane will go with me."

"Oh no, Jane, stay with me." Winnie grabbed my arm as if she had just been thrown off the *Titanic* and I was the only lifeboat. This was a little much, considering I was only going on a short errand, but as weird as it was, it did give me the sense that I was vital to Winnie's very existence. Though I knew it wasn't true, I liked the feeling. I wasn't accustomed to being vital to anyone.

"I won't be long," I said.

Charlie and I got into his Navigator. It was dusky, almost dark, the gloomy hour. The possibility of running into Max again disturbed me. He would certainly be toting some high-fashion girl, and I'd feel dowdy and disregarded.

The evening was crisp but not too cold. Some Christmas lights were already up—too early in my opinion. Christmas was beginning to bleed into Thanksgiving more every year, and I refused to shop in any store that put up Christmas decorations before Thanksgiving. Time passes quickly enough: there's no need to hurry it along, especially in the name of commerce.

After we had been driving for about five minutes, Charlie said, "Jane, your sister is driving me insane."

"Really," I said. I kept my voice neutral.

"I don't know what to do about it. It's both better and worse when you're around."

"How do you mean, Charlie?"

"You're so pleasant, so helpful. You make me see what I could have had. Someone who could help me instead of being so dependent." I tried to resist the urge to feel flattered but was unsuccessful.

"You should talk to her, Charlie."

"I've tried. I don't know what to say anymore. She doesn't discipline the boys. She hardly pays attention to them. My mother is practically bringing them up."

"It couldn't be that bad," I said, but from what I'd seen that morning, it was very likely that bad.

"Couldn't you talk to her?" he asked.

"I probably shouldn't." I was sure that I shouldn't. Winnie didn't take criticism with grace.

"I guess not," he said. "It really is my problem."

"Look," I said, "I'll be with you until Christmas. I'll do what I can."

"I know you will, Jane." He turned toward me and put his hand over mine. "You're the best."

His hand did not feel like it was supposed to be on mine: there was something all wrong about it. He was my brother-in-law and he was just expressing himself, but still I wished he would find some other way to do it. I didn't like to be touched, except when it was socially necessary, and this didn't feel necessary at all.

A light snow was beginning to fall as we approached the restaurant. Charlie maneuvered into a spot in front of a nearby doughnut shop.

I slipped my hand out from under his and got out of the car.

Inside the restaurant, waiters ran up and down steps that led to different levels. Behind the counter a man was taking phone orders and nodding his head with vigor, as if the person on the other end of the line could see him.

Two giant brown bags were set in front of us and Charlie paid with a credit card. We each hauled a bag back to the car. Charlie opened the door for me and waited until I got in. I put my bag on the floor. As Charlie set the other one on my lap, he looked at me—a moment too long.

Maybe I'd figure something out. Perhaps with a series of small shifts, I could turn Winnie into someone else. Not likely. Could I make her a little less selfish? Even less likely.

But Charlie had married her. He must have seen something in her. Though the flush of new love might be over, something else must have come along to sustain them. If not, life would simply be a series of meals, chores, and petty aggravations. True, I didn't have much experience with marriage, but what I'd seen of it with my own parents had not been especially inspiring.

Charlie was quiet on the ride home.

"Food smells good," I said.

"They have really good food there," Charlie said. "I just wish they delivered it out to our house, but we're a bit off the beaten path."

"That's what's nice about it," I said.

"It's an inconvenience, though," he said. "Still, I wouldn't live anywhere else."

Charlie was a man who would always be happy to live in his parents' backyard.

"It's worse when it's Jorie's day off," Charlie said. "Things get done when Jorie is here. You think maybe Winnie is depressed?"

"About what?" I asked.

"I don't know. She has everything a woman could want. A nice house. A couple of good kids and I'm not so bad."

"She wants a kiln," I said. He laughed and shook his head. "You're a great husband, Charlie. I'm sure she just isn't feeling well."

"She's never feeling well. I have married the greatest hypochondriac who ever lived." He smiled, then laughed again. It wasn't exactly a happy laugh.

When we got home, the table was set and ready for us, as if Winnie knew just how far to push Charlie without pushing him over the edge. The boys were in their pajamas and sitting in front of the television in the family room watching a cartoon about a big yellow sponge.

It was the picture of domestic happiness.

Chapter 13

Jane closes the office for the holidays

On Tuesday morning, I drove into the city from the suburbs to close the office for the period between Thanksgiving and Christmas. Tad was leaving to spend time with his family in Colorado.

Jack Reilly's story was sitting on my desk, even though everything else had been tucked away by Tad's organized hand. I fingered the pages.

"Jane," Tad asked, "what are you really looking for? Is it Jack Reilly or is it something else?"

"Jack Reilly, of course," I said. "What's so hard to understand about that?"

"I think you're looking for something else," Tad said. I tapped my nails on the desk.

"You did a nice job of cleaning up the place," I said. "The office has never looked so good." Tad ignored me.

"You're looking for the feeling you had when you were just starting out, when you thought the world was full of possibility."

"I still think the world is full of possibility," I said. I could feel my whole body tense, from my teeth to my toes. He was right. There was something I still wanted, some level of success, some public acknowledgment. Even me, with my shy ways. I wanted a new discovery and, ideally, a new love.

Max might show up at the Maples' for Thanksgiving and I needed him to think that I had done something important with my life. In my head, I knew that I had. I had evidence of it. But in my heart, I felt unimportant, unpolished, and somehow lacking. A woman who doesn't leave home until it is absolutely forced upon her could hardly have something to offer a man who catapulted early into a world of fame and glamour.

"Well, we can't find Jack Reilly," Tad said.

"You can find anyone these days."

"Maybe you should hire someone," Tad said.

"Like who?"

"I don't know. A private detective."

"A private detective? That sounds so silly. It sounds like something you'd do if you were a character on TV."

"People do it. If they didn't, there wouldn't be all these names in the yellow pages." He took the telephone book from the table behind his desk. He'd marked a page with a Post-it. He opened the book and put it in front of me. "I checked it out," he said. His smile was shy, as if he wasn't sure how I would take this. He ran his forefinger over the listings. "This is my favorite," he said. "Hope Bliss Investigations."

There couldn't be too many people with that name. Could this be my childhood friend? We had fallen out of touch years ago, though I couldn't remember why.

Maybe Hope Bliss was a sign.

"Let's think about it over the holidays," I said, ever the girl to grab the bull by the horns. This was something I really wanted and still I held back. Maybe I just had to drag it out a little longer, let the fantasy linger. Besides, I planned to go up to Vermont during the holidays to check out the address that was tucked in my wallet. Wouldn't it be more fun to come face-to-face with Jack Reilly and offer him the fellowship than to let someone else find him?

I pulled an envelope out of my canvas tote and gave it to Tad. Inside was a very large check, a Christmas present.

"We could call now," Tad pressed, without opening the envelope.

"Let's wait. Maybe he'll turn up."

"Not likely."

I shrugged. "Come on. We're finished. Get out of here. Start your vacation."

"Are you sure?" He held the envelope but still didn't open it.

"Absolutely."

"Well, I guess I won't see you, then, until after Christmas." He reached under his desk and pulled out a box. It was wrapped in Christmas paper and had a lopsided bow perched at the corner. "I wrapped it myself," he said.

I smiled. "You didn't have to get me a present."

"I know."

I looked at it.

"Aren't you going to open it?"

"Now?"

"Of course now," he said.

I picked at the tape with what was left of my chewed fingernails.

"Rip it," he said. I looked up. "Come on. I know you can do it."

I made a special point of shredding the wrapping paper with gusto. I opened the box and separated the tissue paper. Inside was a brown leather tote. The leather was so buttery I could have used it as a pillow.

"This is elegant," I said, which was the highest praise I knew how to give any type of clothing or accessory.

"My mother helped me pick it out when she came to visit," he said. "We thought it was perfect for you."

I stood up and put it on my shoulder. "I wish we had a mirror." I thought for a second. "Wait, I do have one." I dug around in my old bag and found a small compact with a cracked mirror. I opened it and tried to hold it away from me so I could see myself holding Tad's present. It didn't work. In the end, I held the bag to my face and rested my cheek on the soft leather. "I'm overwhelmed."

"It's only a bag," he said, but he looked pleased.

He was wrong. It was so much more than a bag. It was a gesture. I felt a little teary but turned away so Tad wouldn't see it. I think he knew, though, because he smiled and kissed me on the cheek.

When he walked out the door, I realized I'd miss him. Funny that it never occurred to me to miss Teddy, Miranda, or even Priscilla.

Winnie's mother-in-law, Marion, came over to the house that afternoon. She bustled over with a basket of homemade cookies like an ancient Red Riding Hood. While she was there, Winnie let the boys eat all the cookies, except for the few we managed to hold back for the adults. Trey spilled a bottle of cranberry juice on the kitchen floor and Theo kept walking through the room like a soldier, saying, "I want a scooter for Christmas. I want a scooter for Christmas."

When Winnie went in to clean up the juice, which I was afraid she wouldn't do—she sat in the family room sipping tea long after we heard the crash—Marion turned toward me. "The children are wild animals. She doesn't discipline them at all."

It was at this moment that Theo came in shouting, "I want a scooter. I want a scooter."

"Theo, get over here, young man," his grandmother said. He came toward her with a look of expectation, but she grabbed him by the front of his collar and pulled him toward her with a rough fist. "Stop it. Stop it right now. We heard you. Do you understand? Go up to your room—

now." He reached for the last cookie, but Marion slapped his hand. "You've had enough."

Theo went upstairs. He wasn't as upset as I would have been at his age. He seemed accustomed to Marion and took her in stride.

"They are wild animals," Marion said again, but she was smiling. "Your sister is horrible with them."

I didn't know what to say to this, because while it was so obviously true, it wasn't up to me to pound more nails into my sister's domestic coffin. I took the last cookie without offering it to Marion—something I would not normally do.

After that whole scene, I could understand why Marion didn't come often. To make it worse, for the whole time Marion was there, Winnie insisted on keeping the television on. The TV was enormous and dominated the family room.

"I can't turn off Dr. Phil," Winnie said when I reached for the remote control. "I look forward to hearing him every day. He is the true voice of common sense. The world would be much better off if everyone listened to Dr. Phil."

Marion turned to me and rolled her eyes. Marion was apparently no fan of Dr. Phil.

I didn't know much about Dr. Phil, but if Winnie would listen to anyone—even to Dr. Phil—it couldn't hurt.

Chapter 14

Thanksgiving at the big house

When I came downstairs dressed for Thanksgiving dinner, Winnie looked at me and said, "Thanksgiving, Jane. Not a wake." I suppose Winnie could have used a little more tact, but that wouldn't have been Winnie.

I already felt awkward. When I went through the clothes in my suitcases, I couldn't find anything flattering. I had the green suit, but I didn't think it was appropriate. I knew how I wanted to look, or had some vision of it. With the possibility of seeing Max again, I wanted to look self-assured. I should have worn the suit. If anyone could make clothes that would instill instant confidence, they'd make a fortune. Isn't that what clothes are really about? I chose a black dress since, as everyone knows, you can wear black almost anywhere. I think the problem was that it was old and shapeless and my stockings were opaque. I usually wore tights, because they were more comfortable and so thick they hardly ever ran. My shoes were flat and sensible, which would have been fine on an ordinary day, but at the moment I was wishing for a bit of a heel. My wardrobe was a consequence of my own indifference. Once I met a woman who joined a Cuban religion, and when she became a priestess, she had to decide on one color to wear for the rest of her life. She chose white. I thought this was a wonderful plan, so simple. Black was my spiritual choice.

"Fashion magazines have just passed you by, haven't they, Jane?" Winnie asked. She didn't mean to insult me; she meant to improve me. Still, I didn't know how she became such an authority, she of the powder blue jogging suit. This afternoon the jogging suit had been replaced by a paisley skirt and a matching sweater set with pearls. Her shoes were flat, but more like ballet slippers than the Doc Martens I was wearing. The pearls made her look very lady-of-the-manor. She wore matching earrings. It wasn't that she looked good; it was that she looked right.

Charlie came downstairs in chinos and a sweater. He was balding a bit at the crown and not especially handsome, but he appeared solid and reliable and there is something attractive about that. You could find Charlie's type in bars all over Boston lifting a beer and rooting for the home team. Max hadn't been like that. He had the kind of good looks other men were wary of. Bentley had even mentioned it and Bentley himself was urbane and polished in his own drunken way. Bentley loved referring to Max as "Hubbell," Robert Redford's character in *The Way We Were*. "In a way he was like the country he lived in, everything came too easily to him," Bentley would say.

"The man was living in a basement," I reminded him.

"Oh, Jane, I never thought you were so lacking in imagination."

"And in the movie Robert Redford was the living, breathing ideal of what the country had to offer, and it was Barbra Streisand, the Jewish one, who had to struggle."

"She could have stopped struggling anytime," Bentley said. "She just insisted on unhappiness. Some people do."

"Maybe a scarf," Winnie said. I hardly thought a scarf was going to turn me from plain Jane into a new, more extraordinary version of myself.

Winnie disappeared for a few minutes and when she came back she had a blue velvet scarf, still in its original package. When she hung it around my neck, I had to admit that it was an improvement.

Winnie stepped back and looked at me. "I'm very good at this," she said. "I should start a business."

Before we left for the big house (which is what Winnie called the senior Maples' five-bedroom farmhouse), I rushed back to my room. It was at the back of the house and had a view of the field between the two houses. The smell of manure didn't bother me. I liked it. It was mixed with the smell of hay, and fallen leaves, wood-burning fires, and autumn. My room in Winnie's house was white and blue, the furniture was Shaker style and simple. It was a calm room, with a desk, a large shabby chair, and a generous ottoman where I liked to put my books, my journal, my glasses, and the stories I was reading.

I sat at the desk and picked up the phone to call Bentley to wish him a happy Thanksgiving. He didn't pick up so I left a message. It occurred to me to call Teddy and Miranda. They weren't there either, and when I spoke to their machine I pretended that it was both of us, Winnie and I, who had thought to call them. Priscilla was at her sister's and I had misplaced the number.

The five of us, Winnie, Charlie, the two boys, and I, walked across the field. The older Maples had placed a walkway of fieldstones between the houses, because without them there were times when you would find yourself ankle deep in mud. I remembered those muddy March days from my years at Wellesley when there was nothing you could do but slog through it. We called it "the ubiquitous mud." That reminded me that I was scheduled to speak at Wellesley after New Year's. It was over a month away and I was already nervous, but that was nothing compared with the way I felt about the possibility of seeing Max again.

Winnie insisted on carrying all five pies, and when they were piled into her arms they reached the tip of her nose.

"I don't want your mother to think we are coming empty-handed," she said.

"We aren't coming empty-handed," Charlie said. "What does it matter who carries them?"

"You know your mother. I don't want her to think I'm being lazy."

"My mother would never think that," Charlie said. Lights were on in every window in the house. It was a chilly afternoon and the sun had given up trying to make an impression.

Marion Maple came to the door and opened it wide.

"Come in, come in. We're all starving," she said.

"But this is what time you told us to come, Marion," Winnie said.

"Yes, dear, of course." Marion kissed Winnie on the forehead. Marion had a substantial body, generous in all areas. She wore an ankle-length velvet skirt. She reminded me of a jolly Mrs. Claus. Marion turned to me. "You're looking especially well, Jane." She had to say it, though I knew it wasn't true. I was looking the same as I always looked—unadorned.

"Thank you," I said.

Lindsay and Heather came rushing toward us from the recesses of the house. They scooped up their nephews and smothered them with kisses that the boys suffered without complaint, though when they were finally left alone, I saw Theo wipe his cheek with the back of his hand.

"Jane, we're so glad you've come," Lindsay said. "Have you met any famous authors lately?" I often met famous authors. Sometimes I published them in the *Review,* but I had no recent stories to tell. "I've been writing fiction at school," Lindsay said. "Experimental stuff really."

I wasn't fond of "experimental stuff."

"That's wonderful, Lindsay," I said. Heather and Lindsay were both wearing short plaid skirts that made them look like they were fresh from the lacrosse field.

"Lindsay can't wait," Heather said.

"For what?" I asked. Charlie handed me a cup of mulled cider.

"Didn't Charlie tell you?"

"Tell me what?"

"That Max Wellman, the famous author, might come for dessert. You know, he wrote that book *Duet for One* that they made into a movie."

"I only said *might*," Charlie said. "He's in the city and might not feel like driving out."

"I hear he's absolutely knock-down, drop-dead gorgeous," Heather said.

"I'm the one with an interest in writing," Lindsay reminded her.

"I'm talking about an interest in men," Heather said.

"Isn't he a little old for you girls?" I asked. They were only in their early twenties and Max was my age.

"What's a few years when a man is gorgeous and successful?" Lindsay asked. "I think a man that age is looking for someone young and energetic."

And fertile, I thought.

"Lindsay, you haven't even met the man and you're ready to marry him," Marion said, laughing. She had two red circles on her cheeks from sitting too close to the fire.

Marion was able to sit because she had hired a woman named Gabriella to make and serve the meal. We were all so used to having help. Sometimes I wondered if it wouldn't be better for us to do it ourselves. I wouldn't have minded having a job to do. I needed something to distract me. Lindsay's argument seemed so obviously true: why wouldn't Max, having exhausted every supermodel in New York, come back looking for the right girl with whom to start a family, and why wouldn't he look for someone young?

Both Lindsay and Heather were good choices. They were the sisters of an old friend and came from a welcoming sort of family. Lindsay and Heather were both very pretty in the way that youth has of being pretty— unself-conscious, lithe, athletic. They were both lacrosse stars at

Wheaton. Maybe Lindsay was the more attractive one, with her straight red hair and green eyes, but Heather had plenty to recommend her. She was a little shorter than Lindsay and her hair was dark and curly. Her eyes were blue with a green tinge and she had a warmth about her. In that way, she reminded me of Marion, and maybe Heather would someday attain her girth, but for now both girls were just as lovely as any man could wish for.

The wine flowed at dinner and I helped myself every time it was offered. By the time we gathered around the fire in the living room I was teetering on the edge of being drunk. It started to snow lightly and we were the picture of a happy family on Thanksgiving. The television was on in the corner so we could watch the football games, but other than that, we looked like a family might have looked before television was invented. We fell into the soft chairs and sofas. I stared at the fire. The snow probably meant that Max wouldn't be coming, so I settled down to what I thought would be a dull but predictable evening.

I felt displaced and melancholy, but as the "extra" woman soon learns, these feelings must be kept to herself. What she turns on the world has to be a false and happy face. A social face. It's what everyone expects, and after a while it becomes what she expects from herself. The role of the single woman when attaching herself to another person's family is to be cheerful and helpful. The idea is to get yourself invited again so you can be just as miserable as you were the last time you were there.

The Maples were open and hospitable and everything a family should be, but I didn't have much in common with them. They weren't a bookish group, despite Lindsay's literary pretensions. And I, for better or worse, always felt most at home in a book. This might have been a social weakness, but it was also my greatest strength. It gave me my purpose. Without my feeling for words, I would have no center. When I started the *Euphemia Review*, I was fairly sure I had no genius of my own, but the irony was that I did have a genius—I had a genius for nurturing genius.

It was important to have a purpose. Winnie had her husband and children, and as soon as you have children, you can stop looking for a purpose in life. Your purpose is always there, running around, messing up diapers, needing food, education, toys, and experience. Children are a built-in purpose. Maybe that's why so many people have them.

Heather and Lindsay were talking about a girl who was leaving school to get married.

"She's only been there two years," Heather said.

"Hasn't even picked a major yet," Lindsay said.

"I don't think I'd do that. Not for any man."

"I don't know," Lindsay said. "I think I'm going to be a writer, and a writer works mainly from experience, isn't that true, Jane?"

"An education never hurts," I said. God, I felt old. I would have liked to agree with her. I would have liked to be silly and frivolous, but I knew few writers—though there were some—who hadn't had good educations.

"Hear, hear!" Marion said, lifting her glass. "Thank God for Jane and her good common sense."

It should have made me feel proud, I suppose, to be known for my "good common sense," but it didn't. It was like being known for your "good sensible shoes" when you hankered after stilettos.

I got up and went into the kitchen where I found some dark rum on the counter and poured it into my hot cider. Gabriella was counting measures of coffee into the coffeemaker.

"Hello, Gabriella. How are you?" I asked. I knew her from other family parties. She was a fixture at the Maples' house, though she didn't live there. She had her own family in a working-class town a few miles away. I wondered what they were doing for Thanksgiving.

"There is more rum in the back cabinet," she said, "for when you run out." It was as if she knew I'd need more than the dregs of that bottle.

"Do you need some help with dessert?" I asked. "I could pile cups on a tray or fold the napkins."

Gabriella turned from the counter and put her hand on her hip. She smiled. In my muddled state, I had the brief fantasy that only Gabriella understood me, that I'd be okay so long as I stayed in the kitchen.

"Are you a little drunk, Jane?" Gabriella asked.

"Not as drunk as I intend to be," I said. I twisted one foot up against the other like a little kid caught doing something naughty.

"You'd better go back and sit down." I left the warmth and brightness of the kitchen and returned to the living room.

"Anyway, I suppose he won't come now," Heather was saying when I slumped back into my chair.

Charlie looked up from the television. "If not this time, there'll be another," he said. "I'm going to sell him a house. He'll be around."

"He *may* be famous," Marion said, "but is he a nice person? Don't you think that's the real question?"

"I'm sure he's nice enough," Lindsay said. "Writers don't always have to be nice. They're artists."

The snow continued to fall. Just as I was settling down to my fourth spiked cider and comfortable with the idea that Max wasn't coming, the doorbell rang.

"It's him," Lindsay said. She jumped from her seat.

"Calm down," Charlie said.

"Really, girls. He's just a man," Charles Sr. said without looking up from the television.

"Well, it's not like we have celebrities showing up on our doorstep every day of the week," Marion said. She adjusted her bulk so that she was sitting straight on the edge of her chair. The girls looked like racehorses ready to burst through the starting gate. Charlie put out a restraining hand and went to the front hall.

There was the noise of greeting. A coat must be removed. A bottle of expensive wine must be handed over.

And then, there he was.

He was introduced to everyone.

I was last.

"Yes, Jane and I have met," he said. He extended his hand. "Hello, Jane." We might as well have been acquaintances who had bumped into each other once at a literary function.

His voice brought me right back to when I'd first known him. It had always affected me like a shot of adrenaline. He didn't look exactly the same; he was thinner. He was more fit than he'd been, but I had liked him the way he was before, a little bulky, not fat, but solid.

"It's good to see you again, Max," I said with all the courage of a stout rum. Good to see him? It was great. It was as if his presence brought back every happy memory I'd ever had. But he was cavalier and distant. He acted as if I were almost a stranger.

Had I expected more? How could I have expected more?

"Well," Marion said, "now that Max is here, I guess it's time for dessert."

"You didn't wait on me?" he asked. This was an expression a New Yorker would use. Some of the Boston in him, even some of his accent, was gone.

"We were so full. We were waiting for dessert anyway," Lindsay said.

We took our seats in the dining room, all of us, except for the boys, who had gone upstairs to play. Max was guided to a chair at the foot of the table. Heather and Lindsay sat on either side of him. Winnie and I were relegated to chairs nearer Charles Sr., who sat at the table's head. Winnie looked sour. I could tell she was annoyed to be exiled so far away from our special guest, but I was relieved.

"So why have you come back to Boston?" Heather asked.

"I'm here for Thanksgiving." Max stated the obvious, which allowed him to give an answer without really giving one.

She colored. "But Charlie says you're looking for a house."

"I am."

"What they want to know, Max, and let's just get it right out on the table with those pies, is do you have a girlfriend?" Marion asked.

"Mother!" both girls choked.

Max smiled. He had a few lines around his eyes. His hair was still thick and still that sandy color that looked greenish in certain lights and brought out the green in his eyes.

"Lindsay wants to be a writer," Heather said.

"Heather. He doesn't want to hear about that," Lindsay said.

"I do," he said. He had developed a way of giving whomever he was talking to all of his attention. I'd heard that this ability was usually found in movie stars and politicians.

Heather cut Max a piece of pie. Between Heather and Lindsay he was supplied with pie for a solid hour and he ate every piece that was put in front of him.

"Well, I'm not a very good writer, not yet," Lindsay said.

"I'm sure that's not true," Max said. "Would you like me to read something?" He was more generous than I was. Of course, he had different motivation. Lindsay was particularly pretty when she cocked her head and smiled at him the way she smiled then.

"I couldn't think of asking that. I couldn't take your time," she said.

"I don't mind." He ate a forkful of pumpkin pie. "I'll be staying with my sister through New Year's. I'm taking a long vacation and I'd be happy to read something."

Lindsay put her hand to her chest. "Oh my God, you are the coolest."

She swung her long red hair. I wondered if he would have been so quick to read something by a chunky girl with bad teeth.

He finished his pumpkin pie and Lindsay supplied him with a piece of apple.

"Charlie, when are you free to go looking at houses?" Max asked.

"Any time, Max. I'm at your disposal." That was Charlie's business voice. I'd heard him use it many times. "We could go tomorrow."

"Tomorrow, then. What will you girls be doing tomorrow?" Max asked.

Winnie, from the end of the table, said, "Jane and I are going shopping."

"You are?" Charlie said. "What for?"

"Christmas, silly. Never too soon to get started."

Max had been addressing Lindsay and Heather, but Winnie wanted to get into the conversation, so she took the only opening she could get.

"We might drive up north to go skiing for the day," Lindsay said.

"You never told me that," Marion said. "I thought you'd be here."

"I just thought of it."

"I think you should stay home," Marion said. "I don't get to see you girls nearly enough." They came home at least twice a month, sometimes more.

"And you're not such a great skier," Heather said. Lindsay shot her a look.

"Why not spend the day writing?" Heather asked. "You have the whole day."

"Yes, that would be fun." Lindsay's enthusiasm was forced, and when she thought no one was watching she gave her sister a dirty look.

"Tomorrow night Lindsay and I are meeting some of our college friends at a club in Boston. Why don't you meet us there," Heather said to Max.

"Why would he want to do that?" Charlie asked.

"It sounds fun," Max said. "What time are you going?"

"We'll be there at ten," Heather said.

"That's a little late for an old guy like me." Max winked.

"Come on. We've read all about you. You go to all the best clubs in New York," Lindsay said. That was an understatement. He had a reputation for being the biggest womanizer in Manhattan. The Literary Lothario.

"So I'm found out. I guess I'll have to come."

"Don't forget," Lindsay said. She put her hand over his and looked into his eyes.

The whole display was nauseating under any circumstance and I might have left the room to vomit, but I was on my seventh rum and cider and I wasn't sure I'd be able to stand up.

I had never wanted to believe Max's reputation. Magazines and newspapers aren't always right. It could have just been a publicist's way of getting him extra attention.

Watching him now, with his eyes boring a hole right through Lindsay's head, I wasn't so sure. He had definitely changed, but there was no way of telling how much.

Fortunately, dessert went on until late, and by the time the pies had been decimated, I could walk without falling over. Max had barely looked at me all evening. The few times our eyes met, we both looked away. Max was the first to leave, so at least he didn't see me hobbling drunkenly over the flagstones on my way back to the house.

The children had already fallen asleep, so they stayed behind with their grandparents.

Winnie let me lean on her as we walked across the field. She gave me an odd look.

"Jane, I think you're drunk."

"Yes."

"You hardly ever get drunk. I can't remember the last time you were." She paused. "That Max Wellman is quite the ladies' man," she added.

"That's what they say." My ankle twisted, but I didn't fall. It was dark. We should have brought a flashlight.

"I thought you said you knew him," she said.

"I did."

"He said he would barely have recognized you."

We were going up the walk when I tumbled into the shrubbery. I started to laugh and couldn't stop. Winnie and Charlie reached down to help me up, but each time they pulled me up, I fell back.

"Jane, I think you're hysterical," Charlie said, but he was laughing, too.

"You're battering our bushes," Winnie said.

I let them pull me from the hedge and help me upstairs. I remembered dragging the drunken Bentley up the stairs that first night with Max. I had no sympathy for Bentley then. I couldn't understand an Evan Bentley who felt, at thirty-five, as if his best days were behind him, but then I hadn't even tried.

Chapter 15

The hair that launched a thousand ships

Winnie came down in her pink quilted bathrobe. She hadn't brushed her hair and she had a rag-doll look to her.

"Oh, good, Jane. You found the hot cross buns. I love the way they smell. She poured herself a mug of coffee, opened the refrigerator, and added a generous quantity of cream to her cup.

"Max Wellman seems to like our girls," Winnie said. My head was pounding and my eyelids felt scratchy.

"What's not to like?" I kept my voice even. I didn't really want Max Wellman to like "our girls." Winnie looked up at me.

"God, Jane, you look just awful."

"Thanks."

"I don't think I've seen you get that drunk for years. Maybe I never have."

"I don't know what happened," I lied.

"Charlie's sisters are nice girls, but they are no geniuses," Winnie said.

This was true. They were silly and young, but Winnie was hardly a genius herself, and it didn't keep her from getting married to a perfectly nice man, maybe not an exceptional man, but a perfectly nice one.

When Charlie came downstairs, he was already dressed for work in a version of what he'd been wearing last night—khakis and a sweater.

"What time are we leaving tonight?" Winnie asked. She stayed seated on the bench at the kitchen island, so I got up to get Charlie a cup of coffee. The important thing about being a single woman in another person's house is to anticipate the needs of others so your presence is constantly equated with positive feelings.

"What?" he asked. He was already looking at his PDA and poking at it with a stylus.

"For the disco. What time are we going?"

"We aren't going," he said, still poking at the PDA. "The papers come?"

I had already retrieved them from the front walk. Charlie took them from the chair where I had left them, pulled up a stool, and started to leaf through each one with great efficiency.

"Of course we're going. Do you want to get old before our time? It's not fair that we never get to have any fun."

"We do have fun," Charlie said, barely looking up. "Anyway, who would watch the boys?"

"Your mother will, I'm sure."

"Don't be so sure," he said.

I took the buns out of the oven, lined one of the array of baskets I found on top of the refrigerator with a linen napkin, and filled it up.

"Well, I got Ariel to watch them today so Jane and I could go shopping, but I don't think Ariel can stay into the wee hours, and if we don't get to the club until ten, then we won't be home until late and the boys should really stay over at your mother's."

"So Ariel will take the boys all day and my mother will take them all night. Is that what you're saying?"

"Exactly." Maybe this was Winnie's modus operandi. If she pretended she didn't understand what Charlie was saying, she could get her own way without making a fuss. "Winnie, they're at my mother's now," Charlie said. "You and Jane can go out tonight. I'll watch the boys."

"I have a better idea," I said. "I'll take care of the boys and you two go."

"Marion won't mind," Winnie said.

"I'd rather watch the boys. You know I hate clubs," I said.

"Right, you are more the lecture type than the disco type," Winnie said. I didn't know if I liked that description of myself. It seemed so spinsterly. It *was* so spinsterly. "Then it's settled. Jane will take care of the boys," she said.

Charlie looked at me.

"I don't think it's right," he said.

"Jane doesn't mind," Winnie said.

Mind? Hardly. If I couldn't extricate myself from their disco plan, I'd have to fake an illness which might not be too difficult considering the state of my hangover.

Charlie finished his coffee while whipping through two newspapers, then left for the office. I was very conscious of what he would be doing that day—driving Max all over suburban Boston to look for the perfect farmhouse in which he could settle with some nubile young thing.

Ariel arrived at ten and by ten-thirty Winnie and I were off to the mall in Winnie's Volvo. The parking situation was so bad it took us nearly twenty minutes to find a spot. I was feeling frayed even before we stepped out of the car, but Winnie, usually so lethargic, became a different person. The crowds didn't bother her. Once inside, she opened her purse and looked at a list. She was on a mission.

Malls make me dizzy. It could be the lighting. I think it is designed to make people crazy so that they lose control of their mental faculties and buy things they neither need nor want. There was a man on the first floor playing Christmas carols on a grand piano. I followed Winnie from store to store. It wasn't long before Winnie could see that I had lost whatever small amount of enthusiasm I had to begin with. The clue was when I sat on something I thought was a bench and it turned out to be a sculpture.

Winnie came out of a store called Scissors and Knives wielding a bag.

"You are sitting on a head," she said.

"A what?"

"A head. I'm afraid you've mistaken this decorative piece of art for a bench. You are sitting on a head, a child's head, as a matter of fact."

I stood up and looked around to see if anyone else had seen me park myself on a bronze head. I thought I was pretty good at recognizing art, but perhaps mall art wasn't my specialty. As a piece of art, the bronze wasn't much, but it wasn't much of a bench either. I might just as well have sat in a flowerpot. There were people looking.

"You were never much of a shopper," Winnie said. "You never understood the health benefits."

"Health benefits?" My head was pounding from the fluorescent lights and my feet hurt from the tiled floor.

"Certainly. You walk, for one thing, briskly in a pleasant environment. You get to express yourself with each and every purchase. Everything I buy is an expression of me. It's one of the most creative acts there is. Come on," she said. I thought maybe she was going to take me into a special room where they indoctrinated you into the cult of shopping. Instead, she took me to the hair salon on the top floor of Filene's.

"I'm going to leave you here," she said. I didn't care where she left me so long as she left me somewhere. Winnie approached the counter. "I'd like to speak to Mr. Marco," she said.

"He's with a customer," the girl said. Her hairstyle made her look like she'd recently been electrocuted. Perhaps a case of the cobbler's children having no shoes.

"Tell him it's Winnie Maple," Winnie announced in a loud voice. The girl disappeared behind a partition and it wasn't a moment before Mr. Marco himself came out. Mr. Marco was about five feet tall and bald on top, but he sported a black ponytail, pulled from the hair on the sides of his head.

"Winnie, my love, what are you doing to me? You are not here without an appointment, are you?"

"It isn't me, Mr. Marco. It's my sister," she said.

"Me?" I turned toward Winnie.

"I suddenly had an absolutely marvelous idea." I noticed that my sister could take on the persona of the person to whom she was speaking. She never tried it with me (maybe my personality wasn't strong enough to mimic), but it worked like a charm on Mr. Marco. "Look at her," she said. "Just look at her." She lifted one of the limp locks that had escaped my ponytail. "My sister is a beautiful woman, but she doesn't do a thing about it. And you know, Mr. Marco"—she bent her head toward him conspiratorially—"when you reach a certain age it's incumbent upon you to bring your best qualities to the fore. Don't you agree?"

"Completely," he said.

"Ah, I said to myself, Mr. Marco is a genius. If anyone can give her what she needs, it's Mr. Marco."

"But without an appointment."

"Oh, Mr. Marco. You know great art must be the whim of the moment. When I come back, I want to see the hair that launched a thousand ships. Let the artist in you take flight."

I wasn't sure I wanted to have the hair that launched a thousand ships, maybe the hair that launched a small lobster boat.

A heavy girl in a white jumpsuit washed my hair. When she finished, she wrapped my hair in a towel and took me to a chair next to the one where Mr. Marco was working. I waited while he chopped and frowned and danced around his subject, an elderly woman with severely thinning hair.

Winnie was right. Mr. Marco could work miracles.

After he took a blow dryer to the old lady's head, she came out looking just like Carol Channing.

He wiped off the chair and blew the stray blond hair to the floor with the blow dryer. Then he motioned for me to sit. He stood behind me and we both looked into the mirror. He put his hands in my hair, fluffed, and puffed.

"You have good hair. Long and thick. I can make you look like Michelle Pfeiffer," he said.

"I doubt that very much," I said.

"Watch me." And he began to snip.

If I didn't look exactly like Michelle Pfeiffer when he was finished, I did look like a much better version of Jane Fortune. My hair, which had been down to my waist since I was a child, was now shoulder length. Mr. Marco had added some blond highlights "to rid the hair of any hint of its inherent mousiness."

When Winnie came to get me, her surprise was almost worth the three hours spent in a series of vinyl chairs.

"Jane, you are a knockout," Winnie said. She paid so much money to retrieve me, I felt as if I'd been ransomed. She was loaded down with bags and I took some of them off her hands.

"Charlie's going to kill me. I'll keep some of these bags in the trunk."

"Why do you buy so much if you know he won't like it?" I asked.

"It's one way to get Charlie's attention."

"I don't know if that's the best way," I said. I was stepping gingerly because I knew I was entering dangerous territory.

"You've never been married." That was obvious and she didn't need to point it out.

"What if he gets too annoyed?" I asked.

"He won't."

"But what if he does?"

"I don't know, Jane. I've never given it much thought."

We packed the trunk of the car.

"He just seems a little discouraged, that's all," I said.

"Then he should say something. Am I supposed to read his mind?"

"Look, it's none of my business, really."

A cardinal rule of being a good single woman—and one I was on the verge of breaking—was never to give advice about someone else's relationship. The trick behind this rule was to remain as inoffensive as possible so that no one could ever have a reason to object to you. That is the foundation of being a good single woman.

"You're my sister. Of course it's your business," Winnie said.

"Then maybe you should pay a little more attention to Charlie. With all of the responsibilities he has as a young father, you wouldn't want him looking around for something that seemed like more fun." I wouldn't normally have said anything like that, or even thought it (this isn't the kind of thought a good single woman can allow herself to have), but it was Charlie's hand placed just a little too long on mine that had started me thinking in that direction.

"He wouldn't do that. Not Charlie. The boys and I are everything to him. And to tell you the truth, I resent the implication." We got into the car. "It's not fair. You haven't been staying with us for even a week and you're suggesting that I'm not a good wife."

"I didn't say that, Winnie. I would never say that."

"That's what it sounded like."

"I only want what's best for you, Winnie," I said.

"I know you do," she said. She put her hand over mine. "That's just how I feel about you."

Chapter 16

Winnie's secret stash

We burst into the house with only as many packages as Winnie wanted Charlie to know about, but since he wasn't home yet, we smuggled everything else inside and hid it with the rest of Winnie's secret stash in the basement next to the laundry room. If you moved the lint-filled wastebasket and the dirty mops, if you had the fortitude to get past the dust bunnies and fallen sheets of fabric softener, there was a secret closet.

"I keep the mess here on purpose," Winnie said as she moved the trash basket to the side. "Voilà!" She pushed open a hidden door and we stepped in. The walk-in closet looked like it was meant to house out-of-season sports equipment and clothes. Instead of old parkas and ski boots, the closet was filled, floor to ceiling, with new things, many of them not even out of their boxes and bags. Winnie added her purchases to the sweaters, ceramic vases, purses, shoes, children's clothes, and toys.

"If you see anything you want, just take it," Winnie said. "Sometimes when I'm depressed I come down here and just pick something. I bring it upstairs and mingle it with the rest of our things. Charlie never notices."

"But what do you need all this stuff for?" I asked.

"Security, I guess. Whenever I need something new, it's always here." She paused and looked at me. "You won't tell?" she asked.

"Of course not." I knew she was trying to get closer to me by sharing her secret, and I would never betray that trust.

"Do you see anything you like?" she asked.

"I get confused when I see too many things at once. That's why I hate shopping," I said.

"Hate shopping?" She said it as if hating shopping was not only implausible but also ridiculous. She walked over to one corner of the closet and pulled out a bag from Neiman Marcus. There was a dress inside and she removed it with a flourish.

It was a wool dress, long with three-quarter-length sleeves, a dress you could wear on a winter evening with tights and ballet slippers.

"This would look good on you," she said. "And God knows you could use a few new things. It looks like you haven't bought anything in years."

I liked the dress, though I had never pictured myself in puce. The garage door opened and Winnie jumped. "He's home." We sneaked out of the closet, closed the door, replaced the trash and cleaning supplies, and rushed upstairs.

Charlie kissed Winnie on the cheek.

"How was your day, dear?" he said. I stood off to the side—single women guests must give couples their private moments.

"Wonderful," she said. "I can't wait to do a little disco." She twirled in a bad imitation of John Travolta in *Saturday Night Fever*.

"Where are the boys?" Charlie asked.

"Ariel took them out to play," Winnie said.

Winnie was assuming that Ariel had taken them out to play. All she knew for sure was that they weren't here when we came home and their jackets were gone from the front hall closet.

"It's getting late." Charlie looked out the window where dusk was falling.

"Don't worry, you can trust Ariel as much as you trust me."

I handed Charlie a short glass of scotch. He thanked me, but he was distracted. I had the uncomfortable notion that he didn't trust Winnie even as much as he trusted Ariel, and Ariel wasn't even the regular babysitter.

"Jane, what's different about you?" Charlie asked.

"She got her hair cut, Charlie. I mean, how could you not notice?" Winnie asked.

"I did notice. Very nice, Jane."

"Thank you, Charlie." I felt self-conscious, a little like a prize poodle just after a grooming.

"I have to go upstairs and change," Winnie said.

"I'll be up in a few," Charlie said.

"Did you find a place for Max?" I asked.

"We looked at a lot of houses, but we didn't see anything he really liked."

I picked up the tea things and started to put them away. Just as I put the last cup into the dishwasher, the door opened and the boys charged in with Ariel.

"I'm sorry we are so late, Mr. Maple," Ariel said. "We went to play in the park and lost track of time. I'll take the boys up and get them changed into warm things."

Trey sneezed. I picked him up and wiped his nose with a tissue. "Got the sniffles?"

He sneezed again. His face was all flushed, but it was probably from playing outside. I kissed his forehead. He was a little warm, but that wasn't how I knew he was sick. It was that he sat, docile, in my arms while Theo galloped up the stairs.

After I tucked Trey into bed, I found a thermometer in the bathroom and we played a game to see how long he could keep it under his tongue. Theo came in and told Trey to stop being such a baby, but after looking at him for a few minutes and finding him so pathetic, he went downstairs and asked Ariel to make some lemon tea. Theo carried it up carefully in an oversize mug.

Trey had a temperature of 102, which wasn't anything to be really worried about. Kids get temperatures, but it would definitely hamper the evening's activities. I was sure that Winnie wouldn't want to leave him.

"We'll have to stay home," Charlie said to Winnie when she came downstairs dressed to go out.

"It's only a slight fever," she said.

"You don't have to stay," I said.

"It's just that I've really been looking forward to this," Winnie said.

"We were only invited last night," Charlie said.

"Well, I've been looking forward to it all day."

Winnie was wearing a rather matronly outfit for a disco. A sweater set, her usual, but in an effort to be hip she had squeezed into a straight black skirt that did nothing to conceal her little round belly.

"Ariel can stay. I already arranged it so Jane could come," Winnie said.

"Ariel is the one who took Trey out for so long that he got sick," Charlie said.

"Don't be so dramatic, Charlie. Kids get colds. It happens. I don't see why Jane should stay. Trey will probably sleep through the night. He won't even know we're gone."

"I want to stay," I said.

Staying with Trey was far from a burden; it was such a lucky break that if I were a different kind of person, I would have introduced the germ into the family myself.

"I'll stay home," Charlie said.

"You absolutely will not," Winnie said. "Max is coming and God knows he doesn't want to be there without you. Your sisters are charming, but even that has its limits."

"He'll be fine without me," Charlie said.

"If you were being honest with yourself, you'd have to admit that your sisters may not have the stuff to entertain Max, but you just idolize those two and frankly I never saw what they did to deserve it."

"Your point?" Charlie asked.

"Forget it."

"I don't want to forget it," Charlie said. "I want to know what you think is wrong with my sisters."

"There's nothing wrong with them," Winnie said.

"I think you're jealous of them."

"Jealous!" Winnie raised her voice. "What on earth of?"

"They have everything in front of them. They aren't saddled with a husband and a family."

"I don't consider myself old and I'm sorry you do. But if I'm old, then you are, too, and if you think I consider you and the boys a burden, then you should look again. Yes, I've made some of my choices already, but I'm happy with them."

As they put on their coats I heard Charlie say to Winnie, "I don't think you're old, honey. Besides, grace is far more important than age."

That was very nice of him to say, since there wasn't anything especially graceful about Winnie.

The next morning, after checking on Trey, who was much better, Winnie sat with me in the breakfast nook and told me all about the night before. Tweedledee and Tweedledumber, as she sometimes called the Wheaton girls, made a big hit with Max. She couldn't tell which of them Max preferred, but it was probably Lindsay. After all, they had the writing thing in common. She said this as if Lindsay's "writing" were on a par with Max's.

"This guy named Buddy showed up. He was Heather's high school boyfriend and he obviously hasn't given up on her. Buddy is at Harvard and I think Heather likes him, but it's hard to tell with somebody like Max around. Buddy's not the best-looking boy in the world. He's got one of those pug Irish noses like Kevin Bacon."

Winnie said that Max danced with everyone, showing no favorites, but he did dance with Lindsay twice, and one of those dances was a slow one.

I stood up to get another cup of coffee.

"I'll have one, too," Winnie said.

Chapter 17

Jane Austen's head

The Maples were having a tree-trimming party. I liked being part of the Maple family, but Max kept turning up, and every time he did, it threw off my equilibrium—what was left of it.

I left the house before the party, claiming that I had business with Evan Bentley regarding the literary magazine.

"What business could you possibly be doing tonight?" Winnie complained. "It's Friday."

"We just have to get some things nailed down before Christmas," I said.

"I never realized, Jane, just how much work you do for this magazine. I'm actually very impressed."

Winnie was making Christmas tree decorations with pushpins and Styrofoam and she was hurrying to finish the one she was making for Marion.

"It's not a magazine," I said. "It's a literary journal."

"What's the difference?" Winnie asked.

"A literary journal is—I don't know—it has a different purpose," I said.

"And what is that?" Winnie asked.

"To promote literature."

Charlie looked up from his paper and licked the corner of his lip.

"Well," Charlie said, "you'll be missed."

"Yes, of course," Winnie said, and returned to poking colored pins into a Styrofoam ball.

It was a pleasure to get into my own car, to set the radio to NPR and listen to *All Things Considered*. Someday soon when they thanked their corporate sponsors and the charitable trusts, the Fortune Family Foundation would be among them. With the help of the bankers, I'd been earmarking money for years, and in the near future there would be enough to make an endowment.

When I finally found a place to park in Harvard Square, I stepped out of the underground lot and into a pre-Christmas flurry. Christmas lights blinked in greens and reds in the trees around the square and car horns blared in the dusk. It was four-thirty and soon everyone would be rushing home.

A skinny Salvation Army Santa rang a bell outside the Harvard Coop and I dropped several bills into the receptacle that stood beside him.

"Merry Christmas," he said.

"And to you," I answered, and smiled. I always liked Christmas and New England winters, especially evenings when the air was so crisp it felt like it might break from the sky like an icicle from a tree.

I went into the Harvard Coop to look for a gift for the Bentleys. I settled on a book of photography that showed writers in their natural habitats—like animals. Max was in the book. The caption might have read: "A native of suburban Boston, this exotic beast has found a home in the industrial-style lofts of Tribeca located in downtown New York City. Tribeca attracts some of the most successful of his species." Instead, it just said: "Max Wellman, Tribeca Loft."

With gift in hand, I walked toward the Bentleys' house. Bentley's wife, Melody, answered the enormous oak door. She took a brief look at me, then pulled me into her ample chest. She smelled of wet clay. She always smelled of wet clay. When Bentley had finally gotten married, he hadn't chosen from his plethora of worshipful students. Instead, he had chosen a woman he met at a party, a woman several years older than he was, a woman who had retired at forty after making her money in fashions for plus-size women. Bentley called it "fashion for fatties."

"Darling, you look horrible," Melody said.

"Thanks," I said.

"I didn't mean it like that. Well, you know what I mean."

I didn't know really, except perhaps that the stress was beginning to show. Melody led me into the kitchen, where Bentley was grinding coffee beans. Since he had given up drinking, he'd become a coffee connoisseur. He gave coffee the same attention he once gave to his brand of scotch.

He asked if I'd prefer Kona, French roast, or a special Brazilian blend.

"I wouldn't know one from the other," I said.

"Jeez, Jane," Bentley said, "you don't look too well. Are you sick?" He looked closely at my face, which was, as usual, devoid of makeup. Melody offered me a plate of Christmas cookies. I took two and sat in a bentwood chair at their pine table.

"I'm not sick," I said. "I'm perfectly well."

"I like your new haircut, Jane," Melody said. "Evan, you didn't say anything about Jane's new haircut." Melody always looked polished. She wore a flowing artistic shirt and slim pants. She was one of those women who always knew how to do the best with what they had, probably a necessity in her former business. Her brown helmet of hair was straight and smooth, and to the untrained eye it looked as if she wasn't wearing makeup. Because of Miranda, my eye was trained. What I was looking at in Melody was not the lack of makeup, but rather the skillful application of it.

Bentley put a cup of coffee in front of me. "Nice haircut," he said. "Try the Kona."

The coffee tasted like sludge. I added several inches of cream from a pitcher on the table.

"He's back," I said. I used an ominous voice and tried to be funny, but it was lost on them. Everything I said or did was lost on someone these days.

"Who's back?" Bentley asked.

"Max Wellman," I said. "I already told you that his sister and her husband ended up renting our house. Bad enough. But it turns out he was a college friend of my brother-in-law's. Charlie—the brother-in-law—is helping him find a house, some perfect place for him and some nymphet to settle down." I took a bite of the cookie in my hand. It was a homemade Christmas cookie, but it was shaped like a Star of David. Melody was Jewish. I think she forgot to add sugar to the batter, but it would have been rude to spit it out, so I kept eating.

"Is that the Max Wellman you're so jealous of?" Melody asked Bentley.

"I never said I was jealous of him," Bentley said.

"You did too. You said he stole the girl you wanted." Bentley turned toward the sink, and when he turned back his face had the flush of a sunburn.

For a few months after Max left, Bentley and I had dated, or I suppose you could call it that. I always thought he was too old for me, and besides, if Max still resided in my heart all these years later, you can only imagine how many rooms he inhabited then. The real difference between my dates with Bentley and our meetings in connection with the *Review* was that on our dates Bentley paid. He kissed me a few times, drunkenly. I hadn't liked the taste of him and his kisses were too wet.

"It wasn't just the girl," Melody said. "I think if Evan were to admit it, he'd like to have the career Max has." Melody sat heavily in the chair beside me.

Bentley had broken out of his writer's slump after the *Review* started to get him attention. He had written two more novels, both to critical acclaim, but neither of them had made much money. It wasn't that he needed money, but if you took money as a sign of the world's appreciation, the world hadn't valued him enough.

Melody sipped her coffee. She took it black, which was either a sign of true love or of a complete absence of taste buds.

"Who wouldn't envy Max Wellman?" Bentley asked. "That hardly makes me unique among writers. Anyway, things always work out for the best. If I got that girl, I wouldn't be here with you."

Though the words were kind, the tone was not. He probably wasn't thrilled to have Melody hanging out his dirty laundry in front of me. And what was more awkward was that she didn't realize that the girl she was talking about, the memory of Bentley's she had to expose in order to save herself from its shadow, was me.

I didn't know that I'd become a piece of Bentley's mythology. He never acted unhappy after I told him I'd rather that we remain friends, yet he had created a story, an imaginary lost love, a struggle between himself and Max Wellman for the love of a woman. The truth was that Max was long gone by the time I started to date Bentley.

This lost love of his was all in his head, a part of the stories we create about ourselves that become our histories. After we tell our stories enough times, they become true for us, and maybe that's all that matters. I had done it with Max, written the role of jilted lover, then played it with the finesse of a Shakespearean actor. Perhaps my suffering was my own creation just like Bentley's was his.

"It's hard to watch him move on with his life," I said.

"When you haven't moved on with yours?" Bentley asked.

"I have," I said, though I didn't feel like I had.

"She certainly has," Melody said. "Look at the work of the foundation. You told me that when you started on it, no one had ever even heard of it. Now, there isn't a bookstore or newsstand in Boston and probably other cities, too, that doesn't carry the *Euphemia Review*. Because of Jane, you get asked to speak all the time."

"I would hope that it has something to do with my books," Bentley said.

"Of course it does," I said, but we both knew that on the strength of his books alone, Bentley would not have the career he had today.

"So what's Jack Reilly like?" Bentley asked. He knew how important it was for me to discover a new talent, especially now.

"I haven't found him yet."

"I guess you'll have to move on to the next one," Bentley said.

"I can't."

"Why not?"

"Because he's the next great thing."

"And you know this how?"

"From the story."

"It's a good story, Jane. A very good story, but it's just a story."

"I'm going to find him," I said.

"I've never heard of a writer applying for a fellowship, then disappearing. There must be something off about him. Maybe he's a criminal. Maybe he's in jail."

This would fit my fantasies about the man from Lynn, the city of sin. But even if he was in jail, he could still be my next great discovery. Literary inmates were all the rage.

"He's not in jail," I said.

"Give it the holidays and then move on. That's my suggestion," Bentley said.

"Evan, you're so practical. Sometimes too practical for an artist. Can't you see that Jane is passionate about this?" Melody asked.

"Passion is something best kept locked up," Bentley said. He had put his passion in a cage when he left the bottle behind. Sometimes I missed the old Bentley, the one who sneaked into a room off the kitchen during a literary lunch at the Ritz and took a torch to an ice sculpture of Jane Austen's head. And although his writing had matured and the reviewers liked it, the verve, the humor of that first book, his first great success, never came again.

"I think he's fallen for Charlie's sister Lindsay," I said. Until I had said it out loud like that, I had kept myself from believing it. I wanted someone, anyone, to come rushing in and say, "No, that's not true."

"Who? Jack Reilly?"

"Max Wellman."

"That's that, then," Bentley said. "Give it up. Sometimes you have to give things up, Jane."

He looked at me with pity, as if I were now, only at this late stage, having to learn the hard lessons of life.

"Come and see my new sculpture," Melody said.

She took me into her workroom. She pulled a wet rag off a lump of clay to reveal the bust of a man.

"It's very bad, isn't it?" she asked.

"It captures him," I said, though I wasn't sure who it was. I hoped that the bust was supposed to be either Bentley or some other recognizable figure.

"You think?" she asked.

"Absolutely."

If it was Bentley and if she had, indeed, captured him, I wondered what the implications of that were. Do we all try to capture the people we love, either in clay, with words, or even just in our imaginations?

We returned to the kitchen. Bentley had made a fire in the brick fireplace and we sat in front of it with our legs stretched out. Melody and I drank snifters of brandy and Bentley held his perpetual coffee cup.

It began to snow, so rather than go back to Winnie's, I decided to stay in the Bentleys' guest room. Melody gave me one of Bentley's oversize T-shirts to sleep in. I felt a bit like a fraud now, knowing that I was a part of a history he remembered so differently than I did. Down the hall the two of them were in bed, chatting the way I imagined couples did before they went to sleep.

I stood by the window and looked out. The flakes got bigger and bigger under the street lamps. I watched for a long time until the street was covered with fresh snow.

Chapter 18

Skating on the Frog Pond

Max invited us to his sister's house—my house—for hot cider and skating on the Frog Pond at the Boston Common.

"Has your sister done her tree already?" Lindsay asked. The girls were home from Wheaton and we were having drinks at the Maples'.

"She doesn't have one," Max said.

"No tree?"

"They're Jewish," I said. Max smiled at me. My stomach did a little flip when he looked at me like that. I was dismayed to find that the more I saw Max, the more I wanted to see him. Even when he was right there, I walked around with a vague longing for him.

Max had changed. There was more of the actor about him. But as long as I could remember what it was like to have him twist toward me in bed, I couldn't pull myself away. I don't think it was hope, exactly, that kept me there; it was more like obsessive fascination—maybe it was hope.

This, if anything, explains why I didn't leave. I had thought, very briefly, about going to Palm Beach, but quickly dismissed it. I even started looking for apartments in Boston, but Winnie said she couldn't do without me. Even though I knew that no one was indispensable, Winnie's marriage was on shaky ground and I felt that the presence of someone else kept it from sliding downhill.

"I know they're Jewish," Heather said. She was sitting on the arm of Max's chair. Those girls couldn't get enough of his physical proximity. They were always snuggling up to him like stuffed animals. "But why don't they have a tree? Don't you even have a Hanukkah bush?" she asked.

Max patted her leg in the accepting way of a man who has become successful and is now ready to round out his world by marrying a silly girl. He couldn't see past their inexhaustible delight in him, past the family embrace. I think some romantic love works that way: you fall not only for the person, but also for a vision of yourself in their world.

The day came for the skating party and I wasn't thrilled about being a guest in my own home. Still, there was enough curiosity in me to make me join the group. We all piled into Charlie's car and headed toward the city.

When we walked into the front hallway of the house, I got ready for a jolt to my solar plexus, but it didn't come. The hall was unchanged except for Max's sister, Emma, who came forward to greet us. After we took off our coats and banged any excess snow from our boots, Emma put her arm around me and leaned in.

"Jane, I want you to feel just as at home here as you would if we weren't here."

That was impossible, but to say so would have been neither gracious nor polite. I tried for an authentic smile and thanked her. Emma had draped our staid sofas with exotic throws and pillows. The look was American Pedigree Meets Casablanca.

Though I had only been out of the house for a little less than a month, it looked more faded than I remembered. Maybe I was seeing it through fresh eyes. It had always had the shabbiness of old money. Did the worn damasks, chintzes, and satins look different to me now because their shabbiness would soon spring, not from old money, but from no money at all?

My college friend Isabelle had been shattered when her parents had sold the family home. It was as if they were selling off a childhood that could never be recaptured. She was thirty-two when it happened, but she still felt as if something was irrevocably lost. I had expected to feel that way, and was surprised to find that my prevailing feeling was relief.

Emma looked at me warily. How much had Max told her about us?

Max's sister, having married Joseph Goldman, was now Emma Goldman.

"What could I do?" she said. "I loved the guy. His name is Goldman, so I took it. I suppose I didn't have to, but I'm traditional about some things."

"I don't get it," Heather said. "What's wrong with the name Emma Goldman?"

"There's nothing wrong with it," Emma said, looking at Max.

"She was a famous anarchist," I said.

"A what?" Lindsay asked.

"An anarchist," I said. "It's someone who believes that government and law should be abolished."

"Good thing we have Jane to translate for us. We'd never be able to cope," Lindsay said.

"Anyway, it would never work," Heather said.

"What wouldn't?" Emma asked.

"You can't get rid of government." Heather said this with great authority. "It's the silliest idea I ever heard."

Joe Goldman joined us. His entrance interrupted the conversation, a very good thing under the circumstances. I didn't know what a producer was supposed to look like, but it wouldn't have surprised me to learn that Joe Goldman was typical of the species. His walk was brisk, his smile welcoming. If there was something anywhere to be produced, he looked fully capable of producing it. We followed him into the living room, where he had contrived the perfect winter scene: a glowing fire, cookies warm from the oven, caramel apples. The cider, both hard and soft, was served in glass mugs and garnished with sticks of cinnamon.

"No food?" Max teased.

Emma smacked him on the shoulder with her palm. "Is this not the perfect winter tableau?" She curtsied and spread out her hands, palms up.

"Did you steal it from the set of *Little Women*?" he asked.

"Steal? Don't be silly. We don't steal, we borrow," she said.

Emma wore her happiness lightly but carefully, like a lace shawl. Even if she hadn't been Max's sister, she was the type of woman I would have wanted to befriend.

Joe and Emma stayed behind by the fire while the rest of us trooped to the Boston Common. Heather's friend Buddy showed up, so there were three couples—and me. I was used to being the odd one out, but it felt worse when Max was there. The Wheaton girls were wearing short pleated skating skirts. I wore black jeans, a little too tight for skating. I'm a good skater and know what to wear to be comfortable, but I was aiming for a little more style than usual, and my aim wasn't good.

Lindsay walked beside me on the way to the Common.

"You used to know Max, didn't you?" Lindsay asked.

"Yes," I said.

"I think he's wonderful. It's amazing that he hasn't tried to sleep with me yet. He's such a gentleman."

"You haven't even been out alone together, have you?" I asked.

"Well, no, but that could be easily arranged." She slipped on a piece of ice and grabbed me to keep from falling. She pulled me off-balance, but I managed to stay upright.

"How is your writing going?" I asked.

"I haven't really done anything during the vacation. We've been so busy. I wanted to ask you. You are so good at figuring things out. You seem to know more than we do, about almost everything. What do you think of me and Max?"

"I'm not sure what you're asking," I said.

"Do you think he's as crazy about me as I am about him?" She looked up at me with a face so young and free from blemish I couldn't imagine a world in which any man wouldn't be crazy about her.

"I don't know," I said.

"He kissed me, you know," she said. "Last night as he was leaving. And it wasn't just any kiss. It was a real kiss, if you know what I mean."

Unfortunately, I did.

We sat on benches around the edge of the pond to put on our skates. I had thrown mine into the trunk of my car when I left Louisburg Square. Not everyone would think that skates would be necessary to their winter, but I usually skated at least once a week.

I watched the three couples, the men kneeling to help the women on with their skates. As I leaned over my own, I pictured Jack Reilly at my feet. Jack Reilly would wear his leather jacket, even though it was too cold to wear only leather. His cigarette would hang from his lips and the smoke would drift past my face as he bent over my skates. He'd make Max look conventional. I had to find Jack Reilly, if only to give me something special to announce to the Wellesley College girls after Christmas.

I finished lacing my skates, flew out onto the ice, and executed a single axel. I twirled, reversed, did crossovers and backward crossovers. I soared in my own little world.

"Look at Jane," Heather said as she struck out with a tentative step. "She's a terrific skater."

Lindsay, who was a little more sure on her feet, skated over to me. "I hope when I'm your age, I'll know half the things you know." She spoke loudly and tilted her head toward Max.

"Me too," Max said.

"You're as old as Jane, aren't you?" Lindsay asked.

"No one is as old as Jane," Max said. With that, he took off and skated to the other side of the pond. Lindsay followed him, and when she caught up to him, she slipped her arm through his.

I took a step, then another. I didn't know what he meant. No one was as old as me? My mother always said I was born old. Maybe that's what he meant.

I started to spin and I spun and twirled in smaller and smaller circles until I got dizzy and crashed on the ice, splayed like an idiot rag doll. The wind was knocked out of me and I couldn't get up right away. When I looked up, it was Max who was staring down at me.

"I'm okay," I said. I must have been blushing right through my clothes. Max took my gloved hand and helped me to my feet. Everyone else who had been skating on the pond, or even sitting on the sidelines, had stopped to look.

"Okay, show's over," Max called out. Max kept my hand in his as if he had forgotten he held it. He wasn't looking at me. Instead, he was gazing toward the Public Garden, which was frozen over now.

Max glanced down at our enjoined hands and let go. He turned toward me.

"Are you sure you're okay?" he asked.

We were standing so close together I could feel the coolness of his sigh on my cheek. If I hadn't known better, I might have thought we were just one breath away from a kiss.

But then Lindsay barreled toward us and, not being too sure on her feet, smacked into Max and he had to hold her to keep her from falling.

"Is Jane all right?" she asked in a loud voice. Everyone was still staring at me, and though I hated to be the center of attention under any circumstance, it was worse when it originated in an embarrassing fall.

Max examined me as if he was trying to read something in my face that had not yet been written. "If you're okay, then." He skated off with Lindsay and slipped his arm around her waist. She beamed up at him.

I stood alone in the center of the pond and watched everyone skating around me.

$\mathcal{C}$hapter 19

$\mathcal{I}$n which gifts are exchanged

Max came to the Maples' on Christmas Eve to give gifts. He gave both Lindsay and Heather Burberry scarves. While a cashmere Burberry scarf is certainly a lovely gift, it's hardly personal. I had expected that he'd give Lindsay a piece of jewelry—maybe not *the* piece of jewelry, but maybe something sparkly to hang around her neck.

Max did have something else up his sleeve, the pièce de résistance. He invited the Maple family to go skiing up north. Everyone was going except for Marion and Charles Sr., who were staying home to take care of the children.

And he hadn't forgotten me. My present was on the bottom of his pile. He didn't look me in the eye when he handed it over.

"Open it, Jane," Lindsay said. She was stroking her scarf absently.

I ripped open the wrapping as I'd seen the Maple girls do. No more careful scraping at the tape with a nibbled fingernail.

Inside the box was a leather journal. The paper was smooth and creamy.

"It's from Italy," Max said. "Do you still keep a journal?"

I lowered my eyes. I placed my palm on the cover of the book.

"I do," I said.

"Oh, that's beautiful, Jane," Lindsay said. "Max, you have such fabulous taste. You really do." She reached out to take the journal so she could look at it more closely, but I didn't give it to her. Instead, I pretended I didn't see that she wanted it.

And what did I get for Max? I bought him a pair of shoes. I couldn't think of anything else, but I thought shoes from Brooks Brothers would hark back to that first pair, the pair that brought us together. It was meant as a soft joke, or so I thought. Maybe I meant more by it.

"You bought him shoes?" Lindsay said when he opened the box. Yes, obviously I had bought him shoes. "How did you even know his size?"

I looked at Max to see what his reaction would be. Shoes were more personal than scarves. He looked at me and smiled.

"You didn't have to do it," he said.

"I know," I said.

"They're beautiful shoes," he said.

"I'm glad you like them."

He reached over, took my hand, and squeezed it. When he received Heather's gift—gloves—and Lindsay's—a Tiffany money clip—he kissed them both, Heather on the cheek, and Lindsay softly on the lips.

"I don't understand the shoes," Lindsay said. She seemed disgruntled.

"It is a bit of an odd choice," Marion said, "though they are very nice shoes."

"Very nice," Winnie said.

*　　*　　*

There comes a time in the course of longing when being with the person becomes more painful than being without them. I didn't have a plan, didn't know where I was going, but I knew I had to go somewhere. I didn't love the idea of packing up my things and heading into the unknown, so I made a plan: I'd go look for Jack Reilly. I was on a quest, and you always have a direction when you are on a quest.

Up in my room I tried to pack, but Winnie kept taking things from my suitcase and hanging them back up in the closet.

"Jane, you have to come with us. Everyone's counting on you." I hardly thought that everyone was counting on me. In fact, I was pretty sure that at least one person—Lindsay—would be thrilled to get rid of me. I wasn't obtuse enough not to notice her eyeing me when she thought I wasn't looking. She seemed to think me some kind of rival, though she was so obviously wrong.

I might still want Max, based on some fantasy of first love, but I had to be realistic. The best thing I could do was go away. I was a bit worried about leaving Winnie, but she had managed her marriage without me all these years.

"Stop that, will you," I said, and grabbed a blouse Winnie had just unfolded. I tried to pull it away from her. "Even if I do come, I still have to pack."

"I suppose," she said, and let go of the shirt. She sat on the bed. "So you might come?"

"Absolutely not."

"You are so stubborn sometimes," Winnie said. I hardly thought so. Too often I was willing to sway to the will of anyone who came within a square mile of me. "But you love to ski."

I looked out the window onto the field and the woods beyond. A light snow covered everything. Winnie was right. I loved to ski. People were so friendly on a mountain. And on a mountain there was nothing wrong with being a "single." It usually meant you could cut the lift lines. So a mountain was one place where you benefited from being alone.

"What will you do?" Winnie asked.

"I'll think of something." I didn't tell her about Jack Reilly—it would have been too much to explain—nor did I tell her I'd already made a reservation at the Inn at Long Last in Vermont, not far from Jack Reilly's last known address.

Winnie stood up.

"I'm sending Max up to ask you himself." If she thought that I wasn't going with them just because I hadn't received an express invitation, she was—half right.

"Don't," I said. "Please, I'm not dressed." I was wearing a flannel granny gown. I had put it on when I came back from a long and chilling walk.

"He'll be right up." She moved toward the door. "Put on a robe."

"No, Winnie," I almost shouted. I had the helpless feeling of a child unable to avoid punishment. Winnie called to Max from the upstairs landing.

My robe was worse than my nightgown. It was pink terry cloth with the nap worn at the elbows. I looked around, panicked. How would it look if I slipped into the closet and shut the door behind me? The indignity of being found cowering behind Winnie's out-of-season coats just about outweighed the potential benefit of hiding. Did I have time to change?

"Jane?" Max was already in the hall.

"Yes?" I yelped like an adolescent boy. I tried to sound as put together as I could, to gather my dignity, to act as if it were perfectly all right for him to see me dressed like a pink polar bear.

Max poked his head into the room as if he were wary about what he might find inside my lair. I wanted to growl at him, but I managed to contain myself.

"Can I come in?" Max asked.

If you must, I thought.

"Of course," I said.

He slipped in and stood by the door. I remained near my suitcase and pushed a pair of frayed underpants to the bottom.

"Everyone wants you to come to Vermont with us," he said.

"Does that everyone include you?" I asked. He stepped farther into the room and sat on an armchair in the corner. He picked up a book from the ottoman, examined it, then put it back down. He leaned his arms on his knees and stared down at the carpet.

"People move on," he said. He didn't look up.

"Of course they do." I kept my voice light and continued to poke at the things in my suitcase.

"Have you?" he asked, and raised his head. I looked at him for just a moment. There was a thud against my ribs, so loud and heavy it felt like a small animal had collapsed inside my chest.

"Of course I have. It's been fifteen years. What did you think?" I lied.

"Then we can be friends." He stood up and came over to where I was standing. He stuck out his hand. My hand, when I extended it toward his, was dry and chapped. I was embarrassed by my own hand.

Friends. How could it possibly hurt so much after so many years? Why had I never gone after him? Why was I so afraid? Why hadn't he come after me?

"I'll meet you up there," I said, and turned back to my packing.

"Fine," he said. "But just know there's plenty of room at the ski house." He seemed disoriented now. He'd done his duty, played the gracious host, and now he was ready to move on.

I watched him leave the room, then walked over to the door, closed it, and went back to sit on the bed.

"Letting go is very difficult for me." I said this out loud, but in a soft voice. Who would hear me? Who would come, sit beside me, and say, "Yes, but, Jane, it's time."

Chapter 20

The Inn at Long Last

The address I had for Jack Reilly was in southern Vermont, not too far from the house Max had rented in Londonderry. Maybe by the time I showed up I'd have Jack Reilly in tow.

I left Winnie's early the next morning and arrived in Vermont before noon. I checked into the Inn at Long Last on Main Street in Chester. The inn was a large white Colonial, complete with burgundy runners on the stairs, Oriental carpets, Windsor chairs in the lobby, highboys, lowboys, overstuffed sofas, and two working fireplaces. It had the flavor of our house, only nothing in it was authentic; everything was a replica.

As I headed up the stairs behind the bellboy, we passed a man who looked familiar. He was soap-opera-star handsome with blue black hair, a chiseled jaw, and a cleft chin. He smiled and nodded. I smiled back. The look he gave me was one of admiration. I was not the type of woman who was always thinking that men were looking at her *that way,* but this look was unmistakable. Even I could recognize it.

I left my things in my room and went back outside. I grabbed a cup of coffee at a diner next door and examined my map. By my calculations, Jack Reilly was about twenty minutes away. I wore my green suit. Unfortunately, my camel overcoat had seen better days, but I could always take it off before I got out of the car.

After a few wrong turns, I found number 3 Briar Patch Lane. A big step up from the Lynn apartment, it was a neat saltbox with a wraparound porch. It even had a picket fence, but it wasn't white. Someone had painted it black. Was this stab at irony the work of Jack Reilly? I opened the gate and went up the icy front walk. Failure to put down rock salt in winter—in my opinion—is a sign of neglect. The mailbox hung crooked beside the door, and when I stepped onto the porch one of the floorboards came loose.

I hoped that Jack Reilly wasn't anything like this house. Though it was pleasing enough on the outside, on closer examination it was in serious need of repair.

After I rang the bell, I heard steps padding toward the door. Unfortunately, those steps were followed by barking. I waited. It wasn't as if knocking on a stranger's door was easy for me. I admired Hope Bliss for going into investigation. I could never do it. I felt nervous and out of place standing out there in the cold. But my desire to find Jack Reilly was strong enough to outweigh even my natural reticence. I waited a few more minutes, but no one came, so I wrote a note and slipped it under the screen door. I could have used the crooked mailbox, but I wanted to be sure that whoever came home saw my note first thing.

I stumbled back down the walk, got into my car, turned the heater up high, and drove back to the Inn at Long Last. It was late afternoon and I was supposed to join Max and the Maples in time for dinner.

*　　*　　*

My car wasn't the best car for the roads of Vermont, and when I finally found the house Max had rented, I had trouble maneuvering up the snowy driveway. I finally parked on the street and trekked up what seemed like a quarter mile to the door. I stopped for a moment on the landing, then knocked.

Max and Lindsay answered the door together. They were wearing sweaters and jeans. They weren't exactly matching, but they might as well have been. Max's arm was draped over Lindsay's shoulder.

It made me want to take the snowmobile I saw in the side yard and drive it onto a lake that hadn't quite frozen over. I could fall into the ice and disappear, never to be heard from again.

"It's so good to be here," I said, and hugged them both.

"Look at this house. Isn't it awesome?" Lindsay said. "Isn't Max incredible?" Her eyes shone with that look some women get when they believe they are looking at something that will someday be theirs. Max didn't own this particular house, but if he married Lindsay, this type of experience would be hers for the asking.

"Hardly incredible," Max said. He tweaked her ear, which I thought a strange thing for a lover to do. He had never tweaked my ear.

Max's friends the Franklins, and a man introduced as Basil Funk, arrived only minutes after I did. Duke Franklin had been Max's mentor. Duke was an extremely popular mystery novelist. His most famous series character, Gideon Thackeray, had been alive longer than I had. Duke was so prolific that he often wrote under several different names. He was rich and had been happy until a year ago, when his daughter, Cynthia, had been jogging along a road near their house and was mowed down by a drunk driver.

Cynthia had been engaged to Basil, a struggling artist. They had been living together on Duke's impressive estate—I'd seen a spread on it in *Architectural Digest*. Basil was so lost when Cynthia died that he had remained in the guesthouse on the edge of the property ever since.

I followed Max into a sunken living room, where he poured drinks from a fully stocked bar.

"How is Inga working out?" Duke said in a low voice.

Inga?

Max looked toward the kitchen. "She seems fine."

"She's an excellent cook. We hire her for all our parties," Nora Franklin said. Nora had an air of distraction about her, and she stared into her glass of wine as if she might find something in it. Basil was not exactly gregarious, either. He sat beside me on what could be loosely termed a love seat and stared dolefully into the fire.

"Mr. Franklin," Heather said, "I've read every one of your books. All twenty-six of the Thackeray novels. I can never wait for the next one."

"I'll have to write faster," Duke said. "And call me Duke."

Winnie, who was sitting with Charlie in a love seat near the fire, looked up as if she'd like to say something, but having nothing to add, sipped her cider.

Basil turned toward me.

"I always read the *Euphemia Review*," he said. "I think it's becoming one of the leading literary reviews in the country, and I'm not the only one who thinks so."

"Thank you," I said.

"Why not put some art in it?" he asked.

I had thought about that. Five-color pages with high-end production value would double the cost of the magazine.

"I don't have a background in art," I said. "I wouldn't know where to begin." I had to remember that I had no special background in literature either, but I had a passion for it, and so far that had made up for any other deficiency. "I don't trust my artistic judgment," I said, and took a sip of red wine.

"You could get someone to help you," Basil said. He put his hand on my leg and leaned toward me. He was closer than I liked strangers to be.

"I could," I said, "but I always thought I'd do better if I concentrated on one thing."

"That's interesting," Winnie said.

"What is?" I asked.

"I never imagined you gave it so much thought. It's like the family foundation is a profession or something."

"You've given grants to artists before," Basil said, ignoring Winnie.

"Usually for memorials and things like that. We gave a grant to Muriel Spiking, who did an AIDS memorial for the median strip on Commonwealth Avenue."

"Muriel Spiking's a hack," Basil said.

I wasn't sure I'd heard him correctly. Even if he didn't like her work, it was rather impolitic of him to say so when he knew I had given her a grant.

"Bronze boxes. That's all she does. Bronze boxes of every shape and size. Bronze boxes. Bronze boxes."

"You see, then, why I don't often give grants to artists. I don't trust my taste."

"Jane, your taste has always been impeccable," Max said.

Lindsay gave him a quizzical look. I glanced at him and he smiled at me. Friends. We were friends now.

Basil took his hand from my leg and put it back on his own. He began to tap his fingers as if an imaginary piano had suddenly appeared on his knee.

"A person of intelligence, such as yourself, can always learn discernment," he said. "I'd like to show you some of *my* work."

"And I'd like to see it," I said. Basil Funk amused me. I didn't know why exactly. Perhaps I needed to be fawned over. He wasn't bad-looking, except for his hair, which was cut in a monkish style and hung in fringes just above his eyebrows.

"Tomorrow night when you all come to dinner," he said.

"I'll look forward to it," I said. He reached out and took my hand. I saw that Max was looking at us. I was too warm and it wasn't from the fire. I got up to get another glass of wine. I offered drinks to the party and everyone accepted, so I spent a few minutes filling orders. Max came over to help me.

"You look flushed," he said. He touched my cheek with the back of his hand.

"I'm a little warm," I said.

I could profess my intention to be "just friends" with Max from now until the end of days, but that wouldn't keep my temperature from rising when he was near.

"Basil seems to like you," Max said.

I glanced over my shoulder to see if Basil could hear us. He was staring into the fire with a inconsolable look.

"Don't be silly," I said.

"Don't sell yourself short, Jane," Max said.

"Let's make a deal. I won't sell myself short if you don't try to sell me off."

Max frowned and chewed at his bottom lip. "Deal," he said.

We passed the drinks around and Max perched on the arm of Lindsay's chair. He bent his head toward her and said something I couldn't hear, but it made her laugh. For a minute I thought they might be laughing at me. Then Inga called us in to dinner.

While we were eating, Max's cell phone rang. When he answered it, he looked flustered. He excused himself and left the room.

We were all quiet for an awkward moment.

"Pass the spaghetti, please," Charlie said.

"I'll have the garlic bread," Duke said.

"This is really delicious. Wonderful, Inga," I called toward the kitchen. I went in to see if she needed any help—or at least I told myself that's what I was doing. Max was in the kitchen.

"I told you," he said into the phone, "I won't be back until after New Year's. And please don't call me on this number." There was a pause while he listened. "Yes, me too." He looked up at me and put the phone in his pocket.

We looked at each other.

"It doesn't matter to me what you do," I said in a low voice, "but you should at least be kind to Lindsay."

He looked toward Inga, grabbed my upper arm, and pulled me toward the mudroom outside the kitchen. "Not that it has anything to do with you, but if you have to know, it's old business," he said. "I'm trying to put an end to it."

"You don't have to explain it to me."

"I know, but for some reason I feel as if I do." His words were clipped. "Please don't say anything to Lindsay."

I looked at the stone floor.

"You must know me better than that—even after all these years," I said.

He shook his head. "I know. I'm sorry."

"God," I said, "I haven't changed that much."

"You haven't really changed at all," he said in a quiet voice.

I must have changed in some ways if, when he first saw me, he said he wouldn't have recognized me, but this probably wasn't the time to bring that up.

"Have you changed, Max?" I asked. I had convinced myself that reports about him were exaggerated, but it looked like he had become the type of man who kept bunches of women like weeds in flowerpots.

"Of course I have. Everyone does."

"You said I hadn't."

"But don't you see. Most people do. My life is much different now than when you first knew me."

"Mine isn't so different."

"I know that."

"All change is not necessarily a good thing," I said.

"You talking about something in particular?"

"You must know your reputation."

"I don't read my own press."

"Now you're being disingenuous."

"We should go back."

I touched his arm. "Max?" He turned toward me.

"Try not to hurt Lindsay."

"That's interesting coming from you."

"I don't know what you mean."

"Aren't you the girl who left me a note and crept away like a thief?"

"It was a long time ago."

"Not really a defense. But don't worry, I have no intention of hurting Lindsay. In fact, I'm thinking of marrying her."

I thought I might not be able to get out of the mudroom before my face melted and revealed my feelings, but I had to, because that was one of the things that defined me. I always behaved properly in every situation (maybe I could have done better when I left Max the note), and to behave properly in this one, I'd have to wear a smile as I followed Max back out to the dining room.

"Don't you think it's a little soon?" I asked. He wouldn't catch my eye.

"I never had any trouble figuring out what I wanted. Time was never an issue with me."

"But it's only been a couple of weeks."

"When you know, you know."

"What if you make a mistake?" I asked.

"Mistakes aren't the end of the world," he said. "They don't kill you." Finally he looked at me.

"Do me a favor—one I know I have no right to ask—give it a little more time."

"Ah, Jane, sensible, practical, levelheaded Jane," he said.

"You used to like that about me."

"That was before I knew what the consequences would be." He turned and left the room.

On the way back to the dining room, I stopped in the kitchen to pick up a bowl of extra meatballs. I didn't know how I was going to make it through the rest of the evening, but I pasted a smile on my face and joined the party.

Chapter 21

Miss Fortune skis as a single

At midnight when I arrived at the Inn at Long Last, it was like a tomb. I didn't see anyone at the front desk. I stood there for a moment, then knocked on the counter. A boy came out from a back room.

"Do I have any messages?" I asked. "Jane Fortune."

He handed over a slip of paper and yawned. I took it and went up to my room.

The paper said, "He's gone and good riddance. You might find him at the Butterfly Museum. Last time I saw him he was working there. Good luck. Maureen Mackey." The Butterfly Museum? I sat there staring at the note, then started to laugh. My bad-boy Jack Reilly was at the Butterfly Museum?

The next morning when I arrived at the ski house only Heather and Lindsay were downstairs. Eventually, Winnie joined us. She sat at the head of the table in a blue quilted bathrobe that made her look like she was eighty years old.

"I have the sniffles," she said, looking sour. "It's so unfair. I really wanted to go skiing."

"You don't seem very sick," Heather said. "You could still go if you wanted to." Heather folded a linen napkin into squares and placed it under a fork.

"And get pneumonia? I don't think so. I really don't. I'll just stay here in front of the fire."

"Lazy cow," Heather said under her breath.

"What did you say?" Winnie asked.

"Nothing." Lindsay and Heather gave each other a look.

Max and Charlie came down. Both were freshly shaven and showered. Max smelled faintly of Old Spice.

Because Winnie wasn't going with us, we were only five and were able to squeeze into one car. I love everything about an early morning on a mountain, from lugging the skis to buying the tickets.

We decided to ski together, which meant that since we were five, one of us wouldn't have a partner for the chairlift. Everyone protested weakly that they would be happy to be "single," but in the end I was the one who skied off to the separate line. I was four from the front when I was paired with another skier. In his hat and goggles, I didn't immediately recognize him. It wasn't until we had been scooped into the air that he turned toward me.

"I know you," he said.

The sun was behind him and I squinted into his face.

"You do?"

"Aren't you staying at the Inn at Long Last?"

He was the man from the stairs, the soap-opera-star man, the man who had looked familiar.

"I'm Guy Callow," he said, and extended a leather glove.

"Jane Fortune." There couldn't be too many Guy Callows in the world. This must be Miranda's Guy. I had met him only once, and briefly.

"Are you related to Miranda Fortune?" he asked.

"She's my sister."

"So you are *that* Jane Fortune," he said.

We reached the top of the slope and were deposited onto the mountain. We skied away from the lift and toward a clump of trees. I pulled to a stop beneath some firs to wait for the others. Guy Callow pulled up beside me.

Since the family mythology regarding Guy Callow was so unpleasant, I was guarded, but then I remembered that the story had come from Teddy and Miranda.

"How is Miranda?" Guy asked.

"She's great. She's in Palm Beach with my father." Even at this late date, I wanted him to think that she'd gone on happily without him. I wished I could have said that she was married to some politician or captain of industry, but Palm Beach was the best I could do.

"Are you here alone?" he asked.

"No," I said, which was technically true, but not in the way he meant it.

"Of course, why would you be?"

I could think of plenty of reasons but was flattered anyway.

Charlie and Heather finally came off the chairlift. Max and Lindsay would be next. Charlie waved at me as he skied toward us.

"Well, maybe we'll see each other around," Guy said.

I nodded. Guy Callow skied away, down an expert slope. I was envious of his freedom to take whatever run he wanted. We were stuck with Heather and Lindsay, who were only beginners. Charlie swooshed up beside me, followed by Heather, who ran over my skis. Both Charlie and I had to catch her to steady her.

"Who was that?" Heather said. "I feel like I've seen him on TV. Is he a weatherman or something?"

"He's an old friend of the family," I said.

"Why didn't he stick around?" Charlie asked.

"We could use another man," Heather added. She pulled out a lip gloss and slathered it on her lips.

"I don't know," I said. I could have asked him to join us, but I wasn't in the habit of doing things like that. And I didn't think I should be too receptive after what he did to Miranda—whatever it was, and no one really knew. There was such a thing as family loyalty.

Max and Lindsay skied over to us.

"Who was that?" Max asked.

"Old friend of the Fortune family," Heather answered for me.

"Coincidence," Max said. He leaned against one of his ski poles.

"Oh, that sort of thing always happens on mountains," I said in a flirtatious voice.

"It does?" Max asked.

"To me." I kept my voice light.

Maybe Max was going to marry Lindsay, but this was my chance to let him see me as something more than terminally single, so I took it.

Jack Reilly wasn't at the Butterfly Museum.

The woman in the office said he had been one of the best employees they'd ever had, except that three weeks ago he left without giving notice. He didn't even leave a forwarding address for his last paycheck.

"If you find him, can you give him this?" She looked up through large red bifocals. She was neither young nor old: she was of indeterminate age—somewhere between thirty and fifty. She gave me a note written on violet stationery. This wasn't an official missive, unless the Butterfly Museum used purple paper. "He's something, that Jack Reilly," she said. "You don't meet many men like him."

How many men had she met at her post at the Butterfly Museum? In a way, she was too much like me, hidden away, single, and of no definite age. No wonder Jack Reilly had made such an impression on her.

"I'll give this to him if I see him, but I may never find him," I said.

"I hope you do. He left so quickly. I never had a chance to say good-bye." Her light blue eyes were watery and distant as she stood by the inner door gazing out. Did I look like her, vague and dreamy and completely out of touch with reality?

"What does he look like?" I asked.

"Oh, he's lovely." She smiled. Even the thought of Jack Reilly made her glow.

"Yes," I said, "but what does he look like?"

She cocked her head to one side, licked her lips, and worried the edge of her Peter Pan collar with unkempt fingernails.

"I suppose he isn't a conventional beauty," she said, "but I like to think of him as a tiger swallowtail."

Her eyes misted over.

I assumed a tiger swallowtail was a type of butterfly—at least I hoped it was. Of course, this description was of no help whatsoever, but then Jack Reilly's looks were not important.

"Could I see a picture of one?"

"One what?" the vague woman asked.

"A tiger swallowtail?"

"Oh, of course." She went back to her desk and shuffled through a deck of cards. She pulled one out and handed it over. "You can keep that," she said.

I thanked her. The butterfly—and it was a butterfly—was large and striped, yellow and black. It was a glorious thing.

I tucked the violet letter and the card into my coat pocket. I was tempted to read the letter, but I would never do that, if for no other reason than that it would be very bad manners. I put my hand in my pocket and fingered the card with the butterfly picture on it like a worry stone, rubbing my thumb and forefinger against it over and over.

*   *   *

The Franklins' estate covered ten acres of prime Vermont real estate. Nora took us on a tour of the main house. It was spacious and modern with many windows.

"We struggled for so long. Book after book. Tiny apartment after tiny apartment. I never even had a dishwasher until we came here. All that time, though, I knew Duke would make it. I always believed in him."

Nora had worked in restaurants and Laundromats. And after all these years, she and Duke were still together. She had the courage I hadn't had. She was willing to throw her lot in with Duke no matter what. It was no wonder that Max still resented me.

All the women—Lindsay, Heather, Winnie, and I—followed Nora outside and down a path to another house. Duke's studio was in a building that sat high on the property with a view that stretched toward the lights of the town below. There were four workstations. One table held an old manual typewriter, another an IBM Selectric, and still another held a computer. The old oak desk was empty except for a sheaf of paper and a fountain pen. Piles of different-colored papers were stacked against one wall. Nora explained that these were "the drafts." She said it with a reverence usually reserved for objects of devotion.

When we returned to the main house, Duke was ladling mulled wine from a pot on the stove.

"It's got vodka in it," he warned. "Wine and vodka. A lethal combination. It's an old Scandinavian recipe." He looked at his wife.

"Scandinavian—my sweet ass," she said.

"And it is, dear." Duke gave her a pat on the behind.

"He made it up. The alcoholic brew. Don't blame it on the Swedes."

"Your mother gave me the recipe when we were first married."

"So you say." She took a mug from the counter and lifted it toward her husband. Duke poured more wine and vodka into the pot. He used no discernible measurements but instead poured with abandon, first from one bottle, then the other.

Basil came in through the back door. He didn't knock.

"Basil," Duke accosted him with a ladle full of wine, "have a drink."

"I think he needs a cup," I said. Duke put the ladle back into the pot.

"Good thinking, Jane. Sensible girl." Duke looked at Max as if he were somehow responsible for my good sense. That was reasonable, I supposed, since all of us were attached to Max in some way or we wouldn't be there.

Basil took the cup Duke offered and warmed his hands with it.

"It's cold out there," he said, "but it's supposed to be clear tomorrow."

"I heard it was supposed to snow," Max said. He stood against the kitchen counter.

"No, clear," Basil said. They stared at each other. Basil looked pointedly at Max, then turned to me. "Jane, I'd like to show you my work."

I didn't want to leave the comfort of the kitchen. Duke's attention was now on another large pot on the stove; he looked up at the kitchen clock. "You've got twenty minutes before the stew is ready."

The other women followed Nora into the warmth of the living room while I was dragged away to Basil's house. He took my arm when we got outside. The moon had slipped behind the clouds, so it was not only cold, it was dark.

"The Franklins should really put footlights in," he said, "so I can find my way home in the dark."

It had been a year since Cynthia died. Maybe they didn't want him to find his way back.

The Franklins' house was hidden from Basil's by a hill and some trees. Basil's was a smaller version of the main house—a little gem. I could understand why he wouldn't want to leave it.

He showed me the first of two bedrooms, which had its own bathroom, complete with Jacuzzi. Basil called the second bedroom his "studio."

He led me in and turned on the lights. This man had been busy. His work was piled against the walls, hanging from ceiling hooks, and there were several pieces, unfinished—or so I assumed—on easels.

"Well," I said. "Well, well." I put my hands on my hips and looked around with as much interest as I could muster.

"I call them 'the art of the word,' " he said, "which is why I think they are perfect for the *Euphemia Review*."

There were words everywhere—stenciled, painted freehand, crayoned, inked—words, words, words on canvas, on watercolor paper, on plywood planks.

One said "L-O-V-E" in pink and green on a plank the size of a door. It reminded me of something I'd seen on a greeting card and I wondered if Basil was trying to make a reference to pop culture. I waited for something in that room to move me. Art is supposed to move you, isn't it? I checked my emotional temperature—nothing.

"That was the one I did especially for Cynthia," Basil said, pointing to the L-O-V-E painting. "I was going to present it to her on our wedding day."

It occurred to me that an accidental death might be preferable to standing in front of all your friends and relatives to accept this gift with a straight face. Still, it was obvious that Basil was serious about his art. Art books and magazines littered the countertops, and I eyed the *Euphemia Review* sticking out from under an *Artforum*.

Basil stared at the L-O-V-E painting. His shoulders drooped and his normal hangdog expression became even hangier and doggier. I thought he was overplaying his hand as the grieving lover.

I looked at my wrist, though I wasn't wearing a watch. I wanted to go back. I couldn't bear the thought of everyone sitting down to bowls of hearty stew while I stood here looking at words. There were other words: U-N-I-T-Y, F-A-I-T-H, P-A-S-S-I-O-N. Many, many words. Trite, sappy words. Maybe I would have liked his work if he had chosen better words.

"Jane," Basil said, lowering his voice to a decibel level even lower than his usual key of grief.

"Yes, Basil?" I tried to make my voice gentle, the kind of voice you might use when visiting a person who had just suffered a psychotic break.

"I think you understand me." He put a hand on my shoulder and we stood there together in awkward silence. Was the grief-man making a move on me? Would I recognize one if I saw one? "I want you to think about these pictures," he said. "Think about adding art to the foundation's work. I could be your emissary, your Evan Bentley of the art world."

Basil had heard of Bentley because, just as everyone interested in that type of thing knew about George Plimpton and the *Paris Review,* they knew about Evan Bentley and *Euphemia.* It was just as I had predicted all those years ago back at Finn's.

Though Bentley had always acted as the front man—he went to the writers' conferences, gave speeches, and performed most of the public functions required of an editor of a successful literary review—my own reputation must have been greater than I knew, because it had preceded me here to this room full of words. I smiled and nodded at Basil. Because I stayed in the background most of the time, I was unaccustomed to being applied to in this way, and I didn't know exactly how to behave. I'd been approached, of course, by the occasional writer who thought I might be able to publish him, but it somehow always took me by surprise. I never felt that I had the power these writers were so quick to give me.

I suggested we go back to the house. Basil turned off most of the lights, leaving one on as a beacon to guide him back. He shut the door behind us.

"You don't want to stagnate, Jane," Basil said when we got outside. He was a head taller than I was and looked down at me in the dim light.

You don't want to stagnate.

It felt like Basil's words were ringing off the sides of the distant mountains—ominous words in a cheap horror film.

"I don't intend to stagnate," I said. My voice sounded loud out there in the quiet of the night.

"Don't be angry," Basil said. He took my arm. I wanted to shrug him off, but it wouldn't have been polite. He was only trying to help me through the dark.

When we came in, the men were still in the kitchen. Max looked up and smiled. If it's true that passion dulls discrimination (and I'm sure it is), my feelings for Max, no matter how I tried to convince myself to the contrary, were still passionate. It didn't matter what I learned about him or who he loved. When he was near, I still followed him with my eyes.

When Duke announced that supper was ready, the women came in with bowls from the dinner table. Max followed me into the dining room to retrieve our bowls.

"How was the art?" he asked when we were alone.

"It depends on what you like," I said.

"Always the diplomat."

"Not always." I looked up into his greenish eyes.

"About last night," he said. "It was all so awkward."

"It's none of my business," I said.

Max chewed on his bottom lip. "Who was that guy on the mountain today?" he asked.

"I told you. Old friend of the family's."

"He seemed very interested in you."

"I don't see how you could have seen that," I snapped. I couldn't tell him how much it hurt me to have him try to make a match for me. I picked up a bowl and he picked up the one beside it.

Everyone started returning with their stew.

"Where are you sitting?" Lindsay asked Max. He pointed to the place where his bowl had been.

Lindsay sat down in what would have been my place.

Ch a p t e r 22

$The\ run\ down\ Hazard\ Hill$

I met the group back at Max's house the next morning. After Lindsay and Heather finished putting on their makeup and after Winnie changed twice, we finally got moving. With Winnie we were six, so I was no longer a single.

Charlie and Winnie skied together, and after the second run we lost them. Winnie was a terrible skier. She had lessons when we were children like I did, but she wasn't crazy about the cold and never took the trouble to learn.

We stayed on the gentle runs all morning because Lindsay and Heather weren't up to anything more difficult. I tried to appreciate the lack of challenge, to enjoy the fine weather, the snow, the trees, and the views of the valley.

We all met up again at lunch, and that's when Basil joined us. He was wearing a ski jacket and jeans. The jeans would get wet, and once wet they'd be frozen S-T-I-F-F.

"Jane," he said, "you look beautiful." I was digging into a bowl of chili when he said it, which I doubt is the loveliest of poses. Max appraised Basil, then looked at me as if checking to see if Basil's vision of me had somehow come to pass. "Don't you agree, Max? Doesn't Jane look great? The mountain air is good for her."

"She always looks good," Max said.

"She looks much better than when she first came to stay," Lindsay said.

"I agree," Winnie said. "You look like a different person."

I supposed that looking like a different person wasn't such a bad thing—considering—but this kind of attention made me uncomfortable.

Guy Callow came in through a far door. He banged snow from his boots and surveyed the room. When he caught my eye, he waved and came over. A smile brightened his too-handsome face.

I introduced him to everyone. He seemed to be calculating the couples, to see who belonged to whom. Winnie vaguely remembered him.

Our table was full and we were almost finished with lunch, so Guy didn't sit down. He just said that he'd probably see us on the slopes and clomped away in his ski boots.

"Handsome," Winnie said. "Remind me. What happened to him? Miranda never talks about it."

"He married a Dutch supermodel named Ooh-Lala."

"So where is she?" Winnie asked.

"Maybe she caught her finger in a dyke," Basil said. He laughed at his own joke.

"That's so disgusting," Lindsay said, but she laughed too.

Max shook his head.

"Oh, Max. You don't have to be all high and mighty. It was funny," Lindsay said. "Don't be so boring." She kissed him on the cheek.

*   *   *

It was on the first run of the afternoon that it happened. I wondered how all seven us would stay together throughout the afternoon. I could be a single again if I maneuvered it properly, but not on that first run. On that first run, Heather was a single because Basil insisted on taking it with me. Basil and I were the first of the group. As we came off the chairlift, Basil fell and I had to pull him away from the path of skiers before they ran over him.

"You are so good at everything, Jane," he said. I was beginning to think that being capable wasn't all it was cracked up to be. A good nurse was capable, but was that the kind of efficiency to which I aspired?

"We don't have to tell anyone I fell," he said.

"I wasn't planning on it."

"Of course you weren't. Discretion is probably your middle name."

"It's Euphemia," I said.

"What?"

"My middle name."

"Like the *Review*?" he asked.

"Like my great-grandmother," I said.

We looked up and there was Heather standing under a tree.

"Hey, guys," she said.

"You think she saw me?" Basil whispered. How could she have missed this six-foot collection of arms and legs taking a tumble at the foot of the chairlift?

"I'm sure she didn't," I said. Basil seemed satisfied.

The others came off the chairlift in couples. First came Max and Lindsay, then Winnie and Charlie. Winnie's nose was running. I handed her a tissue. The problem with skiing with so many people is that you spend half your time waiting around in the cold. And while it was a sunny day, December is still a cold month on a mountain.

"I think if no one minds," Max said, "I'm going to try Hazard Hill. You want to come, Charlie?"

"But it's a black diamond," Heather said. "It's too hard for us."

"We can meet at the bottom," Charlie said.

"I'll go with you," I said.

"If she's going," Lindsay said, "I'm going too."

Max put his hand on Lindsay's arm. "Lind, you can't make it down an expert slope. Heather's right. Why not meet us at the bottom?" He stroked her cheek as if trying to placate a little girl.

"I can do anything you can do," she sang, and before any of us could stop her, she took off.

"Goddammit," Max called after her. "Lindsay, stop."

He was frozen in place.

"We'd better go after her," I said. I pushed at his shoulder and we rushed away with Charlie following behind. Lindsay was wearing a red ski suit, and as I charged on, I focused on that dot of crimson as it receded and eventually disappeared.

We got to Lindsay just in time to see her fly over a large mogul and slam into the mountain. Before she fell, parts of her disappeared into the snow that rose into a wave as she tried to gain control of her skis. Then an arm appeared, a leg. She was a red dot flying into the air. She landed with a bounce and a thud and lay there, a spot of red on the white snow.

She didn't get up. Max reached her first. He knelt in the snow and touched her head. He was afraid to move her. He kept calling her name, but she was out cold. The fall was so bad I thought it might have killed her, but she was still breathing. Charlie came up behind us.

"Holy mother of God," he said.

Lindsay was as white as the snow she was lying on.

"Jane, go for the ski patrol," Max said. "Please. You're the fastest."

I took off. I had never skied so fast before. The hut for the ski patrol was at the bottom of the hill and I skied right through the door. I was breathing hard and could barely speak. I didn't know if my breathlessness was from the speed with which I'd taken the hill or from being scared out of my senses.

"There's been an accident," I said.

Chapter 23

The vigil

"It's my fault," Max said as I followed him toward the waiting ambulance.

"It is not. Don't say that."

"If she wasn't trying to impress me, she wouldn't have done it," he said.

"If she wasn't spoiled and obstinate, she wouldn't have done it," I said.

"Jane, how can you say that? Especially now."

"Because it's true. You shouldn't blame yourself."

"It was selfish of me."

"That's not such a crime. All you wanted to do was take a run on your own. So did I. If you're to blame, then so am I."

He shook his head. "It's not the same."

"You're not thinking straight," I said, and it was the last thing I said to him before he and Charlie climbed into the ambulance with Lindsay.

I didn't know where to find the others, so I started looking in the lodge on the off chance they might have given up skiing, and that's where I found them. After one run, Winnie had complained that she was tired, and they all followed her inside for a cup of hot chocolate.

"Jane," she said when she saw me, "where have you been? I think I sprained my ankle."

I pulled a chair up to the table.

"What's the matter?" Winnie said. "You look all white."

I took Winnie's hand, since she was the one most likely to become hysterical. "Lindsay's had an accident. They took her to the hospital."

"In an ambulance?" Heather asked. Her voice was soft.

"Yes."

"Oh God," she said.

"Look, everything could be fine. Let's not worry too much until we find out how serious it is. Let's just stay calm."

"That's easy for you to say, Jane," Winnie said. "You're not related to her."

"Neither are you," Heather said to Winnie.

"Well, I'm sorry you feel that way," Winnie said. "I think of you girls as my sisters. I'm sorry you don't feel the same way about me." She continued to drink her hot chocolate.

"Let's calm down," I said. "I have Charlie's keys. I think we should go to the hospital."

"Of course," Heather said. "Let's go." Heather started taking off her ski boots. Her shoes were in a bag under the table.

"I'd take you girls," Basil said, "but I don't want to leave my car here.

Why don't I go back to the Franklins' and let them know what happened, then meet you at the hospital?"

We didn't need Basil. He hardly knew Lindsay, but it wouldn't be right to tell him that. Besides, the grief-man appeared to thrive on disaster. He was full of purpose. He gave us directions to the hospital, then told us to be careful because it was beginning to snow. "You wouldn't want to be killed yourselves," he said.

At the word *killed,* I thought Heather was going to faint. I squeezed her arm through her thick sweater and she smiled at me. It was a weak and unhappy smile.

Winnie put her arm around Heather.

"Now, sweetie, let's not get hysterical." Winnie liked to reserve hysteria for herself.

On the way to the car Winnie leaned heavily on me and groaned about her ankle. I carried her equipment and mine and stowed our skis on the roof of Charlie's Navigator.

The snow wasn't heavy, but the car was unfamiliar, so I drove carefully.

"Can't you hurry, Jane?" Winnie asked.

"Let's just try to get there in one piece," I said.

"Let Jane do what Jane does, will you, Winnie? For God's sake. She'll get us there," Heather said.

The ride to the hospital took forty-five minutes, and although it wasn't as long a distance as it might have been, I would have felt more hopeful about Lindsay's prospects if it were shorter.

By the time we reached the hospital, the snow was falling heavily. Heather's eyes were puffy and her nose was running. I pulled out my tissues from an inside pocket and passed one over to her. She tried to smile. As soon as we parked, Heather ran into the hospital. I couldn't run because Winnie, with her pronounced limp, insisted on leaning on me.

We walked into the emergency room. Max and Charlie were sitting on a Naugahyde sofa in the waiting area.

"They took her right into surgery," Charlie said. His eyes were shiny, but he was trying to hide his distress. Max wore such a haunted expression I could barely stand to look at him. Winnie pushed her way into a small space between Charlie and the edge of the sofa.

"Charlie, I think I broke my ankle," she whined. He looked at her but didn't say anything. He turned away. "Did you hear me?" she asked.

"No," he said.

"Charlie!" Her voice was sharp. She got up and hobbled to the counter. A nurse was manning it. "I need to have my ankle seen to immediately," she said. She glanced back at Charlie with a haughty expression.

"We'll get to you as soon as we can," the nurse said.

"Sooner would be better." Winnie looked around. "It doesn't look too busy here." Winnie hobbled away and sat in a chair as far away from Charlie as she could get. He stood and went to the window.

I sat on the sofa beside Max. Without thinking, I touched his leg with my fingertips.

"What does the doctor say?" I asked.

"She has some internal hemorrhaging. They don't know what the prognosis is yet."

Heather gripped the arms of her chair.

"Has anyone called the Maples?" I asked.

"Oh God, the Maples," Max said.

"Should we wait?" Heather asked. "Until we know more?"

"That's up to you and Charlie," I said.

The nurse called Winnie's name and Winnie, without help from any of us, got up and went through the double doors.

Heather walked over to Charlie, then came back.

"Charlie and I think someone should call our parents," she said.

"I'll do it," Max said.

"No, that's okay. I'll do it," I said.

"It's my responsibility."

"No it isn't."

Of course, Charlie or Heather could have called, but I was afraid they'd make the Maples more upset than necessary. Someone calm had to call.

Max put his hand over mine and I felt the warmth and hardness of it. I slipped my hand away and stood up. The phones were down the hall.

I went to make the call. It was a good thing I did, because, as I suspected, Marion didn't take it well.

"We'll leave immediately," she said.

"It's snowing pretty heavily up here," I said. "Maybe you should wait until morning."

"I can't," Marion said.

Charles Sr. got on the extension. "You think we should wait, Jane?"

"I don't know, Charles. The weather isn't very good up here and it's getting worse."

"We're going to leave right now and see how we do," he said.

"What about the boys?" I asked.

"Charlie and Winnie will have to come home."

"I'll tell them."

"In the meantime, we'll call Gabriella. I'm sure she'll come," Marion said. "Heather and Charlie, why didn't they call?"

"They thought it would be better if I did," I said.

"They didn't want to upset us even more," Charles Sr. said.

"That's right," I said.

I hung up the phone and went back to the waiting room. Charlie was still at the window. I walked over to him, touched his shoulder, and told him his parents were on the way.

"Thank you, Jane," he said. "What would we do without you?"

"You'd manage." I smiled. He turned toward me, hugged me, and held on to me. I felt a tear against my cheek. When he released me, I turned from the window and saw Max looking at me.

Basil blustered in. "It's getting almost impossible to drive," he said. "I don't even know how we'll leave the hospital."

"I'm not leaving," Max said.

"How is she?" Basil asked.

"She's in surgery."

"I stopped at the Franklins' and they're ready to take you all in," Basil said.

"We still have the house," I reminded him.

Charlie returned from the window.

"The snow's thick on the ground."

We sat and we sat some more.

Eventually Winnie came back out through the double doors. She was on crutches and her ankle was wrapped in an Ace bandage.

"It's a sprain," she said.

"I'll bet you all wish you didn't wake up this morning," Basil said.

"If we didn't wake up this morning, we'd all be dead," Max said.

Heather laughed, a snort of laughter, short and loud.

Basil looked at the floor. I followed his eyes toward the pocked linoleum.

Three hours later the doctor came down to tell us that Lindsay was out of surgery. He looked at Winnie. "Oh, it's you," he said. No one knew what that meant, but I could only imagine what had gone on behind those double doors.

"We just have to wait," the doctor said. "You never really know with head injuries."

"Can I see her?" Max asked.

"No one can see her yet. You should all go home. You can't see her till morning."

"Thank you, Doctor," Charlie said. He shook the doctor's hand.

After the doctor left, Max said he had no intention of leaving.

"Me either," Heather said.

"Well, I'm not going anywhere," Winnie said, "though I am so uncomfortable." She looked at her ankle. "It would be nice to get into bed."

"We're staying," Charlie said, "at least until morning. Then we have to do something about the kids."

"They're with your parents."

"My parents are coming up right away. They're going to try to find Gabriella to take care of the boys."

"They didn't ask me if I approved of that idea," Winnie said.

"No, they didn't," Charlie said.

I didn't think we should all spend the whole night in this waiting room if no one could see Lindsay until morning. Maybe one of us should stay in case she woke up, but there was no need for everyone to stay, certainly not Basil Funk. I went to the window to check the weather. It was bad.

I returned and spoke to Basil.

"Basil, could you do us a huge favor?" I asked.

"Sure," he said. "That's what I'm here for."

Well, at least now I knew why he was there.

"Take Heather and Winnie back to the house. There's no reason for them to sit up all night."

"I'm not leaving," Winnie said.

"Neither am I," Heather said.

I sat beside Heather. "You're going to need to be strong for your parents and it won't help if you're exhausted. I think Charlie should get some sleep too. Even Max."

"I'm not leaving," Max said.

"Jane's right," Charlie said. "There's no point in all of us staying through the night if we can't see Lindsay, so long as someone is here in case she wakes up."

"I think one of the family should stay," Winnie said.

"We couldn't get Max out of here with a crowbar, so he might as well be the one to stay," Charlie said.

"But what if we get stuck and can't come back? What if the weather's too bad?" Heather asked.

The nurse behind the counter spoke up.

"There's a motel across the street," she said. "Why not stay there?"

So it was settled. Rooms were rented across the street.

They rented a room for me, but on my way out I turned and saw Max sitting there by himself staring into space and I couldn't leave him. The others went on and I returned to the waiting room.

We sat there side by side like two old people waiting for a bus.

"It's all my fault," Max said.

"Stop saying that. It's not your fault."

"I should have stopped her."

"We went after her as fast as we could," I said.

"I wasn't thinking about her, the way she is, what she'd do. I was just thinking of myself. That's all I ever do. I've spent the last fifteen years being a selfish bastard."

"I'm sure that's not true."

"It is. You don't know. Even this," he said, "this Lindsay thing. It was all about me, what I wanted. I'm like that with women. Some of the stories are true. Not all of them, but some of them. I dated a lot of women, but I never got really serious with any of them. Strange, I know. When I met Lindsay, it started the same way, just another conquest. I thought maybe I could change. She comes from a nice, solid family. I thought that maybe this could be it, but I never even really knew her."

He took my hand.

"I don't know what we would have done without you today," he said.

"You would have managed."

At about two o'clock in the morning Max fell asleep with his head on my shoulder. He snored softly. I was wide awake, listening to every breath.

At five, he blinked his eyes open and smiled at me. He seemed unaware of where he was at first and with whom, because he turned to me and gave me a soft half-asleep kiss.

"Morning," I said.

"I fell asleep."

"You did," I said.

He sat up straight.

"Any news?" he asked.

I shook my head. "Nothing."

Chapter 24

Lindsay wakes up confused

Lindsay remained in a coma for three days. In that time, the senior Maples came up and traded places with the junior Maples, and Winnie and Charlie returned home to the children. Winnie was not too pleased at being sent away. She wanted to remain where the action was—even if the action was merely sitting around in a hospital waiting room.

I checked out of the Inn at Long Last and into the Moon Dairy Motor Inn across from the hospital. I tried to be there for Max, but it's hard to be there for someone who walks around like a bombed-out shell. He was a zombie, and all I could think was that his love for Lindsay had blindsided him, that she had become more to him than he imagined.

When Lindsay woke up, she was foggy and confused. She didn't recognize Max. For some reason, she recognized Basil. She didn't know the Franklins or Heather. She knew Charles Sr. but not Marion. She didn't know me.

The doctors said that Lindsay's recovery would take time, that she'd have to remain in the hospital for several weeks, and even after that, she shouldn't travel unless we wanted to medevac her.

"Head injuries are unpredictable," the doctor said. "The patient can experience a complete personality change."

When he said that, Marion, despite her heft, put her head between her knees and started to hyperventilate.

There was no reason for me to delay my return to Massachusetts any longer. I drove back to Dover, packed my things, and went to stay with Priscilla, who had returned to Boston after Christmas. Winnie offered me a home with her for as long as I wanted it, but I was restless. I couldn't remain the unmarried aunt in my sister's house forever. I wasn't sure how Priscilla's condominium would be so much better, but I didn't plan to stay there long. I had to make some arrangements of my own.

I found a parking spot on the street near Priscilla's building—no easy task—and dragged one suitcase up the stairs and into her sunny second-floor apartment.

Priscilla met me at the door.

"Set the bag in the hall," she said. "You can deal with it later."

I put the bag down and followed her into the living room, where I sank into a deep armchair.

"What an ordeal," she said. "Was it very bad?" Priscilla picked up her knitting and turned down the Mozart CD she had been listening to. I looked around at her impeccable apartment, everything in its place. No wonder she had never married again. Everything was exactly as she wanted it. Maybe I could get used to this kind of small and comfortable life, but I wasn't willing to resign myself to it just yet.

I smelled coffee and went into the kitchen to get a cup and brought one back for Priscilla. Her cups were bone china, strong but delicate. I longed for a good hefty mug like the ones in Max's chalet.

"Tell me everything," she said again.

"Being with Max again was hard."

"You did the right thing all those years ago."

"How can you say that? How can you look at the reality of my life and say that? I am alone. I haven't had sex in—I don't know—I stopped counting, but it's probably been about nine years. How can you say I did the right thing?"

"It's just that you never learned about men," she said. "That's all it is." She took a neat sip of her coffee.

I sipped mine. Priscilla made bad coffee. I didn't want to fight with her. I wanted to fall into the safety of our comfortable routine. Looking at her with her chignon, her smooth and beautifully made-up face, her clothes—all from Talbots—I realized there was no going back. I wasn't even sure I liked Priscilla anymore. Her absolute conviction that she was right never wavered. She was an ice queen, never allowing herself to be touched by anything. Maybe that's what she had wanted for me, but now I was sure that it wasn't what I wanted for myself.

"I'm seeing someone," Priscilla said. She looked a little like a teenager with a secret.

"Oh?" I said. I had always feigned interest in her parade of paramours, but I wasn't in the mood to do it now.

"I met him at a self-defense course." She put down her cup and saucer on a side table and punched out her arm as if she were about to take down an assailant. She looked ridiculous. "He was the teacher."

"Why are you taking a self-defense course?" I asked.

"Got my purse snatched. Walking down Charles Street. Can you imagine? This city isn't what it once was. He's coming over tonight. I can't wait for you to meet him."

*   *   *

Jason, Priscilla's self-defense instructor, had a baby face. According to Priscilla, he was twenty-seven. Priscilla, however, was sixty-two, and although I didn't want to let the age difference bother me, it did. Jason wore all black—black T-shirt, black leather jacket, black jeans. He looked a little like I had imagined Jack Reilly might look, only younger. Jason's stomach rippled in a six-pack under his tight T-shirt and I offered him a drink, all the time wondering why a six-pack was still a priority for Priscilla, who had lost hers—if she had ever had one—eons ago.

Though Priscilla had said she had wanted me to meet the karate kid, I felt very much in the way and decided to take a walk, even though it was very cold and windy outside.

"Oh, don't go," Priscilla said. She was snuggled into Jason so securely, she was almost glued to him. But the good single guest never stays when she knows she is in the way, and I was "the good single guest."

I walked around the neighborhood and past my own house. The lights were on inside and I wanted to ring the doorbell, but people didn't just stop by anymore for a visit. It was rude not to call first, especially since I didn't know the Goldmans well.

The light came on in the front hall, and against my better judgment, I started up the walk and rang the bell. I don't think I'd ever rung the bell to that house before. I didn't really know what I was doing there, but there I was.

Emma answered the door.

"Jane, how lovely of you to stop by. Come on in." I followed her into the sitting room. There was a fire in the fireplace. It looked like she had just vacated my favorite chair, because a book and a pair of reading glasses were perched on a table beside it. "Sit, sit," Emma said. She leaned toward me. "What can I get you?" For a moment, it didn't occur to me that she was offering me something as simple as a drink. I had the briefest fantasy that she was offering me something more—a different life perhaps.

"What are you drinking?" I asked.

"Just tea," she said.

"That will be fine for me too," I said.

She went into the kitchen and I sat there waiting to be served in my own house. A new sensation. She brought back a tray with tea and some fancy chocolate cookies.

We sat for a moment and sipped our tea. I stared into the fire, but Emma was looking at me.

"Where's Joe?" I asked.

"He had to fly back to California for a few days on business," she said.

"You must miss him," I said.

"I don't mind having time to myself." She smiled.

"Have you heard from Max?" I asked.

"Yes."

"How is he?"

"He's confused. You know, he's a man, so he doesn't share all that much with me. He feels so responsible for Lindsay's accident."

"He wasn't, you know."

"Oh, I know that and you know that, but maybe if he worries about that, he doesn't have to worry about other things."

"Like what?"

"Like that he might have gotten himself in too deep with Lindsay. She's a nice girl. She's not the kind of girl he's been playing around with in New York. He set out just to play and he got stuck."

"He told me he wanted to marry her," I said.

"We'll see about that," Emma said. "You hurt him badly, Jane, you know. It took him a long time to get over you."

I was surprised that she was being so candid.

"You said he didn't share his feelings with you."

"He was different when he was younger. He used to tell me everything," she said.

"So you know about us," I said. She nodded. "He blamed me." She nodded again. "Well, he had a right to."

She sipped her tea, then looked up at me.

"I'm certainly glad you came to visit," she said. "Oh, by the way, a man came by here looking for you a few days ago. I sent him to Priscilla. Did she tell you?"

Priscilla and—I supposed—Jason were already asleep when I got home.

In the morning, they were eating pancakes with strawberries and whipped cream in the kitchen.

"Where did you go last night?" Priscilla asked. "I was worried about you."

"Did someone come by here looking for me a couple of days ago?"

"Oh yes," Pris said. "I forgot. Someone did come by. I wasn't here, but he left a note. Now, where did I put it?"

Priscilla, in a silk peignoir that made her look a little bit like Auntie Mame in the musical, wafted out of the kitchen.

I looked at Jason. He looked back at me. We didn't say anything to each other. He took a huge bite of his pancakes and stared at me as he chewed. I couldn't tell whether his look was one of mischief or disdain and whether it was directed at me or Priscilla. And I didn't want to know.

Priscilla came back with a thick cream envelope and handed it to me.

"It's from a man. I can tell from the writing."

I took a knife and slit the envelope open. Inside was a note from Guy Callow. He was staying at the Four Seasons and he wanted to see me.

"Well," Priscilla said.

"Well, what?"

"Who's it from?"

"Guy Callow."

"Miranda's Guy Callow?" Pris asked.

"The very same."

"What on earth does he want?"

"Strange as it may seem, he wants to see me."

"But that makes no sense."

"Of course it doesn't." I turned to walk away. Priscilla came after me. She grabbed onto the cloth of my shirt with her right hand and I shook her off. "Please don't grab at me, Priscilla."

She pulled her hand away and looked at it as if she wasn't sure how it had sprung up on the end of her wrist.

"I'm sorry, but I have to know what this is all about," she said.

"No you don't."

I disappeared into the guest room and closed the door. I called the Four Seasons and asked for Guy, but he had just checked out.

Chapter 25

Hope Bliss Investigations

"I don't know if you remember me," I said when Hope Bliss answered the phone.

"Of course I do, Jane. Why wouldn't I remember you?" You could hardly tell a person that you thought yourself unmemorable, so I shrugged, a useless gesture since I was on the phone.

"I saw your name in the yellow pages and I'm looking for an investigator to help me find someone."

I explained my quest for Jack Reilly and she said it seemed like a simple enough problem for a professional investigator. I told her what I had done to find him so far, and she said that no matter how far off the grid someone seemed to be, they were still somewhere, you could always find them, and these days with computers it usually didn't take too long.

Before we hung up she asked if I'd like to get together, and it occurred to me only then that this was the second reason for my call. I wanted to see Hope, to reconnect with someone from my past.

We met at Durgin Park in Faneuil Hall Marketplace. It wasn't far from Hope's office in the North End. We didn't choose the restaurant only for the convenient location, but because, for us, it was nostalgic. When we were in school, our class was taken there on a field trip every year. I remembered watching bins of garbage being pulled past the window on pulleys. It was one of those places where rude waitresses in hairnets were a form of entertainment. I never found impropriety or impolite behavior particularly entertaining, but then I've grown up to be as straight as an architect's ruler, and sometimes just as exciting. Hope told me that she went to Durgin Park at least once a week. She thought the place was hilarious.

I recognized Hope Bliss immediately. If anything, she was fatter than the last time I'd seen her. She probably weighed about two hundred and fifty pounds, but she was one of those women who, despite, or maybe because of, their weight, dressed meticulously. She walked with a light tread, as if she didn't know she could tip the scale on a longshoreman. She broke into a smile when she saw me and I tried to remember why we had fallen out of touch. She rushed toward me and gave me an enveloping hug.

We were seated upstairs and placed our orders with a recalcitrant waitress. She made it clear that she was doing us a favor by deigning to wait on us. Hope thought it was boisterously entertaining. I, on the other hand, like waitstaff to be somewhat deferential.

"It makes the whole dining experience more tranquil," I said.

"Tranquillity is overrated," Hope said. I didn't think so. For years I'd been seeking tranquillity like an obsessive lover, tracking it, stalking it, forcing it to live with me long after our relationship was over.

Hope had been a private investigator for ten years. She had been a lawyer first, in a small suburban firm, and she found herself doing the investigative work not only for herself but for the other lawyers as well. She liked moving behind the scenes and hated going to court because she didn't like the way people looked at her. Weight on a woman was no advantage in a courtroom, she explained.

"A fat P.I. can get away with a lot," she said. "Especially a woman. People generally think fat people are benign."

The food came and Hope dug into her Yankee pot roast. I had a clam chowder that was so thick I was in danger of instant cardiac arrest.

Hope's mother was now living with Hope.

"My dad divorced her, not that I blame him. Unfortunately, he didn't leave her well provided for. By the time they divorced, she had brought him so low he was barely making any money. She made her own bed, as they say. Unfortunately, I have to lie in it with her. The irony is that as soon as he got free of her harping he met a nice woman, married her, and together they started an online dating service for dog breeders, and with all the merchandise tie-ins and advertising they're doing very well."

"Who's getting fixed up, the dogs or the people?"

"The people, for now, but we'll see. So my mother lives with me and I take care of her financially. My father helps a little. And guess what she has to do for me? One thing. She is not allowed to say or do anything about my weight. One word and she's out the door. It's like divine retribution. Do you remember what she was like?"

"I do," I said. When we were young, her mother never missed an opportunity to harp about Hope's weight. Hope's choice of afternoon snack was severely monitored. And even with all the nagging and all the policing, Hope kept getting fatter.

Hope chewed on a large piece of meat.

"Eating slowly is very important," she said between chews. "I have all kinds of health problems because of my weight, but I don't let that stop me. I'm a ballroom dancer, a gourmet chef, and I'm taking Hebrew in a continuing education course. I'm also studying Kabbalah."

How would she have time to look for Jack Reilly?

"I know all about you," Hope said. "I Googled you."

"You what?"

"I looked you up on the Internet. Do you know that you are mentioned on no less than one hundred and thirty-two sites?"

"That's impossible."

"It's true." She choked on a piece of meat and started to cough. She wasn't shy about it, but instead coughed as if the food were caught somewhere between her knees instead of in her throat. Hope drank her water and then sucked down all of mine.

"Well," she said. "I'm going to find your Jack Reilly." I liked the way that sounded. My Jack Reilly. "And probably sooner than you think."

I gave her my friend Isabelle's address on Martha's Vineyard. I had decided to leave as soon as possible. All I had to do was give my speech at Wellesley and I could go.

There was no way I was going to spend the winter with Priscilla and the karate kid.

I considered Palm Beach, but after one phone call with Miranda and Teddy I gave up that plan. They were thoroughly ensconced, doing the rounds, a party almost every night. Miranda said that Dolores was invaluable. I'm sure Miranda counted on her to do the things I always did—to make the coffee in the morning, to take care of the laundry, see to the food shopping.

They obviously didn't need me, so I called Isabelle on the island. She told me to come right out, that she knew someone who had been looking for a tenant for one of the gingerbread cottages in Oak Bluffs. It would be perfect for me.

I paid the bill and Hope and I walked out onto the street.

"I'm so glad you called me, Jane."

"Can I ask you something?"

"Sure, anything." She picked at her back teeth with a toothpick.

"How did we lose touch?"

"I don't know exactly. I guess it was when we went to different high schools. Also, my mother liked you, and at the time, that was a good reason for me to avoid you."

I didn't remember Hope Bliss avoiding me. It wasn't like she had so many friends that she could afford to avoid one. She was fat and eccentric and it took a person who could see past that to befriend her.

"Do you think I've changed?" I asked Hope.

"Not at all. What about me?"

"You've become impressive." That appeared to please Hope, since when we were children she could in no way have been called impressive. She spent her childhood in a constant battle with her weight and her mother.

Though Hope was still fat, she somehow seemed to have won the battle with both.

Chapter 26

Men in briefs

The evening of my speech, I met the dean of the Wellesley College English Department, Lydia McKay, in her office and together we walked across the frozen campus. Dean Lydia was young, in her forties, and she hadn't been at Wellesley when I was there.

I thought Dean Lydia was taking me to an ordinary classroom in one of the Gothic-style buildings I had loved so much when I was a student. Instead, she led me to one of the large auditoriums on campus that were meant to accommodate an audience of several hundred. These types of lectures were rare here (or at least they had been in my time). I was daunted by the size of the room and asked Lydia if this was the only room she could get. Wouldn't a smaller one be more appropriate?

She scratched the side of her nose, pushed up her glasses, and looked at me as if I were a puzzle she couldn't quite figure out.

"Appropriate, Jane? I don't know what you mean."

"I just think this room is a little big, but that's okay, we can have everyone sit up front so it won't seem so cavernous."

"But I chose this room because I think we're going to need all of these seats. We announced your talk in the *Boston Globe*."

"You've got to be kidding," I said. The idea of several hundred people showing up on a Thursday night in late January to see me was not only frightening but also preposterous.

I was wearing my green suit and I'd gone to Mr. Marco so he could trim and tint my hair. My index cards were in my left pocket and I must have looked like someone competent, but I felt like a puddle.

"Anyway," Dean McKay said, "I wanted you to see the venue. We're early so we can grab a cup of coffee in the student union."

We walked back across campus. I poured myself a decaf from one of the huge urns I remembered so well from the all-nighters of my college days. The dean waved me past the cashier and wouldn't let me pay.

As we walked to the only open table we could find at that hour, girls called out to "Dean Lydia." A girl with tortoiseshell glasses and blue-tipped hair approached us. She had a stack of *Euphemia Review*s in her arms.

"Miss Fortune, I'm a huge fan of yours. You're one of the reasons I came to Wellesley. I'd like to be an editor someday. Could you sign these?"

"Jane, this is Sarah Mulcaster," Dean Lydia said, "your biggest fan." I smiled at her. "Sarah, Miss Fortune will be signing after her talk. You can speak to her then."

"Signing?" I asked.

"Some people want you to sign the *Review*," she said. "So we've set up a table in the lobby."

"But I didn't write any of the work in the *Review*. I really shouldn't sign it."

"Why not? It's your *Review*."

"And Evan Bentley's."

"Yes, of course," she said.

When we entered the hall it was almost full and people were still pouring in. I was appalled. I thought I was going to be speaking to a group of about twenty-five girls, not to men and women from God-only-knows-where.

My pile of index cards felt weightless and I had to touch them to make sure they were still in my pocket. Was there a way I could get out of this—feign sickness—or maybe death?

Just as I was beginning to feel like I might vomit (thereby making feigning sickness unnecessary), I looked up and saw Tad sitting in the front row. He smiled and waved. I jumped off the stage to greet him.

"I can't believe you came," I said.

"Wouldn't have missed it," he said. "Even for a hockey game, which, I might add, I had tickets to. You look very nice."

"That's high praise coming from you," I said.

"You ready?"

"For this? I don't think so. I thought I'd be in a little classroom talking to a few girls."

"Oh, Jane, you just don't know."

"Know what?"

"All these girls want to be like you."

"I doubt that very much. Little girls say that they want to be princesses, nurses, sometimes doctors and lawyers, but they hardly ever say that 'when I grow up I want to be a desiccated old maid.' "

"That's only because they don't know what desiccated means."

Dean Lydia beckoned to me and I got back onto the stage by way of the stairs. She indicated a chair for me to sit on while I was being introduced, and as I was about to sit down, I was both surprised and delighted to see Bentley and Melody come through the door. It warmed my heart to think that they would show up just for me. They must have seen the notice in the *Globe*.

Finally, Dean Lydia went to the podium. She tapped the microphone, unable to get it to work at first. Wasn't this always the case? It took a student well versed in audiovisual equipment to mount the stage and press the right buttons to get the thing going. Lydia's voice went from a whisper to a bellow and I thought about how I'd have to modulate my voice to keep from sounding too overwrought.

Just as Lydia was saying, "Generally known as one of the best things to happen to the short story in the last twenty years," the door opened and a man came in. I looked up, registered mild appreciation, as you sometimes do with excessive beauty. Then, as he came closer, I realized it was Guy Callow. What on earth was he doing here? I didn't know he had an interest in literature. "And so I introduce one of our most accomplished alumnae, Jane Fortune."

I couldn't feel my legs, but somehow I got to the lectern. I tapped the microphone as Lydia had done, which made a big popping sound like a gunshot, and everyone broke into nervous laughter.

"Thank you, Dean McKay," I said. "I am Jane Fortune." They knew that already. I took my cards from my pocket and they slipped out of my hand and fluttered to the floor. I stooped to pick them up. Now they'd be out of order. I felt sweat under my arms, between my shoulder blades, and even on my forehead. Okay, Jane. Pull yourself together. I stood up and gripped the podium.

"First, I want to tell you about Euphemia Fortune, after whom the *Review* is named. She was my great-grandmother. How many of you have heard of Isabella Stewart Gardner?" I asked. About nine-tenths of the room raised their hands. In a different audience it would have been fewer, but we were at Wellesley College. These people were bound to know about Isabella. "Well," I said, "my great-grandmother hated her." I paused for the laughter that came pouring toward me. This feeling of making a room laugh was a new one. I took the cards from the podium and tossed them into the audience. "I don't need these," I said. This elicited another terrific response.

I knew the story I wanted to tell. I told about Euphemia's frustration with Isabella, how Euphemia would have liked to be more like her, but short of that, she wanted to create, like Isabella, a monument to her own good taste.

"When I took over the foundation and read Euphemia's journals, I tried to do what she had done. Euphemia had established a fellowship, a place and time for a writer to work. That had fallen by the wayside by the time I took over, so the first thing I did was reestablish it."

I talked until I looked at the clock and my time was almost up. I ended by thanking Tad and Bentley and making them stand and take a bow. I hardly knew what I had said, but whatever it was earned me a standing ovation.

I turned to sit down, but Dean Lydia got up, moved me back to the podium, and said it was time for questions.

The first was from the girl Sarah. She had looked so respectful in the student union, despite her blue hair, but when she stood her voice boomed out with a snide confidence.

"I read somewhere"—she pulled on her tweed skirt and tossed her hair—"that you and Max Wellman were *like* together at one point."

"The question?" Dean Lydia was obviously annoyed. The girl behind the wholesome sweater set and granny glasses had ambushed us—or me. That whole incident still embarrassed me somewhat in that I'd gone on to make such a success of the *Review* and the fellowship, yet falling for the first recipient—especially since it hadn't worked out—made me look like a dilettante even now, just as I'd been afraid it would.

"Is it true?"

"It was a long time ago," I said. I felt like my dignity was draining through a crack in my voice.

"And what's your relationship now?" she asked.

"Friends," I said.

I thought of him holding my hand at the hospital, his face pale and moist.

"Anyone have a more literary question?" Dean Lydia asked.

*　　*　　*

After the speech and after I had reluctantly signed some copies of the *Review,* Tad, Bentley, and Melody said that we had to celebrate. So long as eating was involved, I was fine with that. I hadn't eaten anything before the talk for fear it would make me sick.

Guy Callow approached and tried to hug me, but I put him off by holding out my hand. He shook it and told me I was marvelous, and frankly, for the first time in a long time, I felt marvelous.

Bentley invited Guy to join us at the Figtree Café down the street, and the four of us walked through the stone gates of the college and out onto Central Street. The Figtree was a generic type of suburban restaurant— not high end, not low end, sort of Italian, sort of nothing. It had large paintings of fruit hanging on its brick walls and the tables were a plain blond wood.

Guy looked good enough to dip in chocolate. Still, there was something about him I didn't trust. As soon as we sat down, Guy, though he could in no way be considered the host of the party, ordered several bottles of expensive wine. We also ordered three large gourmet pizzas, and I was so relieved that my talk hadn't been a complete disaster, I drank and ate with the enthusiasm of eight hungry truck drivers.

"You were so terrific, Jane. So smooth, so funny. But you must be used to public speaking by now," Guy said.

"Used to it? I never do it."

"You could never have guessed," Tad said. "You were awesome." There was that word again—a word more appropriate to a sunset or the birth of a baby than to Jane Fortune standing on a stage at Wellesley College.

"I don't know what's going to happen to me," Bentley said. "I was always the public guy—because you didn't want to be. But you are far more entertaining than I ever was. Even when I was flirting with my students, I couldn't hold their attention like that." Melody punched him on the arm. "Of course, that was in the past," he added.

*　　*　　*

By the time we were finished eating, I was tipsy. Guy picked up the check for all of us and I thought this gallant of him, especially since this was a legitimate foundation expense and I would have been happy to pay for dinner. No one, though, not Bentley, Melody, or even Tad, was willing to have me pay on *my special night*.

Bentley, Guy, and Tad all offered to drive me home. There were two problems with that—one was that I didn't have a home, and the second was that I was staying at the Wellesley Inn right down the street.

"I don't have a home," I said. Everyone but Guy, who didn't really understand the import of the statement, looked at me as if I were the saddest case in the world. Even Tad had a home, even if it was a dorm room at Harvard. "Oh, stop with the doleful looks," I said. They all looked like Basil Funk. "I am treating myself to a room at the Wellesley Inn. That way I can walk over and pick up my car in the morning. Now, if someone would be so kind as to drive me that short distance, I would be most appreciative." I was proud of my drunken aplomb.

Guy insisted on being the one to take me.

Guy found a parking spot on the street outside the inn, then turned to me and leaned in close. I knew what was coming and I didn't think I could avoid it: I didn't really want to avoid it. He snaked his hand behind my neck and pulled me in for a kiss. It wasn't unpleasant. I hadn't been kissed in so long. The only thing I really found wrong with it was that it looked like, if I wasn't careful, he might swallow my head. He was that kind of kisser, the type that acts as if they are trying to ingest you. I pictured myself disappearing headfirst into the winding tracts of Guy's large intestine. It wasn't a pretty picture and didn't help me feel sexy. Still, I was drunk, and he was warm, and it was cold outside. I tried to leave the car, but that wasn't his plan. He pulled and tugged at me and kissed and kissed at me, my neck, my fingertips, my earlobe, my elbow—my elbow? It was his constantly taking an unnecessary and unwelcome last step—the tonsillectomy when a gentle probe is sufficient, the elbow when most men would stop at the earlobe—pushing the envelope of love, that kept me in my head, even though I was drunk, and lonely and inclined to be amorous.

Guy asked if he could come in, but I didn't think it was a good idea. The Wellesley Inn wasn't that sort of place. That's what I was thinking, conveniently forgetting that the two of us weren't teenagers sneaking around; we were adults old enough to have teenage children of our own. It was highly unlikely that the night clerk would even look at us as we walked through the lobby.

I stopped Guy with a hand on his sternum and looked into his eyes.

"Let's just catch our breath for a minute," I said. His eyes were shining with the look of a man whose little brain has already taken over. Even with my dearth of experience, I'd seen the little brain take over before.

"Please, Jane," he said. "I've been wanting to be with you ever since the first moment I saw you on the mountain."

I found that hard to believe. People don't look their best in goggles. His enthusiasm eventually swayed me and I told him he could come in if he behaved himself in the lobby so we wouldn't look suspicious.

Inside, Guy kept his hands at his sides as we walked toward the stairs. For all anyone could tell, we were a tired married couple ready to go upstairs to twin beds.

I thought about my sister Miranda and whether I should be doing this at all. She claimed to be over Guy and I believed her, but I felt that people who are really in love never do get over it, not completely.

I unlocked the door of my room and turned on the light.

"Were you in love with Miranda?" I asked Guy.

Guy sat on the four-poster bed.

"You sure know how to deflate a guy," he said.

I wasn't sure whether he meant physically or mentally. Either way, it probably wasn't a good thing.

"No, I was never in love with her," he said.

"But you acted like you were."

"You weren't there. She read too much into it."

I went into the bathroom and got us both a glass of tepid water from the tap. We sat on the edge of the bed. I looked at Guy's profile. As beautiful as Guy was, there was something about him that did not appeal to me and I couldn't figure out what it was. Who knows what makes people attractive to each other? It could be something as simple as smell. Guy's cologne was strong and sickly sweet.

He put his glass down on a side table, then took mine from my hand and put it down beside his. He pushed my shoulder until I was half lying, half sitting, and he started to unbutton my blouse. If I closed my eyes, I could pretend he was someone else, someone I liked more. I closed my eyes, but when I opened them, he was scrambling out of his pants as if his feet were on fire. He wore jockey shorts and I think men in briefs look a little vulnerable, more boy than man.

His penis was purplish and rather enormous. Max wasn't what you'd call diminutive, but Guy was the stuff of which porn stars are made, not that I've seen many porn stars, or any really—but I could imagine. Then I thought of Miranda again, and if I'd had a penis myself it would have collapsed like an empty balloon. I think maybe it was Guy's unbridled delight in the whole process that made me wince. He was like the character Peter Sellers played in the *Pink Panther* movies. There was something so ridiculous in the poses he struck, something so creepy in the amorous glances he threw my way.

Still, I didn't stop him. It was as if I was fascinated into shock, and it wasn't until he was on top of me and his penis was knocking about in an attempt to find the right door that I decided I'd had enough.

I pushed him away. This, at first, had no impact. The mini-brain is so far from the large one that the ears can't easily send it signals. I understood this with a sort of clinical patience.

"What's the matter?" he asked. His voice was husky, almost a second voice, like a science fiction character with an alien living inside him.

"I want to stop," I said. We learned this at Wellesley in our Health and Feminism class. "I want to stop" were magic words, known the world over to mean that if you continue, you do so at the peril of a criminal record.

Guy stalked into the bathroom, closed the door, and in a minute came out with a towel wrapped around his waist. He hadn't lost his tumescence and his penis entered the room before he did.

I had put on my bathrobe, a new one, not the pink terry cloth. This one was black silk, and I don't know why I bought it if not for a moment like this—whatever this moment was. This wasn't going to be a moment of passion. It was more like a moment of passion denied, and you hardly needed black silk for that.

"I'm embarrassed," I said. "Completely embarrassed." And I was, partly because I was ridiculous enough to let this begin and then stop it—what thirty-eight-year-old did that? And the other more compelling reason for my shame was that he had seen me naked. Except for a few extra pounds, I wasn't any more or less lumpy than your average thirty-eight-year-old. It wasn't my body I was ashamed of, it was that I'd allowed him to come so close. The problem was that I didn't want anyone, any man at all, to get that close to me unless I loved him. That was the embarrassing thing. I was a complete failure at promiscuity. It didn't matter how drunk I was or how attractive Guy was. At that moment, I was constitutionally incapable of having sex with someone I didn't love. Only hours ago I hadn't even wanted him to hug me, and now here we were.

I tried to explain it to him—to somehow paint myself out of the picture of prude extraordinaire and into something more along the lines of a woman of great discrimination and dignity. This was made harder by the fact that we had already rubbed around naked.

"You think it's too fast?" he asked. He sat beside me on the bed and massaged my neck. It felt so good I almost reconsidered, but then I thought about the next morning—waking up with him, drinking coffee with him, trying to pretend we were more to each other than we were just because we'd performed a biological function in the night. It was better to stop now. What I didn't know then was that Guy's plans were long term, and his desires, as far as I was concerned, weren't going to be satisfied by a hasty night of sex. "I like you, Jane. I think you're smart, attractive, talented . . . and tonight I found out you were funny."

"You think this is funny?" I asked. He laughed as if I'd just delivered a punch line.

"Not this. Not us, right now. You were funny at the college. You're full of all kinds of wonderful things, and the problem is, you don't seem to know it."

That was a problem, and because I knew he had read me correctly, my heart flipped over. There is something enticing about a man who professes to know you better than you know yourself.

I had to get away.

When I told Priscilla that I'd be leaving for the Vineyard the next day, she tried to talk me out of it.

"Why would you do that? The Vineyard is horrible in winter. I thought you'd stay here until at least May. I was looking forward to it."

She seemed to have forgotten that in the five nights I had been staying with her, she'd been occupied with Jason for four of them.

Still, it's hard to remain angry with someone who likes you well enough to want you to stay with them for four months. Someone who is willing to provide you with a safe haven is as good as family (and in the case of mine, better).

"It's silly. You don't need to go to the Vineyard so early. Let me show you my new outfit," Priscilla said. She was trying to distract me, but she knew me well enough to know that clothes were a bad way to get my attention.

I used to like how Priscilla dressed, but I saw her now with a different eye. Her obsession with Talbots looked less like good taste and more like a lack of imagination.

"Very nice," I said about the outfit, "but I'm still going to the Vineyard."

"I'll see less of Jason. Would that work?"

"I need my own home, even if it's a little box in the wind."

"You'll be very alone there, Greta Garbo, that's for sure."

"There's my friend Isabelle. I've already called her."

"Who?"

"Isabelle from college. The one with the long wavy hair."

"Didn't she leave before graduation?"

"Yes."

"Because she was pregnant."

"You do remember," I said. Priscilla's lack of memory was a ruse. Everyone remembered Isabelle. It was because she had been so promising. She came from a first-generation Portuguese family in Bridgewater. Her father had a bakery and made the best sourdough bread in Massachusetts, but they didn't have much money. Still, Isabelle had won a full scholarship to Wellesley, then, right before graduation, she got pregnant, left school, moved to the Vineyard, and opened her own bakery.

Jimmy, Isabelle's son, was almost seventeen now. He was looking at colleges himself. I saw them often when I was on the island and I suppose you could say that next to Priscilla, Isabelle was my closest friend. I often wished I'd asked Isabelle, instead of Priscilla, what I should have done that summer with Max. Isabelle wouldn't have wanted me to move to California, but she never would have tried to keep me here. In the end, I never told her anything about it. It was silly to be so closemouthed. Maybe if I had talked to a friend about it, I would have gotten it out of my system— or maybe I would have had the courage to track Max down and tell him I had changed my mind.

I kept Priscilla and the rest of the family separate from Isabelle. She was the type of person who would be of no consequence to the Fortunes, and they would end up treating her that way even if they weren't aware of it. I didn't want Isabelle to have to deal with that. They knew about her, but they never asked me to invite her over, and I thought that was reason enough not to.

"I don't know why you'd want to go down and shiver in the cold when you could stay here. We can go to museums, lectures, concerts. We can have a wonderful winter," Priscilla said.

Of course Boston would be cold, too, but in Priscilla's world the winter was one warm fire after another in many different venues. Whether she was visiting a friend, drinking at the Ritz, or rolling with Jason under a down comforter, her winters were sedentary and comfortable. Besides, winter is a wonderful season for a knitter. Wool feels so much better between your fingers when it's cold outside.

All the things Pris offered, the things I had enjoyed all my life, no longer appealed to me. I wanted a windswept shore and my own company. Besides, I needed to get out of town before Guy tracked me down. I didn't want to get into another weird situation. A woman my age should know her own mind, and until I did, I thought it best to stay away from him.

Chapter 27

Jane makes her escape to the island

Seeing Max again had opened up old wounds, and like a sick dog who hides under the porch, I wanted to go someplace I could nurse my injuries.

I drove off the ferry into a blustering island wind. My friend Isabelle had faxed me directions to the cottage. It all happened quickly, because the owners of the house were as desperate for the rent as I was to disappear.

Even on a cold gray day, the gingerbread cottages in Oak Bluffs make you think of fairy tales. If your life were a toy, this is where you'd live. The small houses are multicolored—lavender, white, green, orange, yellow, and purple. I drove past one with heart-shaped cutouts around the trim and another with intricate scrollwork. My house was blue with cathedral windows—a sanctuary. I parked the car, went to the door, and, as instructed, pulled the key out from under a ceramic garden gnome. The house was miniature but complete. I walked through the front room, decorated in wicker and white denim, and into the kitchen at the back. Someone had turned on the heat and filled the refrigerator with groceries. Isabelle.

I spent the afternoon unpacking. Instead of acting with my usual efficiency, I took it slow. I put my clothes into closets and drawers with a dreamy disregard for time. I listened to the radio for company. A commentator was reviewing Max's new book. It wasn't the first review I'd heard, but it was the nastiest. He called the book a "puerile puddle of palaver." Obviously the critic was in love with the sound of words in his own mouth.

Max had been widely reproached for *Post* because, though Max was known for his humor and social satire, this time he had attacked a serious subject. They said he was obviously trying to write his "important" novel. Thirty-nine is a good age to try to write your "important" novel. This one was about a family on Long Island in the aftermath of 9/11. I could have told him this was a subject that should be avoided, if only because of the slew of stories I received that tried to say something about it and failed. Only time would make that subject somewhat manageable, and there hadn't been enough of it. Maybe there never would be.

The book was selling well, based on Max's reputation alone. There was also some talk of awards, so not everyone agreed that he'd reached over his head.

I took my copy of *Post* from the pile of books I'd brought to the island and put it on my night table.

That evening I met Isabelle and her son Jimmy at the Black Dog for dinner. Isabelle's thick curly hair was tied back with a silver clasp. She didn't look much older than she had on the day she left Wellesley. She had an innocence and an energy about her. Though her life had not been easy, she always put a positive spin on it. Being bright and resourceful, she had known just what to do with the bakery to attract the wealthy islanders and tourists. Isabelle had been serving cappuccino and espresso long before expensive coffee chains became a blight on the landscape.

"I can't believe you filled the refrigerator," I said before even saying hello.

"Why not?"

I gave Jimmy a peck on the cheek. Last year when I saw him, he was a boy, but now he had the look of a man. He even held out my chair. I smiled at Isabelle. She gave me a proud-parent smile in return.

"No one in my own family would ever think to do anything like that for me."

"No offense, Jane, but your family brings new levels of meaning to the term *self-centered*."

I laughed. Jimmy looked at me like he didn't know how having your family insulted could be so funny.

"How are they anyway?" Isabelle asked.

"Teddy and Miranda are in Palm Beach for the winter. Or, as they put it—they are wintering in Palm Beach. The truth is, they spent so much money we had to rent out our house to rebuild our capital."

"The only reason I'm surprised," Isabelle said, "is that I was under the impression that there was so much money to begin with, to go through it all would take a real effort."

"That may be the only real effort they ever made," I said. "Let's just say that they had few frugal habits."

We ordered hamburgers and clam chowder.

"We should keep that between ourselves," I said. "They think they're putting one over on everyone." I felt foolish even as I said it, but Isabelle knew everything about everyone on the island, and although she never had bad intentions, she could sometimes be indiscreet.

"Who do they think cares?" Isabelle asked.

"Society at large," I said in an overblown voice.

She laughed. "A family that believes they are living in a Henry James novel. How picturesque. So, Jane, what brings you here in the dead of winter? Not that we aren't delighted to have you."

Both Isabelle and Jimmy looked at me with the same expression. Jimmy was a handsome kid, dark hair, olive skin, dark eyes. He had Isabelle's coloring, but otherwise he didn't look much like her. I had wondered, at times, who his father was, but it wasn't the kind of question I'd ever ask, even of a close friend like Isabelle.

"Could you picture me in Palm Beach?" I asked. "Lime green is not exactly my color. I don't play golf. Besides, I'm sure they rented a nice apartment, but still, we'd be on top of each other."

There was one more important reason, a reason I hadn't even admitted to myself—and that was that they hadn't asked me. Miranda had replaced me with Dolores as easily as she might have replaced a Gucci loafer with a Jack Purcell sneaker.

I had built what little self-concept I had on certain bricks, and one of them was that I was essential to my father and sister. Essential? I wasn't even necessary.

In my little gingerbread house I had time to think—too much time. I had never lived alone. I spent time alone, but Miranda and Teddy were always coming and going and just having them in the house changed the quality of the solitude.

Every morning I went to Isabelle's bakery for coffee and muffins. Once a week I received a package from Tad. Even though we had chosen the winner of the fellowship, we still had to fill the *Review*. Mornings, I sat at my desk on the second floor of my little house looking out onto the other cottages, most of which were empty in winter, and read the stories, made the choices, and sent them back. I also took care of other foundation business—wrote checks and personal rejection letters for the stories we wouldn't be using. Several weeks passed this way and I still hadn't heard from Hope Bliss. She said it wasn't going to be difficult to find Jack Reilly. He couldn't be that hard to find.

I grieved for Max as if the loss were new. I don't think I was grieving just for him, but for a past I might have spent better. Was my life going to end like this? The *Review* twice a year, the contest, the business of the foundation? I could do it all with my eyes closed. I wasn't even forty. And stories like Jack Reilly's, the ones that really excited me, were so few and far between. Maybe Basil Funk was right. I should incorporate more art into the foundation's work. Somehow, though, I didn't feel that was the answer.

And while I had made my retreat to the island, what had been happening up in Vermont? My source of information was Winnie, who unfortunately had no idea what really interested me.

Lindsay still wasn't supposed to travel long distances, so she had moved in with the Franklins. Her prognosis was good, though according to Winnie, she seemed a bit odd.

"At least she remembers everyone now. We were really worried there for a while. But I don't understand Max," Winnie said on the phone. "I would have thought that he wouldn't leave her side, but he only stayed until just after she woke up. Then he left on a book tour. I hope he's not one of those guys who will get a girl's hopes up only to drop her flat."

"I don't think he's one of those guys," I said, despite all the evidence to the contrary. Maybe he had gone back to the girl who had called him that night on his cell phone. Who knew what he was thinking? He was a different man from the one I had first fallen in love with.

But I, too, was surprised that Max had left so soon. He might have canceled a few dates of his tour. I had always thought that he was unlikely to leave the woman he loved in a precarious condition.

Charlie lifted up the extension. "Basil's been asking about you," he said.

Winnie said, "What are you talking about, Charlie? I didn't hear Basil say a thing about Jane."

"You weren't there," Charlie said.

"When wasn't I there? I'm always there," Winnie said.

"Well, you weren't."

Charlie hung up.

Winnie called every week. She complained of the sniffles during each call and the boys were always misbehaving.

"Anyway, Jane, you're so lucky to be on the island by yourself. No responsibilities. You could have stayed with us for the winter, you know. We liked having you. Charlie and I fight even more when you're not here."

Considering how much they fought when I was there, this wasn't a good sign.

One morning in mid-February I arrived at Isabelle's, as usual, and she said she had a message for me. A Hope Bliss—what kind of name was that—had called her house looking for me. I remembered that I'd given Hope Isabelle's number because at the time I didn't have one.

I ate my cranberry muffin quickly and rushed back to the house to call Hope.

"Did you find him?" I asked as soon as she picked up the phone.

"Are you sure there is only a story involved here?" Hope asked.

"It's a very good story," I said.

"It was one of the strangest cases I've had lately," she said. "Sorry it took me so long, but I had to do it the old-fashioned way. I trekked around all over the Boston area from one person to another to find anyone who had known him, or seen him. You want to know where I found him?"

"Of course I do." What was she talking about—why would I have hired her if I didn't want to know?

"He's been under your nose the whole time."

"Is he here on the Vineyard?"

"Yes."

"Where does he live?"

"Oak Bluffs."

"I'm in Oak Bluffs."

"I know."

"He's in a gingerbread cottage four doors down from yours."

195

"That's crazy."

"Isn't it? You want to hear the craziest part?" I didn't say anything so she continued. "He's squatting."

"What?"

"He found an empty house, got it open, and moved into it. He's squatting."

"That's not too honest," I said. I had seen Jack Reilly as an outlaw, even hoped he would be one, but the reality didn't excite me as much as I thought it would. I was basically an honest person and expected other people to be honest. I'd imagined a bad boy, not a parasite.

"Damn straight. It's stealing," Hope said. "Anyway, that's why he was so hard to find. He has a post office box in Lynn, but other than that it doesn't look like he pays taxes, or has a bank account, or even has a telephone."

When I told Isabelle about Jack Reilly, she said I should call the police, but I didn't want to get the police involved. What if—and I was beginning to doubt it—Jack Reilly was all I'd dreamed him to be. What if when I opened the door, love hit me like a bucket of water from an upstairs window? Would I want the police shifting around at the bottom of the front walk waiting to drag him away?

It may have been ridiculous to put myself in jeopardy in pursuit of something I couldn't even name, but I was determined to do it because if I didn't, if I let the police go in and haul Jack Reilly away, I'd never know if, despite his antisocial behavior, he was the one.

Chapter 28

Jack Reilly: squatter

I wasn't sure how to approach Jack Reilly. At first, all I did was watch his house, but I never saw anyone come out or go in. Since the house was on the same side as mine, it was harder to keep an eye on it than it would have been if he had lived across from me. I decided that if I didn't see anyone go in or out in three days, I'd go and knock on the door.

The day my surveillance would have ended, I was going out for a walk, and as I locked my door, I turned and there was a man coming out of the house where Jack Reilly was squatting. This man was almost bald, with a scrawny chicken neck. He held a notebook in his hand and he was wearing a lumberjack jacket and the type of black-and-white-checked pants chefs wear.

Since I was only going for a walk and had no special destination, I didn't see any harm in following him. He wasn't the Jack Reilly I'd pictured, but maybe he was a friend of Jack's. Maybe he, too, was squatting in the neighbor's house. Perhaps I could find something out about Jack Reilly from him.

The man huddled against the wind and walked toward the center of town, where he went into a seaside restaurant and sat at the bar. I followed him in and took a booth. I wished I had brought something to read so I wouldn't look conspicuous. I would have made a terrible detective, and every time I tried anything remotely related to detection, I appreciated Hope Bliss more.

I ordered a beer for stamina and worked up the nerve to send one over to the man at the bar who was now scribbling in his notebook with a cheap ballpoint pen.

The man took the beer, looked at the bartender, then turned toward me. The look he gave me was both wolfish and questioning, which may be the appropriate look to give a strange woman in a virtually empty restaurant who buys you a beer.

He got up and came over. He held his beer up in a toast and thanked me. I bowed my head and smiled shyly. I didn't know if I was feeling shy or if I felt that this was the look I must produce, like some misguided Nancy Drew. I was proud of myself for tracking him to a public place so there'd be less chance for trouble. And I was still hoping that this man wasn't Jack Reilly, that the whole thing was some mistake.

"Would you like to sit down?" I asked.

"Sure," he said, and slipped into the booth across from me.

"I'm . . ." And then, of course, I paused. He had applied to the foundation. He'd know my name. "Lindsay Maple."

"JR," he said.

"JR what?"

"Just JR," he said. "Like Cher or Madonna."

I nodded and sipped my beer. Where to go from here? Now I was stuck with an unattractive squatter who was wearing two different patterns—plaid on top and checks on the bottom. At least if this JR wasn't my Jack Reilly, there was still hope.

"I see you're writing," I said, and pointed to his notebook.

"I'm a writer," he said.

"What kinds of things do you write?" I asked.

"Stories."

"You living here for the winter?"

"It's quiet here."

"Where do you live?"

"Gingerbread cottages."

"Amazing, me too," I said. His teeth, when he smiled, were nicotine-stained, and he pulled out a packet of Nicorette gum. "Look, I have to ask you something. I heard that a guy named Jack Reilly lived near us in the gingerbread houses. Ever heard of him?"

He looked up, pressed his lips together, then smiled.

"I'm Jack Reilly," he said.

"You said you were JR," I said.

"JR, Jack Reilly."

"Oh," I said.

"And you're Jane Fortune," he said. "You make a terrible sleuth if that's what you were trying to do."

I blushed.

"How do you know me?" I asked.

"How do you know me?" he answered.

"I've been looking for you," I said. "You submitted a story to the *Review*."

"And that's how I know you. I saw your picture on the Internet."

"There's a picture of me on the Internet?"

"Several. I knew you were living a few doors down. I knew who you were when you followed me in here and bought me this drink."

"Why didn't you say so?"

"I thought I'd let you play out your game. Didn't want to disappoint. Why were you playing it anyway?"

"I thought you might be dangerous."

"Why?"

"Because you're squatting in that house."

He nodded. "It wouldn't be the first time. I believe that empty out-of-season homes should be used by the people who need them. Doesn't make me dangerous."

"But it's stealing," I said.

"Depends how you look at it."

"I look at it as stealing."

He smiled. I could see how the woman at the Butterfly Museum might have been taken in by him. He had a way of talking that made you feel like you were a precious stone sitting in the palm of his hand.

"I have some of your things," I said.

"What things?"

"A letter from a nice lady at the Butterfly Museum, a couple of books, and a notebook."

"My notebook. I've been looking everywhere for it."

"The woman in Lynn gave it to me."

"She's a piece of work, isn't she?" Then he paused and his brows came together. "Why were you there?"

"I told you. I've been looking all over for you," I said.

"Why?"

And then I said it, though it didn't come out the way I wanted it to: it wasn't the grand announcement I had planned. Grand announcements didn't feel right with this Jack Reilly.

"You won the damn contest—you won the fellowship," I said.

"That's great," he said as if it came as no surprise. "But why didn't you contact me at my post office box?"

"Believe me, if you'd put it on your story I would have. I wouldn't have spent the winter tracking you all over New England."

He hit the side of his head with the flat of his hand.

"We artists," he said as if this were some sort of excuse for being a flake. "You gonna turn me in for squatting?" he asked.

"It's none of my business, I guess, but I already told my friend Isabelle, and she's not so forgiving about things like this. She's a year-round resident, and I think she feels personally responsible for the entire island."

"I'm screwed," he said.

"Maybe not. The fellowship doesn't usually start until June, but there's no reason why it couldn't start earlier. It is for the struggling artist."

"That would be me," he said.

Jack Reilly packed up his stuff that afternoon and came over to say good-bye. So it hadn't been love at first sight. The hope I'd been holding broke into shards and I spent the afternoon walking carefully around them to keep from getting cut.

Maybe he wasn't going to be *my* next big thing, but that wouldn't keep him from being the next big thing in literature. I could help him. Wasn't that my job?

By the time he walked away to the ferry with his battered backpack, I was feeling better. My Jack Reilly fantasy was gone and now I could get on with my life, whatever that meant.

Life on the Vineyard, if I were to admit it, was too quiet for me, and without my fantasy for company, lonely. When I walked down the street I looked with longing at "Help Wanted" signs and tried to picture myself answering phones in an insurance company or slinging scrambled eggs across a counter in a diner. I imagined myself as a bookseller or a sales-clerk in a gift shop that sold scrimshaw.

One afternoon I went down to Isabelle's bakery and asked for a job.

Isabelle wiped her palms against the front of her apron. She had a dusting of flour across her cheek.

"I need a job," I said.

"You have a job, Jane," she said.

"What job?"

"The foundation. You have the foundation. You don't need to work in a bakery."

"But you're wrong. I do. I need to get my hands dirty."

"Maybe you should try to write. You're so good with words. There would be no Max Wellman without you—and how many others—Jessica Lowe, Marylou Patter, Axel Bonner."

"They all would have made it without me," I said.

She shrugged. "We'll never know for sure, will we, because they had you."

"Please, I want a job."

"I think you've lost your mind."

"That's okay with me. I'm tired of my mind."

"I can't pay you much."

"Don't pay me at all."

"I have to pay you something."

"When do I start?"

"Tomorrow, I guess." She looked skeptical. "We start at four, but you can come in at five."

"Five?"

"In the morning."

"Yes, of course," I said. I was somewhat deflated, but no matter. I could wake up early. If Isabelle had done it all these years, then so could I.

It was dark when I woke for my first day on the job, and I questioned my earlier impulse. I felt groggy and headachy. I bundled up against the cold and walked through the dimly lit streets until I saw the lights of the bakery. When I arrived, Isabelle was already there with her workers, Doris and Salvador. The ovens were burning and the kitchen smelled of brown sugar and cinnamon. It was all so warm and cozy, I could have nodded out right there, but Isabelle set me to work filling muffin tins. Most of the jobs I did at the bakery were monotonous, but after a few weeks I got used to the work and began to like it. I'd let my mind wander. Sometimes stories would come to me from things I saw in the shop. I imagined a relationship between Doris and Salvador. As far as I knew, they were barely acquainted, but in my mind I created a love story of passion mixed with impediments. Poor Doris in her hairnet and Salvador with his stormy eyebrows—I doubt they would have liked it if they'd known what I was thinking.

I established a routine. I woke up at four and got to the bakery at five. I worked at the bakery until noon, covered the morning rush, then walked the island all afternoon. At first, one mile of walking in the cold wind made my throat feel like tin and I'd rush home to a warm fire and woolly socks. After a while, though, I was hiking all over the island, mile after mile. Between that and my work in the bakery I could feel my body getting firmer, trimmer, stronger. I wouldn't need to cover anything this summer.

Early evenings I worked on foundation business, and when everything was finished for the day, I took out the journal Max had given me and I wrote. Yes, it was my dirty secret. At first, I wrote only journal entries, but then I started writing this story.

Jack Reilly kept in touch. He had fixed the front steps of the house in Hull. He was building some bookshelves and he was writing. He said his book was going to be great. Sometimes he sent me pieces through the mail, pieces typed on an old manual typewriter, even though there was a computer in the house. Jack asked for advice, but he rarely took it. I envied Jack Reilly his unrestrained confidence. He was so sure of his greatness. Did that make him greater?

I dutifully called Priscilla once a week. She still couldn't understand why I'd prefer the loneliness of the island to a winter in the city.

"I met the Goldmans at a party," she said. "I've been spending some time with Emma. She's a knitter. She says that knitting is very popular with Hollywood celebrities, not that that matters to me, of course. I can take a celebrity or leave one alone. Speaking of celebrities, her brother Max came by once while I was there. He's not very talkative, is he? I would describe him as morose."

"Morose?" Max was many things, but that wasn't one of them.

"Was he alone?" I asked.

"Yes. Emma says he's been acting strangely—not like a man in love—if any of us can tell what a man in love is supposed to act like. But Emma says he's either engaged or close to it. That girl Lindsay is home with her parents now. They say she's had a complete personality change. Of course, I didn't know her before and a head injury can be a serious thing. Maybe that's why Max is upset. You know, you throw your lot in with someone and then they change. It could be disturbing."

If I had been managing to keep even a sliver of hope alive, it died then, gasping on the little matchbox bed I had so carefully crafted for it.

"And Charlie found Max a house. Just what he wanted. That Charlie is a genius. I read a review of Max's latest book. The reviewer used the word *excrement*. Hardly a compliment. Have you read the book?"

"No."

"I think I'll pick it up. See what all the fuss is about. Good thing you didn't hitch your wagon to his star."

Over the years, I had often told myself that Priscilla had the best of intentions. After all, Pris was my mother's best friend and I assumed they'd think alike as far as I was concerned. When my mother died Priscilla was like a bandage I placed over my grief. At first, I relied on Priscilla's judgments and opinions with a blind faith, but I was beginning to see that Priscilla had her own agenda. It was important to Priscilla that I never change. So long as I remained the same—a somewhat inept, dependent spinster—she could be the savvy one, the worldly one, a lady of great taste and sophistication—and even a femme fatale. These undermining quips of Priscilla's weren't new, I had just refused to notice them, because if I did, it would change how I felt about her. Now I couldn't help noticing them and each little jab drove us farther apart.

The next week I didn't make my call to Priscilla. I was tired of the duties of good breeding.

At the end of the week, Pris called me.

"I haven't heard from you," she said. I knew she didn't like to pay for long-distance phone calls, even though she could easily afford them. It was a vestige of a time when long distance was considered a luxury. "Jane, is something wrong, dear?"

"Why would you ask that?"

"You don't sound like yourself." I hadn't said anything, so how could she suggest that I didn't sound like myself? "Maybe you should come home. Maybe you're lonely out there."

"I have Isabelle."

"She isn't a good friend."

"Yes she is."

"If you say so."

It was just like Priscilla to knit up her own version of my life and toss it over the real one like an ugly throw. I tapped my fingers on the desk and stared out the window. It was a gray and cold day.

"How's Jason?" I asked. It was a question born more of courtesy than curiosity. The more I thought about Priscilla's relationship with Jason, the more it worried me that I had allowed this woman to guide me in the ways of men.

"I met someone new," she said. "Kent Bracken. We have so much in common." Like their age, I hoped. "He's married, but it's all so romantic, I can overlook that for now." She might be able to overlook it, but his wife was likely to have more difficulty with the arrangement. It was none of my business. "He's one of the greatest scientific minds of the twenty-first century—stem cell research. He could find a cure for diabetes, even Alzheimer's. What a mind. We talk poetry for hours. We met at the symphony. He's just crazy about culture."

"Great," I said. "I have to go. I'm expected at Isabelle's." I said Isabelle's name very loudly.

"Well, keep in touch. I'm worried about you."

"Don't be." Her worry demeaned me. It assumed that there was something wrong with me and there wasn't.

"I don't see how you could be fine on that godforsaken island in winter," Pris said.

If she said anything after that, I didn't hear her because I had hung up. I know it's extremely impolite to hang up on someone when they are talking to you. This behavior certainly wasn't in keeping with the Fortune family code, but maybe I was coming to the point where I could live with that.

Chapter 29

The Fortune family returns

"May I ask you why the hell you are working in a bakery?" my father asked.

It was late May and he, Miranda, and Dolores had just arrived on the island.

Before they came, and after our winter tenants left our Vineyard Haven house, I got it cleaned and moved my things from the gingerbread cottage. Though I would have liked to stay in the cottage, the owners were coming for the summer, so I moved into our family's two-story Colonial on William Street.

Isabelle helped me find a girl who was home from college to come in daily to cook and clean. I imagined that this girl,

Bethany, must have been very much like Isabelle when she first left Bridgewater.

"Do you think that we are poor, Jane?" Teddy asked. "You haven't asked for any money. Do you need any?"

Though it had taken him months to ask, I was still grateful that he thought of it.

"I don't need money," I said.

"Then why?"

"I like it at the bakery."

"Jane, you just can't do it," Miranda said. "Think of how it looks."

"I don't think anyone cares how it looks."

"I care," she said.

She was tanned and wearing a green Lilly Pulitzer dress. Miranda's face was lined from excessive sun exposure. She should know better. What were all those expensive beauty products for if not to protect her skin? I was surprised Teddy hadn't said something to her.

"You look better, Jane," Teddy said. "What have you done to yourself? You look thinner. Have you lost weight?"

I was wearing formfitting jeans and a T-shirt, not one of my usual tent dresses. I'd given them up. I didn't miss them much, but occasionally I missed their shapeless comfort.

"I got my hair cut," I said. I thought this might be enough of an answer to satisfy him and make him change the subject.

"Good for you. You look terrific. And your face. You must be using Crème de la Mer. I've always said it's the best."

"Soap and water," I said. This wasn't entirely true. I had invested in some kind of beauty regimen from the drugstore, but I didn't have to tell him.

"I'm impressed. Very impressed. I'm so proud of you, Jane. Taking a little initiative with yourself."

"You do look good," Miranda said. "Different somehow. Maybe even younger. But you'll have to give up that job. I can't imagine it will be much of a sacrifice." Her nasal voice wandered up and down the scale and finally ended on a C-flat.

"I'm not giving up the job," I said.

"That's just patently ridiculous," Teddy said. "I can't have a daughter of mine working in a bakery."

"Why not?"

"People will talk. The Fortunes just don't do that sort of thing."

"They do now," I said.

"Someone will have to get the luggage," Miranda said.

"Have you sprained something?" I asked. She was holding her Louis Vuitton train case. She wore large sunglasses and she looked chic in a *Breakfast at Tiffany's* kind of way.

"No," Miranda said. "Why would you ask that?"

"There's no Astrid here, Miranda. I hired someone to come in and clean and cook, but she's not coming until later. I guess you'll have to get your own luggage."

Dolores, from her place at the door, said, "I'll get it."

"Jane can help you," Miranda said. "I'll make coffee." I didn't even think she knew how to make coffee.

"I'll go," my father said, putting his hand on Dolores's arm to hold her back.

"I don't mind helping, Teddy. You know that." She smiled up at him in a soft and kittenish way. I looked at Miranda, but she didn't seem to notice.

Though Miranda had come to the island looking as polished as burnished wood, Dolores was a little the worse for wear. The sun had given her freckles and she had gained weight. Since Dolores wasn't tall, the weight didn't sit well on her. Some people gain weight all over, while with others, weight gravitates to one place. For Dolores, it was her thighs, and this year she'd be one of the women who would be using every artifice to cover up the one spot on her body over which she had lost control. Dolores also needed a trip to the hairdresser to take care of the dark roots in an otherwise brassy head of hair.

My father didn't seem to notice any of these changes in Dolores, which was very unlike him. If anything, he paid more attention to her than before they went away. I supposed it was only natural, since they had been living together for months.

I had planned a lobster dinner to welcome them back, and since we didn't talk anymore about my work at the bakery, we had a pleasant evening. Bethany came over, and together we boiled the lobsters, melted the butter, set the table, and cleaned up afterward.

After the meal, Teddy pushed himself away from the table.

"Thank you, Jane," he said. He patted his stomach. "This meal was a very nice gesture, and I, for one, appreciate it." He stood up and took a cigar from his pocket.

"It was very nice, Jane," Dolores said.

"I don't know about shellfish," Miranda said. "Didn't I read something recently?"

No one answered her.

"I'm going up to the widow's walk to smoke. Anyone want to come?" Teddy asked.

"I will, Teddy," Dolores said. She followed him upstairs. Did Miranda understand that if Dolores exchanged Mudd for Fortune—which would no doubt be a happy exchange in name alone—Miranda would be shifted to the role of stepdaughter to a woman over ten years her junior?

"This island air must be good for you, Jane," Miranda said. She shifted in her seat and stretched into a yoga pose.

"I've always liked it here," I said.

"You and Mom," she said. "The two of you. You always liked the same things."

"We did," I said, and smiled.

"I miss her sometimes," Miranda said. She stretched backward.

"Me too," I said. "How long is Dolores staying? I didn't even know she was coming."

"Oh, Dolores will stay as long as she likes. We do everything together. I don't know how I could have coped without her. Not everyone likes to be alone all the time"—she paused—"but you don't seem to mind it."

Bethany brought us coffee.

"I wasn't alone," I said.

"Oh yes. You've been working at that bakery." She picked up her coffee and thanked Bethany. "You'll never guess who we ran into in Boston." They had stayed over a few nights in a hotel on the waterfront on their way to the Vineyard.

"Who?" I asked.

"Guy Callow. Remember him?"

"Your old boyfriend," I said. This would have been the time to tell her that I, too, had seen Guy Callow. I don't know why I didn't, but I didn't.

"I guess you could call him that. He looks good. He's coming down here in a few weeks. Daddy says—Daddy called Guy's father right after we ran into Guy—that the Dutch girl settled a lot of money on Guy when they split. He never even ended up practicing law."

"That must make you feel better," I said. "There must be something wrong with a man who lives off a settlement from his ex-wife."

"Something wrong? Like what?"

If I was going to say anything about seeing Guy, I should do it now. The longer I waited, the more awkward it would become.

"Anyway, I don't care at all about Guy Callow. He was a mere mosquito bite to me." Miranda sighed and looked toward the window. "Daddy and Dolores get on so well, don't you think?"

"I guess so," I said.

Miranda turned back toward me. "Guy told us he ran into you in Vermont," she said.

"That's right. I almost forgot."

"How you could forget about running into Guy Callow is really beyond me, Jane. He's such a beautiful man. Don't you have any feelings about men at all?"

"Not about Guy Callow," I said.

"Well, that makes sense, I suppose. He was my boyfriend—and sisters, well, they just don't do that to each other, do they?" I felt that somewhere in there was not exactly a threat but a warning. "I'm not interested in him anymore, of course. I'm not the type of woman to go mooning around after the same man forever. He made his bed, now he can just lie in it. Still, if he wants to be friends, that's fine too. Either way, it doesn't matter to me."

If Miranda was telling the truth, I was glad, because it hardly seemed like she had made a lasting impression on Guy's heart. And if she really had such a careless attitude toward love, perhaps she could bottle it and share it with me.

After everyone went to bed, I went out onto the widow's walk. From there, you could watch the boats bob in the bay.

Guy Callow's imminent arrival didn't thrill me. If it hadn't been for Max, maybe I would have found Guy more appealing, but I'd never know because my feelings for Max, no matter how hopeless, were too deeply anchored. Maybe after he married Lindsay, I'd be free. At the moment, though, when I compared Max with Guy, the former always left me wanting more, while the latter was always too much.

At four-thirty the next morning I crept out of the house. I had farther to go now that I was in Vineyard Haven and I had to drive to work. I rolled the car out of the driveway and started the engine when I got to the street. The noise of the engine was jarring in the still of the morning.

When I arrived at the bakery, Isabelle took me aside.

"Have a muffin," she said.

"What's the matter?" I asked.

"Nothing," she said. She paused, took a bite of blueberry muffin, and chewed. I waited. "I was thinking, though, now that your family is back, you might want to stop working here."

"Why?" I asked.

"I doubt they'd like it very much. I might not know them, but I know what they're like." She took a knife and smoothed a slab of butter onto her muffin, then took another bite.

"I don't care what they think," I said.

"You've always cared what they thought, even when you thought you didn't."

"Well, I don't anymore."

I felt that there was something more she wanted to say.

"Soon the kids will be coming back for the summer," she said.

I nodded. Miranda and Teddy had come to the island early, before the season had officially started. Florida was getting too hot and it only made sense for them to move into the only house they had left. There was also the hint of a scandal involving Miranda and a Kennedy cousin, but I couldn't even bear to think about that.

"Are you firing me?" I asked.

"Of course I'm not firing you. It's just that the kids will be expecting the job. In the summer I usually hire a few kids so they'll make money for college."

I was embarrassed to think I'd almost taken a job reserved for a college kid who really needed the money.

"Okay, and I could use someone to work on the *Euphemia Review*." I tried to redeem myself by making a new job for a needy kid. If Isabelle did it every summer, then so could I.

"Can you pay them?" she asked.

"Of course," I said. I'd have to talk to the bankers, but I didn't want her to think that I'd hire someone and not expect to pay them. While I was at it, I'd get a stipend for Tad.

"How about Jimmy?" she asked.

"It won't be much money," I said.

"That's okay. He has odd jobs." Her mother-mind was ticking away.

"Then Jimmy it is," I said. I hoped he had some feeling for the written word. "You need me today?"

Isabelle looked at me and I realized that she had never needed me. She had made room for me and I was grateful.

"I'll be going along, then." I smiled. I wanted her to know how much I appreciated what she had done, but I didn't know how to say thank you. "You want to have dinner Friday night?" I asked.

"Love to," Isabelle said.

She turned and walked back into the kitchen. I bought some hot rolls and muffins, left the warmth of the bakery, and walked out into the chilly morning.

When I got home I set out the bread and muffins and made some coffee. Teddy and Dolores came downstairs together, both dressed in tennis whites.

"Jane, what are you doing here? I thought you had that job," Teddy said.

"Not anymore."

"Well, thank God for that. You took my advice. Good girl. Never known you to do it before, but it's a welcome change."

I poured the coffee.

"The tennis club probably isn't open yet," I said. It was too early in the season.

"We'll find a public court," Dolores said.

"Isn't she resourceful," Teddy said. It wasn't a question so much as a compliment, the type he'd been throwing her way since they'd arrived.

"Dolores is very resourceful," I said. I didn't mean what Teddy meant by it. I glanced at Dolores, who smiled innocently back at me.

Teddy picked out a banana nut muffin and took a bite.

"These are wonderful," he said after wiping the crumbs from his mouth with a linen napkin. "Who would ever think that the best muffins anywhere could be found on an island?"

He put the muffin down, half eaten, and went outside, as he did every morning, to pick up the newspaper from the front walk—or the shrubbery, depending on the aim of the paperboy. He came back to the kitchen, took a sip of coffee, and laid the local paper out on the table. He licked his forefinger before turning each page. His squint revealed that he probably needed reading glasses but was too vain to admit it.

"Look here," he said. "The Buffingtons, Veronica and Glenda, are coming down this summer. It says that Veronica has taken that lone house overlooking Menemsha Pond, up-island."

The Buffingtons hadn't been back to the island since Michael Buffington had died.

"I wonder how I can get Veronica to forgive me. They always have the best parties. Since my first note of apology didn't work, I'll have to prostrate myself. I know it was very rude not to do anything when Michael died, but is she really going to punish me forever?"

Dolores turned her head with a sharp tweak and looked at Teddy. Who was this Veronica Buffington? Was she a rival?

"I'm going to write her another note," Teddy said.

"Are you sure you want to do that?" I asked. I had nothing against the Buffingtons. I liked them, but I hated to see Teddy humiliate himself just for an invitation.

"It can't hurt. When Michael was alive, they had the best parties. All the really interesting people were there. We wouldn't want to be left out this summer. Jane, you never did know the value of the right friends."

Dolores looked up again. She might have realized that there was nothing especially "right" about her when it came to the scale on which my father measured friends. She might have managed to turn his head with flattery, but that was nothing compared with a Veronica Buffington.

"Why don't you just call her?" Dolores asked. I think she thought that by offering a suggestion she could retain some control.

"No. I know what I'll do. I'll write her a downright obsequious note," Teddy said. "Jane, where is that paper?"

We kept a stack of cream cards in a secretary behind the sofa in the living room. I went to get them and brought several back to the kitchen.

While Teddy was writing, Miranda came downstairs, still in her bathrobe.

"What are you doing, Daddy?" she asked.

"I'm writing to Veronica Buffington. She's coming back to the island."

"Will she have that insipid Glenda-the-Good-Witch with her?" Miranda asked.

"They're both coming."

"You'd think they wouldn't want to do everything together. Glenda's at least thirty-five. Why doesn't she want a life of her own?"

*   *   *

215

Several weeks later, the four of us, Miranda, Dolores, Teddy, and I, were having lunch at a restaurant that claimed to serve the best fried clams on the island. We were seated at a table with a view of the harbor. It was a warm June day and we had just entered the summer season.

"The Buffingtons' party is next Friday night and we're all invited," Teddy said. He pulled out the invitation with a flourish. Apparently he had just received it that morning.

"I can't go," I said.

"Why not?" he asked.

"I'm having dinner with Isabelle," I said. "We get together every Friday night." It had become our ritual.

"If you have dinner with her every Friday, then you don't have to go on this particular Friday. I'm sure she'll understand," Teddy said.

"The Buffingtons will have other parties."

"Jane, I can't believe you'd give up the first good party of the season for something you do every week. Besides, how could the baker be anywhere near as interesting as the people who will be at the Buffingtons'?"

Dolores looked into her clam chowder. Though she'd managed to amuse Miranda and Teddy for months, she couldn't claim to be as "interesting" as the kind of people you'd find at the Buffingtons'. Dolores had never painted a picture, played a concerto, or danced with the Boston Ballet. These were the type of luminaries you might find at a Buffington party. I'm sure the only reason they invited us is that we were somewhat related to them.

I picked up a fried clam and popped it into my mouth.

"I'm going to dinner with Isabelle," I said.

"I never could understand you, Jane," Teddy said.

"No, you never could." I smiled and lifted my face toward the ocean breeze.

Teddy had a spot of tartar sauce on his chin and Dolores reached over with her thumb and wiped it off.

"Daddy," Miranda said, "you're not usually such a mess."

Dolores came to his defense. "It was just a small spot of tartar sauce."

"Yes, but it was on his face, and perhaps he should be the one to wipe it off, don't you think?"

Dolores reddened, but instead of looking down like she usually did, she looked straight at Miranda with an expression of defiance.

"Girls, girls," Teddy said. "It was only a spot of tartar sauce. Let's not blow it all out of proportion."

Chapter 30

Beach blanket bingo

At eleven o'clock in the morning on the day of the Buffingtons' party, I watched from an upstairs window as Guy Callow strolled up our front walk carrying a bouquet of flowers so large it concealed his head.

Miranda answered the door.

"Hello, Guy," she said. She used her bored, aristocratic voice, but there was a hint of the flirt in it. "You should have told us you were coming. I would have dressed." She was wearing a bikini with a sarong draped around her waist.

I couldn't very well stay upstairs, so I went down and hovered outside the sunroom where my father was reading the paper.

When Miranda led Guy into the room, Teddy stood and held out his hand. "Come on in, son," he said. "Good to see you. What brings you to this neck of the woods?"

Whatever rift had kept them apart all these years had apparently been repaired in that one meeting up in Boston.

Guy was still holding the enormous but unlovely bouquet, which made shaking hands with my father awkward.

"Sit down, Guy. Bethany will get you some coffee." Bethany, for some reason I could barely fathom, was always happy to do my father's bidding. Of course, she was getting paid for it, but she was so agreeable you'd think Teddy Fortune was the most likable man she'd ever met. I could imagine her, at night, discussing our foibles with her family, not in a malicious way, but as if we were an anthropology project.

I slipped into the room as Bethany was leaving to go back to the kitchen. She winked at me and mouthed the word *hunk*.

"Hello, Jane," Guy said. He pushed the flowers at Miranda. I was glad to see that he knew what was correct. He'd have to pay homage to my sister before he was going to get any attention from me.

"Thank you," Miranda said.

Miranda handed the flowers to me. "Jane, if you are going in to help Bethany, can you put these in water?" She perched on a wicker chair. "Sit down, Guy," she said.

Guy looked at me. It was that look, that look of admiration, but now it was also the presumptuous look of a shared secret. In the sunlight, Guy's blue eyes had a violet ring around the irises. His hair was shorter than when I'd last seen him. His white tennis sweater showed off his tan.

I took the broom of foliage into the kitchen to look for a vase. Bigger is not always better. I finally found a large glass vase hidden behind some bottles of olive oil in the pantry.

The flowers looked top-heavy, but it was the best I could do. I took a tray from a low cabinet and set out the willow-pattern cups and saucers, creamer and sugar bowl.

"Thanks, Jane," Bethany said, "I can do that."

We both leaned against the kitchen counter and waited for the water to boil.

"You are not like the rest of your family," Bethany said.

"I'm not?"

"They think that the world was made to revolve around them. You're not like that."

"Oh, don't be so sure," I said.

She shook her head. While we were making the coffee in the French press, Guy came into the kitchen. He gave Bethany an appraising glance. His eyes took a short vacation in the cleft between her breasts. He was so accustomed to that type of looking he probably didn't realize he was doing it.

"Can I help?" he asked. He came toward me and stood too close. Bethany backed away a little, looked at him, then at me, finished plunging the coffee, picked up the tray, and took it into the sunroom. She didn't come back. She must have decided to make the beds.

"I wanted to make sure you were okay with everything," Guy said.

"I don't know what *everything* is," I said. I turned and poked at the flowers, trying to make the arrangement more aesthetically pleasing. "Look, I'm sorry about it."

"You have nothing to apologize for," Guy said. His hands met mine on the vase. He smiled at me with those violet-rimmed eyes. The kitchen was sunny and warm. Other than the hideous bouquet and perhaps the wolfish look at Bethany, he hadn't done anything that was so unpleasant it couldn't be forgiven. I stifled the feeling that he wasn't all he appeared to be. I gave him what I hoped was an unself-conscious smile and removed my hands from the vase. I took the chance that he would continue to hold it and not let it crash to the floor: his grip on the vase was firm.

"You look beautiful, Jane," he said.

"Don't say that. It makes me feel ridiculous."

"Beautiful women are never ridiculous."

"That's where you're wrong. They are often ridiculous."

Guy looked like he might have reached out to me then had he not been encumbered by the mammoth vase. I walked toward the sunroom and there was nothing he could do but follow.

It was a beautiful day, breezy and not too hot. Someone had opened the windows and the silk curtains blew against the panes.

"We were just saying that you should come to the Buffingtons tonight, Guy. I'm sure I could get you an invitation," Teddy said.

Teddy had barely procured an invitation for himself and his two cohorts. Was he now going to call Veronica and ask if he could bring another guest?

"Actually," Guy said, "Glenda invited me."

Miranda sat up straight and turned to Guy.

"You know Glenda?" she asked.

"I met her a few years ago at a cancer benefit."

"Really. What do you think of her?" Miranda leaned forward. This pose showed off what minimal cleavage she could muster.

"She's a little quiet for my taste," Guy said.

"That's exactly what I think. She reads too much, just like Jane."

"Reading's not a bad thing," Guy said.

"Of course not, per se, but really there is so much to do in the world." She sat up and lifted her chin. "Of course, I like to keep up with politics and the like."

"I should loan you my new *Foreign Affairs*," Guy said. "There's a good article in it about Rwanda, ten years later."

"Ten years later than what?" Miranda asked.

Guy poked at the inside of his cheek with his tongue and I poured him another cup of coffee.

"Cream?" I asked.

"Black," he said.

We had magazines fanned out on the coffee table, and I wished, for a moment, that I had scooped them up and put them away. *Town & Country. Martha Stewart Living. People. Vanity Fair.* But the worst one was the *National Enquirer,* Miranda's guilty secret, but it must not have been too secret, nor must she have felt too guilty, because there it was, sitting right on top of the pile.

Those were the magazines. This was my family. We were who we were. If Guy didn't like it, he could leave. In his Brooks Brothers sweater with his three-hundred-dollar sunglasses hanging around his neck, he didn't look like he spent too much time worried about Rwanda either.

"Jane's not coming to the party tonight," Miranda said.

"Really, why not?"

"Previous engagement," I said.

"Is it a man?" Guy teased. He looked at me and his smile was mischievous.

"Are you kidding," Miranda said. "I can't think of the last time Jane had a date. She's having dinner with the baker."

Guy held his coffee with both hands and took a sip. He stretched his legs and crossed them at the ankles. Though the rest of him was still, his feet moved in small circles. Priscilla had once told me that moving your feet like that was just like wringing your hands. It had been a habit of mine, but I'd broken it.

Dolores came in. She had been to the hairdresser and her hair was back to its unnatural blond. She had bought, as I'd predicted, just the right sundresses and cover-ups to camouflage her thickening thighs.

"Hello, dear," Teddy said. Guy looked at him. He was obviously trying to gauge where Dolores fit into this picture.

"So this must be Winnie," Guy said. He knew this wasn't Winnie. He'd met Winnie, however briefly, on the mountain.

"No, no. This is our friend Dolores Mudd," Teddy said.

I noticed that he hadn't called her Miranda's friend.

Dolores held out her hand in a limp way, as if waiting to have it kissed.

Miranda introduced Guy. I was waiting for Dolores to pull out something as antiquated as "charmed," and I'm sure she would have if she thought she could have gotten away with it, but Guy exuded an intelligence that didn't sanction Dolores's synthetic charm.

"Nice to meet you, Guy," she said. She looked at the coffee tray. "Should I make fresh coffee?"

"Dolores, you are so thoughtful. What would we do without you?" Teddy said.

"I just made it," I said.

Teddy leaned over and poured coffee for Dolores. He poured the milk in, then handed it to her.

"Thank you, Teddy," Dolores said. She sat in the chair closest to his. She was careful to pull the short sarong she was wearing as a skirt into a flattering position.

"So are you all going to the beach today?" Guy asked. "My suit is in the car."

"Jane never comes with us," Miranda said.

Guy turned so his knees were facing me.

"Won't you come today?" he asked.

I didn't like going to the beach with a crowd. I had a quiet, hidden place where I went alone with my books, my journal, and a thermos of iced tea.

"She's such a spoilsport," Miranda said.

"I'm not as bad as all that," I said.

"So you'll come?" Guy asked.

Bethany packed a picnic, and I joined the family, the chairs, the coolers, the beach umbrellas, the towels, and the multiple tubes of sunscreen.

As we walked down the beach to find a spot, Miranda and Teddy waved to people, pausing here and there to chat. Miranda stopped to talk to a stocky man in a Speedo. It's debatable whether American men should ever be allowed to wear Speedos in public, but I don't think there's any debate as to whether fat men should wear them, and this was a fat man.

"That's Joe Tonic. He has a Learjet," Miranda said when she rejoined us. My father and Guy looked over at Joe Tonic. That explained a lot. A jet could make up for any number of unsightly bulges.

When we were finally settled on the beach, we took up considerable space. Between us, we had four blankets, three beach umbrellas, five chairs, and two coolers.

I settled in a low chair on the edge of our encampment. I was wearing a new bathing suit, a blue one-piece, and since I didn't often wear a bathing suit in public, I kept my T-shirt on over it. I pulled a book from my bag and propped it on my knees. Guy sat down beside me. He wasn't wearing a Speedo, though he might easily have gotten away with one. The sun beat down hard and the morning breeze disappeared with the afternoon.

"I'm going to fry," Miranda said. She slathered herself with sunscreen, then took an enormous black hat from her bag. The hat shaded her diamond necklace, but her tennis bracelets sparkled in the sun.

Dolores took a thermos from the picnic basket.

"Lemonade, anyone?"

"Dolores is so thoughtful," Teddy said. "Don't you think she's thoughtful, Guy?"

"Very," Guy said.

Miranda reached out a languid hand and Dolores deposited a plastic cup into it. Miranda took a sip, then spit it into the sand.

"This is nonalcoholic," she complained.

Dolores looked at my father and he nodded.

"We have some vodka," Dolores said. She took out a plastic bottle.

"Well, give it here. What are you waiting for?"

"Lemonade, Jane?" Dolores was playing the lady of the house. Guy looked at her. He reached over, took a cup, and handed it to me. When his hand touched mine, his fingers lingered. I hadn't received this kind of attention in some time and couldn't help but find it titillating.

"What are you reading?" Guy asked.

I wasn't reading anything because, though that had been my intention, Guy was sitting too close and talking too much.

"Jane is antisocial," Miranda said before I had a chance to respond.

"Are you, Jane?" Guy asked.

"I don't think so," I said.

"So what are you reading?" His two-toned eyes hooked mine and for a minute I forgot what I was reading.

"Jane Austen, Jane Austen, Jane Austen. Every summer, the same damned thing," Miranda said.

"She's right," I said. "Every summer I read a book by Jane Austen."

"Even if she's read it before. Can you imagine," Miranda said. "You could use a little variety, Jane."

"I don't want variety," I said.

"That's news," Miranda said.

"What do you want, Jane?" Guy asked.

I paused. I didn't like where this conversation was going.

"Constancy," I said.

Miranda let out a long groan. "Could you be any more boring?" She pulled the brim of her hat farther down. Dolores offered up a plate of cookies from Isabelle's. "Not me," Miranda said. "I'm off sugar this week."

I took a cookie. Guy retrieved a copy of *Newsweek* from his backpack. He began to read, but not before asking me to "do" his back with sunscreen.

As I massaged his smooth and muscled back, I waited to feel something. I had done this for Max years ago on Nantasket Beach. Then it had made me feel possessive and feminine. I had none of those feelings now and I couldn't understand it. There was nothing visibly wrong with Guy. I had been alone for a long time. He seemed to like me. Wasn't it only natural that I should like him back? What if I had truly gone past the point of no return when it came to love and sex? Maybe I'd lost whatever chance I had at love and my spinsterhood was permanent.

Since this idea horrified me, I layered the sunscreen onto Guy's back with more enthusiasm. He turned his head toward me and smiled. He had good teeth, so straight and white they didn't look real.

I finished his back and opened my book. I couldn't concentrate, not because I was aroused by the nearness of Guy, but because I wasn't and I was sure I should be. But with all of his overt appeal, he didn't move me.

There was something about this man that I didn't trust. How could the same man who wanted Miranda ever want me? No one could change that much.

That night Isabelle and I sat on two Adirondack chairs out on her porch. The island restaurants were getting crowded, so we preferred to sit on her deck and eat homemade spaghetti out of soup bowls.

"I can't believe you came here instead of to the Buffingtons'. You could come here any time," Isabelle said.

"It's our ritual," I said. "And I'm not missing anything. There's never been a party I couldn't live without."

"What about Guy Callow?" Isabelle asked.

"What about him? Do you know him?"

"A little. I heard you were out with him today," she said.

"You heard wrong. He came to the beach with us. With the whole family. He just showed up on our doorstep this morning. Do you have spies all over the island?"

"Of course," she said.

"How well do you know Guy?" I asked.

"I knew him when we were at Wellesley."

"What was he like?"

"Charming."

"He's still charming," I said. Isabelle slurped her spaghetti, then took a sip of her gin and tonic. The lime floated around the edges. She looked up. "What? Do you know something about Guy?"

"Dessert?" she asked.

"Isabelle, tell me."

"Look, it wouldn't be right for me to say anything—not now. I think he might be really interested in you. Let's wait and see."

"Who told you he was interested in me?" I asked.

"Maddie. She works at the Buffingtons'. She's Jimmy's girlfriend. Guy told Glenda."

"But he only came to the island today." I thought back. Hadn't he said that?

"He's been on the island four days," Isabelle said. "I brought an apple pie home. You want it with ice cream or without?" She was up and already standing by the door.

"With," I said.

She disappeared into the house and I sucked up the last of my spaghetti. Of course Guy had every right to come to the island and not come over to visit us.

But what was this besotted act of his? Besotted people usually can't wait to burst in on their beloved. They don't wait four days, then amble over, pretending they've just arrived. What was he about? Isabelle, and her vague allusions, only made it worse.

I could have tried to convince her to tell me more about Guy, but I knew that once she made up her mind, she wouldn't say anything more until she thought the time was right.

Chapter 31

An island storm

The rain had been falling hard for days and we were all bored and grumpy. Of everyone, I was the least bothered by the weather because I had my books and the foundation work. I loved my room, especially with the wind and rain beating on the windows. But the bad weather didn't allow for the tennis, golf, and trips to the beach that usually kept the family out of the house most of the day. We were all holed up together and even I was feeling the strain of it.

What made it worse was that Guy came every day at around lunchtime. I felt that no matter how comfortable I was upstairs, the only polite thing to do was to go down. The thing I didn't like about Guy was probably the thing my family liked most—his constant prattle. He could talk about anything for hours. The only word that wasn't in his vocabulary was *silence*. Sometimes, if I didn't go downstairs right away, he'd come up to get me. He'd shout from the landing, then I'd hear his feet on the stairs. He had a jaunty way of taking the steps two at a time, and somehow he always caught me unprepared. I might be pulling a shirt over my bra or zipping up my pants, and he'd burst right in as if he had a proprietary interest in me.

I entered the living room just as Miranda said, "I'm so bored, I think I might die of it." And she did look like she was about to expire from something. She was draped over the sofa like a wet rag.

"I could go out and rent us some movies," Dolores offered.

Teddy looked up from his paper.

"That's not a bad idea. Very nice of you to go out in this rain just to get us some movies."

No one moved.

I took a seat and looked out the window. I liked the island bluster, the dark skies and gusting wind. There was something primordial about the roughness of an island storm. It made me feel like cozying up with a good book. Of course, as anyone would have been quick to point out, just about anything made me feel like cozying up with a good book.

"What did you think of the Buffingtons' party, Guy?" Miranda asked. That was several days ago and I wondered what made her bring it up now.

"They always have good parties," Guy said noncommittally.

"And what about Glenda, what do you think of her?"

"She's on the thin side," he said. "Makes her look a little pinched."

"I've never heard a man complain about a woman being too thin," Miranda said. She ran her hand over her eighteen-inch waist.

"Some men like a little meat on the bones, don't they, Guy?" Teddy said. Unlike Charlie, Teddy was not a natural man's man. Whenever he made a reference to anything remotely sexual, it made me feel queasy. Maybe it was because he was my father.

"Glenda told me that she volunteers at a home for battered women. It sounds very cloak-and-dagger. They can't tell anyone where the house is in case the husbands find out," Miranda said.

"You can't fault a woman who does good works. Don't you think so, Jane?" Guy asked.

"Of course," I answered, but I was barely paying attention. I was looking at a wren flitting about trying to find some shelter from the wind and rain.

"I don't know what all the fuss is about," Dolores said. "When my husband hit me, I just hit him back." Her voice was so casual she might have been talking about what she had for breakfast. She obviously had no idea what effect her statement would have on this group. Everyone in the room stared at her in shocked silence. Dolores worried the edge of her blouse with a manicured nail.

"Howard Mudd?" I asked. I had a hard time imagining a gay makeup artist taking a whack at Dolores.

"No," she said. "My first husband. It was a long time ago. Let's just forget I said anything."

I was sure we would all be happy to forget she'd said anything—if we could. Teddy spoke first.

"I'm sure if Michael Buffington were alive, he wouldn't like Glenda to do that. People could imply things."

"Like what things?" I asked.

"That she has a special interest, so to speak. So many people get involved in causes for personal reasons. Someone gets cancer and they become a cancer research advocate. A brother dies of AIDS and suddenly homosexuality is no longer a problem. In fact, it's a cause célèbre. People are like that. They are basically self-interested," Teddy said.

"Do you think that, Guy?" I asked.

"I wouldn't want to disagree with your father, but I don't think all people are self-interested."

"What about you, Miranda?" I asked.

"I agree with Daddy."

"And you, Dolores?"

"I don't think much about it. All I was trying to say before is that women have resources. That's all I was trying to say. Not all women are helpless."

I was beginning to see that Dolores was one of the least helpless of them all. It might look like, as a family, we were in a downward spiral, but we still lived like rich people. She had seen something she wanted, a man or a lifestyle—I wasn't sure which—and she was doing everything in her power to get it. And it looked like her powers were considerable.

"Whatever happened to your first husband, Dolores?" I asked.

My father shot me a look. I was treading on the thin ice of decorum. I felt a little like the probing Priscilla.

"I haven't the slightest idea," she said. "He was a very unusual man— a boy, really. He wanted to be Hemingway and he drank a lot and read *A Moveable Feast* over and over again until he could recite it by heart." She smiled as if this memory was not unpleasant.

Guy walked over to where I was sitting and perched on the arm of my chair. I felt stifled. I couldn't make him out. For all his chatter, good looks, and general attempts to please, I still felt that there was something missing in him—something hollow at his core. He read the books everyone was reading, saw the exhibits that were reviewed well in the *Boston Globe*, went to Symphony Hall in winter and Tanglewood in the summer. He grabbed for all the beautiful things the world had to offer, but I felt that he did so only because he wanted to be able to make effective dinner-party conversation.

"Let's go out," I said.

"In this?" my father asked. He barely looked up from the paper. "Not me. I'll leave that to the young and foolish."

"You'd have to include yourself, then," Dolores said. "The young part, not the foolish part, I mean." She blushed and it was a pretty blush.

"Nonetheless, dear, I'm not going," my father said.

Guy, Miranda, Dolores, and I put on rain gear and headed out to a pub in Oak Bluffs. Guy insisted on driving in his small BMW sports car, which required me and Dolores to sit in the back with our chins resting on our knees.

The rain pelted down, the windows fogged, and Guy kept playing with the defogger. Finally he opened a window which sent a wedge of rain back onto Dolores.

"I'm soaked," she said. "That's just great. Just add that to what I said to your father and my day is complete." She squeezed her wet hair with a fist.

"Teddy understood what you meant," I said.

"I never want to look stupid," Dolores said.

Miranda and Guy were in the front seat, and because of the wind, they couldn't hear us. I felt sorry for Dolores. What she didn't understand was that it didn't matter whether she looked stupid or not. It was the fact that Teddy and Miranda felt Dolores was inferior that endeared her to them. Should she suddenly find the cure to a deadly disease—as unlikely as that appeared to be—they'd want nothing more to do with her.

The pub was crowded. We were not the only people on the island who were going stir-crazy. On a sunny afternoon, the place would have been deserted, but that day the pub felt like a party of wet survivors who had made it to a place where they thought they might have some fun. The jukebox was playing "Brown-Eyed Girl."

Miranda, Dolores, and I slid into a booth while Guy, ever the gentleman, went to the bar to get us drinks. I had a view of the front window and I saw something that made me, for a moment, unable to catch my breath.

Miranda asked me if I was feeling well. She said that I looked green, which I'm sure was hardly an exaggeration. My mind was playing tricks. For just an instant, I thought I saw Max Wellman walking across the street under a golf umbrella. It couldn't be Max. What would he be doing here? He was still on his book tour.

Before I had a chance to flog myself mentally for being such a complete ass—now that the fantasy of Jack Reilly was gone, I was subject to delusions—the door opened and Winnie and Charlie burst in.

"Surprise!" Winnie shouted from across the room as if she weren't just surprising us but every other person in the pub. Winnie was bedraggled from the rain, but her face was smooth and pink, and she was smiling. Charlie wore a yellow rain slicker and had the air of a person who never let the weather stop him. They charged over to our table and squeezed into our booth, even though it was made for only four.

"Daddy said we'd find you here. We just missed you by a hair, didn't we, Charlie? Nasty day. Couldn't be worse. Almost upchucked on the ferry."

Charlie put his hand on Winnie's arm.

"She's fine now, though," he said. Charlie got up to get drinks. As soon as he left, Miranda turned to Winnie.

"Are you staying with us?" she asked. She tried to keep her voice light, but she sounded nasal and inhospitable. We had an extra guest room, even with Dolores staying, but it was a small one, under the eaves, with just a single bed. Miranda's room was the largest in the house, a master suite, with a California king. This was the room to give the Maples if they were staying, and it would mean that Miranda would have to move into the small room.

"We took a couple of rooms at a B and B. Hard to get, but some people canceled and voilà! We came down for a little romance and we're not likely to get it if we stay with you, now, are we? Besides, we brought Heather and that boyfriend of hers, Buddy," Winnie said.

Charlie and Guy, who met up at the bar, came back with the drinks, distributed them, and crowded into the small booth.

Dolores had been sitting there, unintroduced, and Miranda introduced Guy first, then Dolores.

"I remember you, Guy," Winnie said, ignoring Dolores almost completely. "We met you on the mountain."

He nodded.

"How's Lindsay?" I asked Winnie.

"You'll never believe it. Not in a thousand years—not in a million," Winnie said.

"She's okay, isn't she?" I asked. She was doing well the last time I'd asked.

"Well, she's fine, if undergoing a complete personality change is fine—and in her case, well . . . " Charlie gave Winnie a sharp look. "I haven't told you the best part. She's getting married." I felt as if my heart were contracting into a fist. "You won't believe who she's marrying—not in a million years, not in a zillion."

"Who's marrying who?" Miranda said, obviously bored.

"Lindsay is marrying Max Wellman," I said, putting it out there on the table. It was my way of taking control of the inevitable.

"Oh, right, that famous author. You already told me that, didn't you, Jane?"

Winnie looked at me.

"No she isn't," Winnie said.

"She isn't what?" I asked.

"She's getting married, but not to Max Wellman. That's what's so strange. She's marrying Basil Funk."

I couldn't make sense of this right away so I drank my beer, swallow after swallow, without saying anything. I think I had gone completely blank.

"The thing is," Charlie said, "Basil went to the hospital every day. He sat by Lindsay's bed and read to her. He was the first face she saw when she woke up—very Sleeping Beauty and all that. Max had gone downstairs for a cup of coffee. They shared that moment and then a bunch of others. Basil was there every day, every hour, at the hospital. Even more than Max. When Lindsay went home, Basil went with her. He wouldn't leave her side."

"Isn't it romantic?" Winnie asked.

"I think it's bizarre," Charlie said. "Lindsay was, supposedly, in love with Max. Where did that go? Did it just disappear? It's embarrassing to have such a fickle sister, despite the head injury. And Basil, how do you explain Basil? He was supposed to be so grief-stricken over Cynthia that he couldn't even leave the Franklin estate. I don't think it makes the slightest bit of sense. I can tell you, it wasn't easy to explain it to Max."

"Was he very upset?" I asked. My drink was empty and Guy, seeing that, got up to get me another.

"That was another weird thing," Charlie said. "If anything, Max seemed relieved, so relieved that he couldn't even hide it, though it would have been nice for him to hide it from me, her brother, if only for show."

Guy came back with another beer, put it on the table in front of me, and shoved in beside me.

"And Max's gone. We haven't heard from him since," Winnie said.

"He did buy a house before he left," Charlie said.

"There's that," Winnie said.

Max, however, was not as gone as Winnie had led us to believe, because at that moment he came through the door, closed his enormous umbrella, and walked up to the bar. If a person's heart can actually stop beating, I'm sure mine did, though I breathed on, smiled and nodded at the appropriate places in the conversation, and pretended I was still alive.

Guy was sitting on my outside and I needed to get past him with a desperation I've rarely experienced. I nudged him and he turned and smiled at me as if I were looking for some intimate physical contact.

"I need to go to the ladies' room," I said.

"Oh, sorry, of course," he said. He slid out of the booth.

I didn't even pretend to go toward the ladies' room at the back of the pub, but instead went straight for Max at the bar and tapped him on the shoulder.

"Hi," I said. He did not seem very surprised to see me, but his smile was welcoming. "May I sit down?" I asked. There was a stool beside him and I hoisted myself up without waiting for his answer.

"Can I buy you a drink?" he asked.

"I'll have a white wine, please." Guy had bought me a beer, but I preferred wine. Max motioned to the bartender. We sat quietly side by side. "What are you doing here?" I asked.

"I have a book signing at the Bunch of Grapes tomorrow night." I usually kept track of who was reading at the local bookstore and I hadn't seen anything about Max. More silence. Then, "You look good, Jane," he said.

"I'm the same as I always was."

"Maybe that's what it is." His smile was warm and knowing.

As tempting as it was, this was not the moment to mention that the first time he saw me after fifteen years, he had said I was so changed he would never have recognized me. "I just heard about Lindsay," I said.

"Can you believe Basil. That dog. Who would have believed Basil had it in him? Lindsay's turned into a freak for modern art."

"I guess she doesn't write anymore, then. Did you ever end up reading anything she wrote?" I asked.

"Of course. I was sleeping with her."

I laughed, a short bark of a laugh in which mirth was joined with mild hysteria.

"How was it?" I asked.

"The sex or the writing?"

"The writing, of course. I don't want to know about the sex."

"Wretched."

"Oh, Max. Did you think that at the time, or only after she left you."

"I thought it at the time." He turned toward me so his knees were touching my hip. Max's hair was longer than usual and it flopped into his greenish eyes, but he stared out from under it as if keeping eye contact with me was one of the most important things he'd ever done.

"How are the Franklins?" I asked.

"They're a little shocked by all this," he said. "Duke's meeting me down here tomorrow. He wanted a change of scene. He has a book he needs to finish so he checked into a hotel. We won't see much of him, but I'm glad he's coming."

Max's hand was on the bar. It was the same hand I'd seen on the table at the cottage in Hull, the same hand that would stray occasionally to my knee while we were talking. Max moved his hand to my knee now and I looked down, then up.

"I'm so glad to see you," I said. I wanted those words to say everything I felt, but they were only a few words and could only say so much.

I felt a tap on my shoulder and turned around. It was Guy.

"Oh, Guy. Hi. Max, this is Guy Callow. I think you might have met him briefly up in Vermont." Guy offered his right hand and put his left on my back, laying claim to me. Max removed his hand from my leg. I turned toward Guy and shrugged him off the best I could, but he was slow to take the hint and I had to do it twice.

"Very nice to have a real chance to meet you, Max. Love your work." He turned to me. "We're going now."

"That's okay," I said. "I'll come along later."

I turned around and saw that the whole table was staring at us.

"No, I really think you should come now. Must leave with the girl you came in with—isn't that true, Max?" Guy was mock jovial.

I looked at Max, willing him to say that he'd drive me home.

"I don't have a car. I didn't bring one to the island," he said.

"How are Winnie and Charlie getting back? Are they going to our house or to their bed-and-breakfast?"

"I think they're going to the bed-and-breakfast. Either way they have to go back to Vineyard Haven. Max, where are you staying?" Guy asked.

"I'm in Vineyard Haven too."

"How about this? My car is small and seven of us won't fit, so why don't I take two trips. I'll take three people now, and then come back for three more. The rain hasn't let up and it's for shit out there."

"That's very nice of you, Guy," Max said. What else could either of us say? Guy was being so agreeable. He was the ultimate manipulator— you couldn't even see him doing it. He didn't even insist on taking me first.

"How about if I leave Dolores with you and start with the family?"

"Fine," I said. "We'll go over to sit with her." What else could we do? It would be impolite to leave her there all alone.

Max and I took our drinks and went over to the booth. We didn't have much to say to each other with Dolores as chaperone. Maybe that's just what Guy had planned.

When Guy came back to get us, he was all flushed from the cool wind. He loved taking charge, just like that night at the Figtree in Wellesley. At the car, he opened the front door for me and tried to stick Max in the back with Dolores.

"Max is too tall for the back. He should sit in front," I said.

"It's okay," Max said.

"No it isn't." I insisted that he take the front seat. He and Guy made small talk on the way back to the inn where Max was staying. The rain was letting up. When Max got out of the car and waved goodbye, I told Dolores to get into the front. Guy looked back at me. He obviously thought that the seat beside his was my rightful place.

Too bad I didn't want it.

Chapter 32

The Bunch of Grapes

I didn't tell anyone about Max's book signing because I wanted to go alone. I dressed carefully—cargo pants, a white blouse, and sandals with a small heel. It was still raining, but it looked like it might be letting up. I hooked my Burberry raincoat into the crook of my arm and tiptoed downstairs. It was a stealth operation.

Guy was visiting, as usual. The whole family was sitting around the fire in the living room, and to get to the front door, I had to slip past the open French doors that led from the living room to the front hall. I could try the back kitchen door. That was a possibility. I went into the dark kitchen. Our habit was to lock it from the inside and leave the key in the door, but the key wasn't there. I fished around in the closest drawer and found nothing. I checked my watch. I didn't want to be late. My sandals made clicking sounds on the tiles of the kitchen. I should have worn sneakers. I turned and started toward the front hall.

I was almost at the door when I heard "Jane, where are you going?" It was Miranda.

Guy stood up and came toward the French doors.

"You look very nice," he said.

"Thanks." I turned to go out without saying anything else, then Miranda came up behind Guy. She put her hand on his shoulder.

"Where are you going?" she asked me again.

Since this group wasn't the type that would rush to go to a book signing in the rain, I might still be safe even if I told them. In ordinary circumstances, they wouldn't be quick to follow me. But they'd been lounging around all day and almost anything would be better than more lazing about.

Even Teddy left the stifling living room and followed Guy and Miranda out to the front hall, where I stood with my hand on the doorknob.

"Jane, for a minute there you looked just like your mother."

This compliment, probably the highest my father could give, was bittersweet, but I had no time to get tripped up on emotion. I had a mission.

"I'm going to a book signing," I said.

"That's so boring," Miranda said. She turned and started back toward the living room.

"I don't think it's boring. Not at all. Jane, if you can wait just a minute, we'll go with you," Guy said.

"I don't know," Miranda said.

"I'm going," Guy said.

"Well, then." Miranda was on her third martini. One more and it might have been impossible to pry her from the house. Oh, for one more martini.

"You know," Teddy said. "I think I'd like to join you. Veronica mentioned something about a book signing when I saw her the other day. It's that Max Wellman, isn't it? Our tenant's brother?"

"Yes," I said. I looked at my watch, a thin diamond heirloom I'd inherited from my mother. Why did my family choose this, of all times, to be interested in books?

"Oh, him," Miranda said. "He's very attractive. Didn't we see him at the pub the other day?"

I kicked one foot against the other. "Look, I'll go on ahead and save seats. You can meet me there."

"We'll be ready in a minute," Guy said. "In fact, I'll come along with you and the rest can come when they're ready."

"I don't want to rush you. Take your time and I'll see you there."

Before he could say another word, I was out the door, and despite the strappy sandals, I walked at a brisk pace toward Main Street. Usually when I enter a bookstore, I feel immediately calm. Bookstores are, for me, what churches are for other people. My breath gets slower and deeper as I peruse the shelves. I believe that books contain messages I am meant to receive. I'm not normally superstitious, but I've even had books fall from shelves and land at my feet. Books are my missives from the universe.

This time, when entering the Bunch of Grapes, I was far from calm. I must have looked like a bird pecking for feed, head turning here and there in short nervous bursts. Then there he was. He was sitting at a table at the back, signing extra stock.

He looked up when he saw me and smiled. I gathered my nerve, took off my coat, and hung it over my arm. The storm was ending in a soft drizzle that probably left me looking bedraggled after my sprint up the street. Still, I walked straight toward Max. There were other people milling about who looked like they might want to talk to the famous author, but his literary escort, a small woman with a linebacker's shoulders, blocked the way. I lifted my chin and said in my most Miranda Fortune voice—haughty and dismissive—"personal friend." The little spark plug of a woman moved aside.

"Will you sign one for me?" I asked.

"Signing's later, Miss Fortune. You'll have to wait in line like every-one else," Max said. I was stunned. The little lady smirked at me. Then Max broke into a smile and laughed. "Just kidding. Jane, you used to know when I was kidding."

"You haven't been so funny lately," I said.

He reddened. "I suppose not," he said.

The little woman sidled up to the table.

"Everything okay, Mr. Wellman?"

"Fine, Janice. This is the woman who gave me my start. Jane Fortune."

Now, Janice turned the same fawning expression on me that she used on Max. It was as if I were suddenly someone important.

"Oh, Miss Fortune," she said, "you've done so much for the new writer. It's an honor to meet you."

"Call me Jane," I said.

I picked up a book from the table and handed it to Max. He wrote in it, closed it, and handed it back. I wanted to know what he'd written but didn't have the nerve to open it right there.

"We can get that book comped for you, Miss Fortune," Janice said.

"Jane. Please call me Jane. Thank you, but I'd be happy to pay for the book." I already had a copy, of course, but buying extra books never bothered me. Buying a book is a vote for the author—a direct contribu-tion. Max didn't need my contribution, but nonetheless, it can be awkward to go to a signing without buying a book.

"No, no. We couldn't let you pay." She took the book and disappeared toward the front of the store.

I turned and looked behind me. The room was filling up, and if I didn't choose a seat, I might not get one. Max looked up also, and just as he did, Guy, Miranda, Teddy, and Dolores came in. I hadn't saved seats for them and now seats were scarce.

Guy saw me and smiled. He came up to us, put his hand on my upper back, and kissed me on the cheek. He always staked his claim in the way climbers put flags on the top of Mount Everest. It infuriated me, not only because he had no claim but also because since he'd come to the island, I'd given him no reason to think he did. I stepped away from Guy, hoping that Max would see and understand my feelings, but I was not good at communicating in general, and I was, apparently, worse at communicating through body language. Max greeted Guy with a calm, distant smile, then went back to signing books as if I weren't there.

"Did you save seats?" Guy asked.

"I forgot."

"I'll get us some." Guy was airy and pleasant as always. "Looking forward to your reading," he said to Max, then Guy took my arm and led me away.

Guy found five seats, two in one row and three just behind them. He took one of the front seats, then patted the chair next to him to indicate that I should sit there. I moved toward the other row, but just as I did, Dolores, Miranda, and Teddy shoved by me and sat down, forcing me into the seat besides Guy.

Janice came back with my book in a paper bag and gave it to me with a bit of a flourish as if I, not Max, were the celebrity. The itch to open the book and look at the inscription was severe, but I couldn't open it, not with everyone watching.

"So what's this book about?" Guy asked.

"A family coping after September eleventh," I said.

"Sounds absolutely dreadful," Miranda said from behind us. "Why don't people write about happy things?"

"I hear it has some humor in it," Dolores said. "That's Wellman's signature style." This coming from Dolores was a surprise. "I read a review," she added.

"Jane's such a great reader," Guy said, ignoring Dolores. "It's wonderful. So few people really read anymore. Someday writing will be a lost art."

"I certainly hope not," I said. "People will always have to communicate." I sounded like a librarian in a 1950s musical.

"E-mail, text messaging—it's the way of the future. It's a sound-bite culture," Guy said.

"Not yet," I said.

"Ever hopeful. You're such an optimist." Guy turned such a benefi-cent smile on me it made my stomach turn.

The reading was about to begin. A cozy-looking woman from the bookstore walked to the podium. She wore a shiftlike dress, had long brown hair and green-rimmed glasses. She reminded me a little bit of me before I'd started to pay more attention to my appearance. She introduced Max as one of the finest writers of his generation. Yes, well, I was the first one to see that, wasn't I? At least that was something.

Guy leaned toward me and tried to say something, but I shushed him. Max stood. He towered over the podium. He looked out at the audience and caught my eye. I smiled and lit up. No matter what Max did or where he went, no matter how many years passed, there would always be a link between us. Maybe it wasn't the same for him, but for me, there would al-ways be a spark that never went out.

"Before I begin," Max said, "I'd like to thank someone in the audience without whom I don't think I'd be the writer I am today." He paused. My stomach did a little flip. I hated to be acknowledged in public. "Duke Franklin," he said.

Everyone turned and there was Duke standing at the back. Duke was a rock star of the written word. He was far more famous than Max and the room went into an immediate buzz. Cameras flashed.

"No cameras. No cameras." Little Janice jumped up and waved her arms. A few more flashes went off, then everyone sat down and waited in hushed anticipation.

"Some people have criticized me for taking on this subject," Max said. "There were days when I criticized myself." He looked down, then up again. "It's been said that I've exploited something I don't really under-stand. And that might be true. It's been said that I lost my sense of humor when I wrote this book—and that might be true—though I hope not. We all want to express ourselves, don't we? Not just writers. We all want to say something when we are in pain or when we feel joy. I don't believe any subject is taboo. Not really. Anyway, this is just a family story when you come down to it. I didn't want to write in a vacuum. I wanted this book to live in the world of today. We live in a certain time in history and I wanted to reflect that. I only hope I've done it well."

The room broke into applause, and when it became quiet again Max began to read. Because I'd never read the book, I could listen with fresh ears. I'd been predisposed to dislike it, like most of the critics. The scene Max read was a little domestic scene, but within the frame Max had built for it, it glowed with significance.

I knew I was no longer objective. I was, as I had always been, besotted.

When Max finished reading the crowed cheered and clapped. When they quieted down Max spoke.

"Before I take questions, there's another person in the audience I should thank. She usually prefers to remain in the background and I wanted to honor that. Still, I'd like to thank Jane Fortune of the *Euphemia Review,* who is here tonight. She gave me my start, and I am forever grateful. Jane, do you want to stand up?"

I did not, but I stood, smiled, and sat down again. My hair follicles itched. I wasn't accustomed to public acknowledgment, but I had to admit I was glad he hadn't forgotten me.

Teddy leaned over and whispered, "Well, well, Jane, what do you know?"

"At least that *Euphemia Review* was finally good for something," Miranda said in a loud voice.

A lady behind Miranda asked her to be quiet.

"Oh, mind your own business," Miranda said without turning around.

"I'd like to hear what he's saying," the lady said.

"Then get a hearing aid," Miranda shot back.

Teddy put his hand on Miranda's arm.

"Now, dear, that isn't very gracious of you."

Teddy turned to apologize and there was Veronica Buffington with a sour look on her face.

"Veronica, what a surprise. We didn't even know you were coming. You must have slipped in behind us. And where's Glenda tonight?"

"She's off-island."

"Maybe you'd like to have a drink later?"

"Fine." She cut him off. "Please, I want to listen."

I turned to see Dolores, who was sitting on the aisle seat, put her hand on Teddy's leg and give it a squeeze. Everyone was laying claim to territory tonight.

Miranda had once told me that you can usually make a person catch your eye if you stare at them long enough and with enough force. She was staring at Max with an intensity that far outweighed her minimal devotion to literature.

Chapter 33

Without you . . .

I could hardly wait to open the book and look at Max's inscription, but Guy insisted on coming back to the house, and every time I made a move to go upstairs, he called me back.

Teddy had gone off with Veronica Buffington, and in an unprecedented move, he hadn't asked anyone else to go with them. Miranda, not a great fan of Veronica's, was happy to come home, but Dolores's usual veneer of helpful good cheer was showing cracks. Normally she would have offered to go make coffee or pour drinks. Nothing.

"I'm going to bed," she said.

"So early?" Miranda asked. She didn't seem to care what Dolores did anymore. I think they were getting tired of each other. As I mentioned before, Miranda's friendships were usually seasonal, and this one had lasted almost a year.

I couldn't help feeling a little sorry for Dolores. She'd spent many months tracking her prey and now it looked like he was about to trip off into the wilderness with a more exotic animal.

Miranda sat on a large chair with her feet tucked beneath her. She smiled at Guy.

"That Max Wellman is something, isn't he?" she said. "So well-spoken, so talented, so incredibly good-looking."

Why didn't Guy ever go home? I was sick of his constant chatter: he was beginning to sound like mood music played off-key.

"I'm going to bed." I attempted another escape.

"It's too early." Guy grabbed my arm.

"Not for me. Good night."

I extricated myself and went upstairs without saying another word. There was no way I was going to wait for Guy to say his goodbyes, which usually started in one century and ended in the next.

Upstairs, I sat at my desk, opened the book, and ran my hand over the inscription. All it said was "Without you . . ." That was it—cryptic.

What could I do but write the end of the sentence myself. It was time I did something on my own behalf. I'd have to make sure that those words held a world of possibility rather than a lifetime of disappointment. If given the opportunity, I'd tell Max how I felt, how I'd always felt. I'd wasted so much time trying to protect myself, and where had it gotten me? I was plagued by a dull ache that never went away, a tumor of regret, not exactly benign but not terminal either.

In the morning when I went downstairs, Winnie and Charlie were already there. Someone had gone to Isabelle's for muffins and croissants. Winnie had chocolate on her chin.

"Win, you've got chocolate . . ." I pointed to her chin and handed her a napkin.

"Thanks," she said, and wiped it off.

"Our sister was the star of the evening last night," Miranda said. She licked some strawberry jam from her lips. She was, apparently, no longer off sugar. "Jane is a patroness of literature."

"I knew that," Winnie said in a matter-of-fact voice. "Everyone knows that. I'm surprised you didn't. You've got to look past your own nose once in a while, Miranda. What on earth do you think Jane's been doing all these years?"

Miranda stared at her. "Piddling about," she said.

"Hardly," Winnie said.

"Let me get you a coffee, Jane," Charlie said.

"I'll get it."

"No, sit down. Let someone do something for you for a change."

He brought it over. He remembered how I liked it, with cream and sugar.

I sat at the table and picked out a cranberry muffin.

"We're having a party," Miranda announced.

"We are?" I asked.

"We are?" Teddy echoed.

"We absolutely must. Winnie and Charlie are here and we must have a party for them. We'll have it on Saturday night—just something casual, a few friends. We haven't had a party this summer and it's high time."

"In honor of us," Winnie said. "That's fabulous, Miranda. What a great idea."

"It's the least I can do," she said, leaning back. "You know it is the thing I do best." She paused, looked up toward the ceiling as if pretending that she wasn't thinking of anything in particular. "That Max Wellman, he's very attractive."

"You've mentioned that before," I said.

"And rich," Dolores said.

"We should invite him," Miranda said. "Do you think he'd come if *I* asked him?"

I didn't see how an invitation from Miranda Fortune would mean anything to him, but Miranda was sure that her invitations were special and would be accepted by anyone who received one. All Max knew about Miranda was that she was my rather dismissive sister who didn't even remember having met him once years ago. He'd been a nobody then, just a struggling writer without money or reputation. She hadn't noticed him.

"We'll invite the Buffingtons," Miranda said. "I'll even suffer Glenda-the-Good-Witch for the sake of the party. She'd better not bring one of her battered women, though. She doesn't ask if she can bring them; she just drags them along as if they're her date. Do you think Sylvia Piorello, the opera star, wanted a woman with a whopping black eye at her beach soirée. I think not."

"It might be nice for those women to have a chance to go to a party," Dolores said.

"Well, you should know," Miranda said.

"Dolores never fails to see the good side of things." Teddy patted her on the shoulder.

"I think the idea of the party is delicious—battered women or no battered women," Winnie said. "And we appreciate the gesture, don't we, Charlie?"

He nodded. Charlie and Winnie seemed to be getting along much better than when I'd last seen them. I'd been worried, but I was sure Winnie was right—I didn't know anything about the way long-term relationships worked; it was inevitable that they ebbed and flowed.

"That's Miranda all over. She's always so thoughtful," Dolores said. We all looked at her. We were not completely unaware of our faults, both as a family and individually. Dolores usually managed complete sincerity with her compliments—it was her gift—but this one was so patently ridiculous that it flew up like a balloon, popped, and emitted an unpleasant gas.

"Thank you, Dolores," Miranda said, pulling herself up straight.

Charlie said that he and Winnie had an announcement.

Oh no, it was what I feared. They were getting a divorce. This romantic vacation was a ruse. But Winnie was beaming. If something was wrong, she didn't know about it.

"I got a job," she said.

"A what?" Teddy asked.

"A job." Her voice was full of excitement. "I really did."

Miranda slumped back on her chair, Cleopatra among her attendants. "What kind of job?" she asked.

Winnie stood and looked to Charlie to provide her with fanfare. He drummed on the table with a spoon.

"You are looking at the next . . ." Charlie paused and drummed on the table some more.

"Personal shopper at Barneys," Winnie said.

"What?" Miranda asked.

"I didn't even know they had a Barneys in Boston," Dolores said.

"It's a small one. And I already have a few private clients as well. I'm a natural." Winnie had managed to get chocolate on her chin again, and this time Charlie reached over to wipe it off.

"Congratulations, Winnie," I said. "It's perfect."

"I don't see why you have to do something like that," Teddy said. "Are you having trouble with finances?" He said it as if he would be willing and able to help her if she were.

"Not at all," Charlie said. "Winnie needed a purpose."

"And buying stuff for other people is a purpose?" Miranda asked.

"It's *my* purpose," Winnie said. "And Charlie's been so supportive." She kissed him on the cheek.

"Well, dear, if you're happy, I'm happy," Teddy said. Teddy was mellowing.

"Anyway, I'm going shopping this morning to look for things for my private clients. Would anyone like to go with me?"

I think she was expecting Miranda, or even Dolores, to volunteer, but I offered to go. I was restless and wanted to get out of the house. I went upstairs and put on a sundress and sandals.

Winnie was alone in the kitchen when I came down. She said that everyone else had dispersed to do their own things. Teddy was reading the paper. Miranda had gone off on party business. Dolores was upstairs doing whatever it was Dolores did, and Charlie had gone for a walk.

We strolled toward Main Street. A soft breeze tickled my bare arms. The flowers along the front walk sparkled with drops from the previous night's rain and everything smelled fresh, earthy, and new.

$\mathscr{C}$ h a p t e r 3 4

$\mathscr{F}$ ive for lunch

On Main Street, groups of people gathered outside corner coffee shops to enjoy the good weather. Winnie wanted to go into a certain boutique she liked to visit every year.

The owner, Sally, was lying in wait for her. Before we even made it through the door, Sally came outside and pulled Winnie into the type of hug reserved for old sorority sisters.

"Some things have come in that are perfect for you," Sally said as she led Winnie inside. "And there's a face cream that's just flying out of the store."

Those were magic words. Anything that was flying out of

the store was a sure choice for Winnie. "See my skin?" Sally said. "Don't I look years younger?"

"Ten years, at least. It's like magic," Winnie said.

I wandered around the store looking at things. There was no point in trying to save Winnie from this woman who was little better than the type of charlatan you might find in a book by Mark Twain.

Shopping was Winnie's way to hope. She had to have something to hope for and she chose magic potions that promised to make you thinner or younger. To tell her that nothing would make her thinner but exercise, and nothing at all would make her younger, would be like trying to convince a true believer that there is no God.

We left Sally's shop with many packages, most of them Winnie's. I bought a stiff white blouse with a large collar that belted in the middle and a pair of black silk pedal pushers that I thought would work well for Miranda's party.

Even though I had an eye out for Max, I didn't see him until I almost walked into him outside a restaurant where people were gathered on the street waiting to get in. Duke was with him.

"Hello, ladies. You must come and have lunch with us," Duke said.

"We barely finished breakfast," Winnie said. She looked anxiously down the street at all the stores she had yet to visit.

"I'd love some lunch," I said.

"I'm afraid it's a bit of a wait," Duke said. "I'll go in and tell them it will be four."

"I'm going to the little girls' room," Winnie said, and followed him in. That left me alone with Max.

"I liked the inscription in the book," I said.

"You did?"

"A bit cryptic," I said. He smiled. "I decided to fill it in for myself."

"Did you."

"Yes. Without you, I wouldn't be the man I am today."

"That works," he said.

He seemed colder this morning. I tried to think of what I might have done last night to bother him. Then I remembered his look when I turned to wave goodbye and he saw me walking out with Guy's hand resting on the small of my back.

The idea of Max being jealous of Guy was ridiculous, but I couldn't think of another reason for his sudden coldness. Still, it couldn't be that.

I looked up at Max. He was standing in the sun and I had to squint. Most women don't look attractive when they squint and I'm sure I'm no exception. Max was just about to say something when I heard my name being called. I turned around and there, coming down the street, dressed for tennis, was Guy Callow. He smiled, waved, walked up to us, and kissed me on the lips. He rested his hand on my shoulder and I lifted it off. Then he looked up at Max as if he'd just seen him there.

"Hello, Max. Jane, you promised to have lunch with me," Guy said.

"No I didn't," I said.

"Don't you remember, honey?" he asked. I might be preoccupied, but I was hardly demented. I knew when I made a lunch date and when I didn't. And why was he calling me "honey"?

I looked down the street and saw Dolores slipping into an ice cream store.

"Isn't that Dolores?" I asked.

Guy shrugged. "Why would I know where Dolores is?"

"I thought I saw her, that's all. Look, Guy, Winnie and I have just been invited to join Max and Duke for lunch. I'm sorry, but I don't re-member making a lunch date with you."

"You must have been drunk last night," he said, and raised an eye-brow toward Max. It was a we-guys-are-all-in-this-together look.

I tried to remain calm.

"I most certainly was not drunk," I said.

"I don't know why you would have forgotten, then," he said.

Duke came out.

"Reservation for four," he said. Guy turned to Duke.

"Duke Franklin, sir, I've read every book you've ever written." He put out his hand and Duke shook it. I knew it was wrong and extremely impolite not to introduce Guy, but I chose not to. "I'm Guy Callow, Jane's boyfriend."

"My what?"

"Oh, Jane. You don't have to be so shy about it."

"You are not my boyfriend."

"Semantics, semantics," he said. "Jane promised to have lunch with me today, but it seems she forgot. Do you mind if I join you?"

I looked up at Max, who was scowling, the type of unconscious scowl you'd never make if you were aware you were doing it.

"Of course you can join us," Duke said. "Any friend of Jane's is . . . as they say." He gave me a curious look and disappeared back into the restaurant to change the number of the party.

Winnie came out.

"What a crowd. Oh, hello, Guy."

Duke came back to tell us that our table was ready and we snaked our way through the restaurant to a booth for four. The waiter put a chair at the end of the table to accommodate a fifth. Duke took that chair. Winnie slid in first. I slid into the other side. Max and Guy bumped shoulders as each tried to slip in beside me without making it obvious. Max won.

After we ordered, Duke started talking about Basil and Lindsay.

"I was disappointed," he said. "Basil was so destroyed by Cynthia's death. He claimed to love her so much that he couldn't even leave our property. I don't say he's a bad person. He's a friend, after all—almost family." Duke paused and pulled something from his pocket. It was a ring box. He opened it. Inside was a large and sparkling square-cut diamond. "He asked me to get this ring reset. There's a specific jeweler in Oak Bluffs."

"I'll do it," Max said, and took the box from Duke.

"It just seems to me that Cynthia wouldn't have forgotten him so fast," Duke said.

"Women are different," I said. "I think they love longer."

"How can you say that?" Max asked.

"Easily. I don't want to denigrate Basil or his love for Cynthia, but I believe that true love lasts."

"Even if the person you love is gone?" Duke asked.

"Even then," I said.

"Oh, Jane, you're such a romantic," Guy said. His voice was light but derisive, as if being a romantic was a silly thing to be.

My hand was resting on the table and Max raised his until it was just above it. For a moment I thought he was going to bring it down over mine, but he didn't.

"I'll be back," Guy said. "This is getting a little heavy." He slipped out of the booth and I didn't see where he went, but he never came back. We finished our food and ordered coffee.

Winnie looked up.

"Isn't that Guy and Dolores walking by the window together?" Winnie asked.

"Why would he disappear in the middle of his meal? And Dolores isn't exactly his best friend. He doesn't even like her," I said.

I realized, too late, that I sounded like a spurned and jealous girlfriend. Max finished his coffee quickly and said that he'd better go to Oak Bluffs to find the jeweler.

Duke paid for lunch and we all walked into the street.

"That was strange," Duke said.

"What?"

"That Guy character getting up and leaving like that without even a goodbye."

I was about to say that he must have had a good reason, but I stopped myself. I didn't know if he had a good reason and I didn't care. If I said anything, it would only make it look like I did care, so I kept my mouth shut.

Chapter 35

In which Isabelle reveals all

That evening I went to see Isabelle. She had a summer cold and was bundled up in a large chair. She had a box of tissues nestled in her lap. Jimmy was waiting on her, but she kept waving her hand at him and telling him to go out with his friends.

It took both of us to convince him, but finally Jimmy got ready to go.

"I'll be back in an hour," he said.

Isabelle smiled.

"Fine, fine," she said. As soon as he was out the door, she said, "He's a good kid, that Jimmy."

"You've done a good job."

She shrugged.

"I'm not sure that I had much to do with it. Kids are what they are. I've been lucky." She paused. "Listen, Jane, I'm glad you came by. I have something I need to tell you." I waited. "I hear you've been seeing a lot of Guy Callow. There's talk on the island that you're a couple."

"Who would bother to talk about me?"

"Everyone talks about everyone. That's not the point. Is it true? Are you and Guy a couple? I would have thought you'd say something to me, but you were always pretty closemouthed about that sort of thing."

"We are not a couple. First, I don't really like him, and second, he used to be Miranda's boyfriend. I've never even slept with him." I felt a little guilty saying this, since I'd come so close, but the fact was, I hadn't slept with him and had no intention of sleeping with him. In this day and age, how much of a couple could that be?

"You don't like him?" Isabelle looked incredulous.

"Not much."

"But he likes you."

"That may be, but if you want to know the truth, he's a thorn in my side. He's always where I don't want him to be. I don't know what he wants from me, but I think whatever it is, he's getting a little desperate. I used to think he was just a benign annoyance, but today he showed up in town and insisted we'd made a plan for lunch when I knew we hadn't, and then, right in front of everyone, he said that I must have been drunk—that's why I didn't remember."

"Oh God," Isabelle said. "Thank God you finally told me. It makes this easier. That Guy, that manipulating little prick, is the Guy Callow I know."

"Why didn't you say anything before?"

"I thought he might have changed, that something good might be happening for you and I didn't want to ruin it."

Isabelle moved in close to me and peered into my eyes.

"What on earth are you doing?" I asked.

"I'm trying to see if you're telling the truth, if you really have no feelings for Guy."

I appreciated that she was trying to read me, but I'd be grateful if she would keep her cold to herself.

"Why would I lie? I never lie."

"That's true, you never do—not about the important things."

That was true. I didn't lie about the important things, but I had told Winnie that her painted pottery was beautiful.

"Anyway, where are you getting all this information?" I asked.

"From the girl who works for the Buffingtons."

"I still don't see why anyone would care."

"You wouldn't." She sneezed into a tissue. "You're fairly well known on the island. Not just because your family has had a house here for so long. People like you, Jane. They know you from the *Review* and you're a bit of a celebrity. You've been single all these years and now this absolutely breathtaking man is hitting on you—people are talking."

"Whatever," I said. "It's silly."

"So you really aren't in love with him?"

"Isabelle, do you want me to write it out in blood?"

"Okay, then this is what I want to tell you: it's about Jimmy's father." In all these years, she'd never said anything about Jimmy's father, and I was afraid now that she was going to reveal that it was Guy Callow, that he'd been the man who'd impregnated her, then left her with a child to support.

"Guy?" I asked. I must have looked like a wide-eyed caricature of surprise, because Isabelle started to laugh almost uncontrollably. When she caught her breath, she continued. "No, of course not. Jimmy's father is named John Boyd. Guy was his best friend. We spent a lot of time together, the three of us. John and I were in love—you know, the way you are with first love—nothing else matters. This was just after Guy and your sister, but before the supermodel. When I got pregnant with Jimmy, John asked me to marry him. John came from an old Virginia family. His father was in politics and John was slated for politics too.

"John's parents, with the help of Guy, talked John into walking away from the 'whole mess.' John's parents paid Guy to talk John out of marrying me. That was the money Guy used to go to Europe. They said that marrying me would ruin John's life—and it might have—the life they'd planned for him."

"How did you find out about this?" I asked.

"From John—years later. He'd gotten sober and was doing something called 'amends.' He was going around to all the people he had harmed and apologizing. He came to the island and cut a substantial check for back child support. I had never taken him to court. I couldn't. I was so ashamed. Not because I got pregnant, but because he didn't love me, not the way I loved him."

Isabelle sat back and blew her nose.

"Why didn't you ever tell me?" I asked.

"Aren't there important things you haven't told me? We're both the type of people who tell things when we're ready, when we think it's time. Maybe that's why we get on so well."

"Where's John now?" I asked.

"He's a state senator in Virginia. Married with two kids. And this is the part I have to tell you so you'll know exactly what kind of man Guy Callow is. Every time Guy needed money—before he ran into Ooh-Lala—he tapped John. It was an insidious sort of thing. He'd ask John for a loan, knowing that he couldn't refuse. There was always an implied threat that Guy would tell his secret. John told me this—almost in passing. It was so long ago, and after Ooh-Lala, Guy didn't need him anymore."

"What do you think Guy wants with us?" I asked. I could hardly breathe.

"From what I hear, he is really crazy about you, Jane."

"That's ridiculous. Does he know about our 'reduced circumstances'?" I asked.

"Honey, the Fortunes in reduced circumstances live better than ninety-nine percent of the population—but that's not it. He has money. He's not interested in your money."

"Then what?"

"He's written a novel."

"What?" I was having trouble taking this in. Wasn't this the man who said that writing was dead or soon would be? Maybe his novel would be the thing that would ultimately kill it.

"He has money, but what he doesn't have is fame. Guy Callow, even when we were in our twenties, always wanted a fast and famous sort of life."

"Why has he been hanging around me, then?" I asked.

"You don't get it, Jane, do you? You never have. If you were to put your stamp of approval on his novel, you could get it published. You could take him from obscurity into the limelight."

"I doubt that very much," I said.

"You could," she insisted.

"Not if the novel isn't any good," I said.

"Even if it's marginal, you could. And if he were married to you, the door to that world would be open to him, and that's what he wants."

"I don't even live in that literary world," I said.

"But you could. All you'd have to do is accept a few more invitations."

I smiled. "Well, you and Guy have thought it out much more completely than I ever could."

I remembered, in Vermont, thinking that if Lindsay married Max, she could walk into his world. It had never occurred to me that someone would want to walk into mine.

The evening was chilly.

"You warm enough?" I asked Isabelle.

"I'm okay. You?"

"I'll be fine," I said. Despite Isabelle's cold and her rumpled tissues, I sat on the arm of her chair. "Thanks for this."

"You're very welcome." She paused and looked toward the window. "God, Jane, I'd better go to bed. I feel like shit."

"I'll take you up."

"I can manage on my own."

"But the thing is," I said, "you don't have to."

Chapter 36

Max makes a confession

Midmorning the next day, I picked up Priscilla at the ferry. Though Priscilla didn't have a summer house of her own, she made liberal use of those of her friends. She was coming to stay for a few days and I was giving her my room and taking the small one under the eaves. Priscilla brought three suitcases and a carpetbag for her knitting. It was a lot of luggage for a short visit.

Priscilla and I came up the front walk lugging her well-worn but elegant suitcases. The rest of the family must have been able to see us from the sunroom, but only Teddy got up to greet Pris and help us.

"Welcome," he said. "You've come just in time. Miranda's having a party."

"Lovely," Priscilla said. She dropped her bags on the front walk and started toward the house.

"On Saturday," I said. I picked up two of her suitcases and followed her in. Teddy took the other one.

"How long does the woman think she's staying?" Teddy said to me in a low voice. "She's got enough luggage for weeks."

We followed Priscilla toward the house. She walked into the sunroom and looked around.

"I hear you're having a party, dear," Priscilla said to Miranda.

"Just a small party," Miranda said in her nasal mock-English accent.

"Hello, Priscilla," Dolores said from her chair in the corner. Priscilla wouldn't expect Dolores to call her by her first name unless she had specifically given her permission to do so, which I'm sure she never did.

"Hello, Dolores. You're still here, I see," Priscilla said.

"The Fortunes have been so wonderful to me. We've become just like family." Dolores reached over and poured a cup of coffee for Priscilla from a tray that was perched on an ottoman.

Miranda eyed Dolores. Miranda would think it presumptuous for Dolores to proclaim herself one of the family.

"You must want coffee, Priscilla," Dolores said.

"Thank you, dear." A simple "Thank you, dear" from Priscilla could hold a wealth of kindness or be the coldest, most patronizing words ever heard. This particular "Thank you, dear" could have frozen lava.

Guy came over with a bunch of daisies for Priscilla. He didn't knock. He was becoming too familiar for that. He opened the screen door and called into the house to warn us he was there.

"I heard you were coming," he said, handing the flowers to Priscilla. "I don't know if you remember me. I'm Guy Callow."

"I remember you," Pris said in an unpleasant tone.

Guy sat with us for over an hour, which was not at all unusual. What was strange was how easily he was able to charm Priscilla in that time.

After he left, Miranda said, "He comes around so often. As far as I'm concerned, it's over. I don't mind him coming around, but he should know he has no chance with me."

Priscilla looked at Miranda, then back at me. I shrugged.

"Well, Miranda, would you like me to tell him how you feel?" Pris asked. "So he'll know. You wouldn't want to hurt his feelings."

"His feelings?" Miranda laughed. "That man doesn't have feelings to hurt. Never did."

Dolores looked up.

"I don't think you're being fair to him," Dolores said.

"Dolores always sees the best in people," Teddy said.

"Oh, please. I've had enough of this Saint Dolores business, Daddy," Miranda said.

Dolores looked down, hunched her shoulders, and for a minute I thought she might cry. Teddy walked over to her and took her hand.

"Come on, Dolores. Why don't you and I go for our walk."

She smiled and followed him out of the house.

"Well, that worked beautifully, Miranda," Priscilla said. "Why not just ask her to leave if that's what you want?"

"I don't know what you mean."

Priscilla pulled out her knitting. She was working with ribbon and mohair and her fingers moved with great agility as she twisted and turned her needles.

"Emma and I are making this same scarf, only in different colors," she said to me.

"Who's Emma?" Miranda asked.

The next morning I got up early and sneaked out of the house before anyone else was up. Guy had taken to coming earlier and earlier, and if I wanted to avoid him, I had to be out with the sun. I put together my bag with my hat, sunscreen, book, journal, and towel. The morning was cool and dewy, but it would warm up. I walked to my secret and favorite spot near the ocean, a small gathering of rocks that served as both backrest and windscreen.

I knew I shouldn't have left Priscilla alone on her first day on the island, but she was the whole family's friend, not just mine, and they could entertain her for one day. I left a short note saying that I'd gone to the beach and would be back in the afternoon.

The beach was deserted that early in the morning. I settled into my little cove and looked out at the ocean. I took out some pages Jack Reilly had sent me. The work he was producing was good and he liked to get my editorial input even if he rarely took my advice. It wasn't the same relationship I'd had with Max, of course, but it was a good working relationship and I was satisfied with that. Allowing Jack to move into the cottage in Hull had been the right decision.

When I finished the pages, I took out Max's book and began to read. Though it was not my favorite of Max's books, it was still engaging. I read until the sun moved higher into the sky and the heat of the morning made me drowsy. Eventually I nodded off and the book must have fallen from my hands.

I felt a shadow fall across me. I was afraid it was Guy, so I didn't open my eyes. It would be just like him to track me down when I wanted privacy.

"Jane?"

It was Max's voice. I blinked my eyes open. Max picked up his book from where it lay in the sand and brushed it off. "Hasn't anyone told you not to leave books lying around in the sun?" He smiled and sat down beside me.

"How'd you find me?" I asked.

"I went to your house and they said you were at the beach. I've been looking for you for the better part of an hour. Miranda gave me an invitation to your party tomorrow night."

"It's her party," I said, "not mine. I think my sister has a crush on you."

He smiled. "She's out of luck," he said.

"Why is that?" I asked.

He looked out toward the horizon.

"I have to ask you a question." He dug his hand in the sand.

"Go ahead."

"Are you in love with Guy Callow?"

I turned toward him.

"Is that what you think?"

"I wouldn't have asked if I didn't think it could be true." He was very serious. He twisted his fingers in the sand.

"No. I am not in love, nor have I ever been in love, with Guy Callow," I said. "I don't even like him."

Max stopped twisting his fingers. He looked at me.

"I have some things to explain," he said. I waited. I realized I was wearing a two-piece bathing suit and moved to cover myself with a towel. "You don't have to do that."

I crossed my arms over my stomach. "I wasn't expecting company."

"I want to ask you another question," Max said.

"Go right ahead."

"Before, when we were together, if I hadn't run off after I got your note, if I had tried to change your mind, do you think you would have come with me to California?"

"That's an easy one," I said. "I knew I had made a mistake almost before I made it, if that's possible. I was afraid. I was stupid. When I look at Nora, how she believed in Duke, how she stood by him all those years, when I compare myself with her, it makes me sick."

He took my hand, which required that I uncross my arms. I felt exposed. A shiver slid along my legs and up my thighs. It was nothing like the housefly buzz of titillation given off by Guy Callow. This was a different feeling entirely.

"I should have come back for you," Max said.

"I could have come after you," I said.

"When I first saw you after all those years, I was still angry. I hardly knew it, but it was like a stone in my stomach. I was willing to do almost anything to get away from the feelings I had about you."

"Lindsay?"

"I don't even know what I was thinking. By the time we were in Vermont, I had decided I didn't even really like her, let alone love her, but I had led her on and the Maples are such good people. I don't know why I told you I was thinking of marrying her. I guess I wanted to hurt you. Then there was the accident. If Basil hadn't come into the picture and Lindsay had wanted to marry me, I probably would have married her for a whole lot of reasons, none of them having anything to do with love."

"You would have been very unhappy."

"I know."

"Tell me about the girl on the phone that night," I said.

"I dated her twice. I met her at a signing and she turned into an obsessed fan. I know. Sounds silly. An obsessed fan."

"Did you sleep with her?" He blushed and looked into the sand. I nodded. "You slept with everyone," I said. He bit his lip.

"I wasn't as bad as my press, but I was pretty bad."

"I always felt a little sorry for Glenn Close in *Fatal Attraction*," I said. Max laughed and kissed me on the lips. His mouth tasted of Listerine and apples. I pulled away. "I was afraid you had become the type of man I wouldn't like."

"Have I?"

"I don't know. It doesn't matter. Some feelings are so tied up in who you are, you can't get rid of them, even when you know you should."

"If I have turned into the kind of man you wouldn't like, I'll change," Max said.

Even though I'd felt a shift in Max since he'd come to the island, I never expected this. It was all so romantic and my life was not romantic; it was pedestrian, even mundane. But here he was. And here I was.

And he was kissing me and kissing me again and it was the same kiss from when I was twenty-three and the years peeled away and the two of us were on the beach in Hull and we were young and nothing had happened to us yet.

"How long have you known?" I asked, pulling away.

"I knew in Vermont. That night at the hospital. You were the only one who made sense. You were the same Jane Fortune I had always known, the one I fell in love with. It was as if no time had passed. I came here looking for you."

"No, you came here for a book signing."

"It was just an excuse. I scheduled it myself. They were happy enough to have me. Then I saw you and it looked like you were with Guy."

"I wasn't," I said.

"Anyway, Guy or no Guy, I decided I had to risk it. This time I don't want to screw it up with half measures. I don't want there to be any confusion. This time we're older and I want the whole thing. I want you to marry me."

"I can do that," I said.

If possible, I was happier at that moment than I had been fifteen years ago. There was no ambivalence. Not for an instant did I think I might be doing the wrong thing. There is great comfort in being sure of something. And I was sure of Max.

Chapter 37

Miranda Fortune is off her game

I floated into the house. Miranda was sitting at the kitchen table going over the list for the party and supervising Bethany's dinner preparation.

"That bee-a-utiful Max Wellman came by looking for you," she said. "Very convenient for me. I gave him an invitation to the party. He's just the kind of person you want at a party—handsome, single, a celebrity. Did he have some literary business to discuss with you or something?"

"Or something," I said.

Max wanted to announce our engagement at Miranda's party. He thought it would be the perfect place—with the family all around. I agreed. Miranda's party would be the perfect place to announce my engagement to Max Wellman.

We had stayed at the beach as long as we could, but at three o'clock I couldn't put off going home a minute longer. Priscilla would be livid at being left alone with Teddy, Miranda, and Dolores all day.

When I mentioned Priscilla's name, Max pulled away. He knew she had a hand in my decision all those years ago.

"Priscilla's not so bad," I said. "She gave me the wrong advice about you, but it's no crime to be wrong. And I didn't have to listen to her."

He nuzzled my neck.

"I'll try to open my mind to Priscilla."

"Thank you," I said. "I'm not sure I was completely wrong to listen to Priscilla. I thought she was standing in for my mother. She tried, but my mother was a nicer woman. It took me a while to figure that out."

Max walked me to the end of our driveway. He started to kiss me goodbye, but I pulled away. I didn't want anyone to see us. I wanted to keep our feelings private, at least until the party.

"Let's keep this a secret until tomorrow night," I said.

"Come out for dinner tonight," he said.

"I can't. We're having a family dinner. Why don't you join us?"

"I think it would be hard to keep our secret," he said. He reached out and touched me on the arm with his fingertips.

"Come for dessert, then," I said. "Nine o'clock. Bring Duke. If we made it through all these years, we can make it through dessert."

He reached over, took a strand of my hair, and twisted it gently between his thumb and forefinger. Then he let go, turned, and walked down the street.

Priscilla, as I predicted, was annoyed with me for staying out all day. My absence, though, had given her an opportunity to warm up to Guy, who had spent the day with the family. Fortunately, by the time I got home, he was gone. Priscilla was up in her room. Miranda warned me that she was in a snit.

"I've invited Max Wellman and Duke Franklin to join us for dessert tonight," I told Miranda.

"I wish you had said something," Miranda said. She spoke as if she were doing the cooking herself, but it was Bethany who was up to her elbows in bread crumbs and flour.

"I'm saying something now."

"I didn't know you and Max Wellman were such good friends. I guess it's okay, but we're already having Guy and Priscilla, Charlie and Winnie. I didn't buy enough cheesecake."

"I'll go pick something up."

"You can't leave again. You just got here. I've been trying to entertain Priscilla for the last three hours."

Though I appreciated her efforts, I couldn't picture Miranda entertaining anyone, least of all Priscilla.

"I'll just go get some extra dessert. I'll be right back."

My feelings were too big for the house. In the car, I played love songs as loud as I could and sang with the radio at the top of my lungs. It was ridiculous—and thrilling.

I pulled up in front of Isabelle's and went inside. Isabelle still had the last traces of her cold, but she was back at work.

"I need something for tonight," I said.

"I thought the Fortune family party was tomorrow night," she said. "I have the order right here." She pulled a paper from a sharp peg.

"Yes, but I need a little something extra for tonight." I was breathing very fast.

"Have you been running?"

"No." I paused. "Isabelle, I want you to come to the party tomorrow night."

"Me?"

"Of course. You're my friend, aren't you? You're one of my best friends. And isn't it fair that I get to invite some of my friends to the party?"

"Miranda won't like it."

"I couldn't care less."

"Jane, you seem a little strange." Isabelle came around to the front of the counter. "Why don't you sit down and catch your breath. I'll get you a cup of coffee." I sat, but I could barely stay still. Isabelle put the back of her hand on my forehead as if checking for a fever.

"Sit down, Isabelle, I have something important to tell you," I said.

She sat, put her hands together on the table, and waited.

"Max Wellman and I are getting married," I said. She just sat there, staring at me. Of course, it must have come as a shock to her. She hadn't known anything about it, but then, neither had I. "It's a secret. We're going to announce it at Miranda's party. That's why you have to be there."

"Where did this all come from?"

I tried to explain as best I could, and when I was finished she continued to stare. I stood up. She went back behind the counter and put together a box of cookies.

"Now, promise not to tell anyone," I said in a sober voice. "Isabelle." I snapped my fingers at her. She was stunned. "You okay?"

"Of course. Congratulations."

"The party starts at six. Cocktails and desserts. That's Miranda's idea of elegant but not expensive. I hope there'll be enough food. I think Miranda is a little off her game."

Isabelle handed over the box of cookies and I pulled out my wallet.

"On the house," she said. At the door, I turned around and Isabelle was still staring.

Guy didn't seem too happy when Max and Duke arrived after dinner. They pulled chairs up to the decimated dinner table and Guy had to scoot over to make room for them.

"Tell us everything about your new book," Miranda said. She leaned toward Max in the pose she used to show off her minimal cleavage.

"The best way to know about my book is to read it," Max said. He leaned his torso away from her. "I'd be happy to drop off a copy."

Duke looked at Max and smiled. Both of them were obviously used to this type of professed interest from people who didn't read.

"Guy," I said, "there's a rumor that you're writing a book." He looked around with a surprised expression. He pointed to his chest with his thumbs and said, "Me?" with feigned innocence. His blush, however, seemed genuine.

"I don't know where you heard that, Jane. But the fact is, it's true."

"Why didn't you say anything?" I asked.

"I didn't want you to think I was trying to take advantage of you," he said.

"Advantage? Of me? What kind of advantage could you take?"

"What's the book about, Guy?" Max asked.

"I don't know if I should let the cat out of the bag," Guy said. If that phrase hinted at the style of his prose, we shouldn't expect much.

"Tell us, Guy," Dolores said.

"Well"—he paused—"okay." He held back as if he needed more encouragement.

"Come on, Guy," I said.

He took a sip of his coffee and bit into a vanilla cookie. "It's autobiographical. It's about a man who marries a supermodel. The style is kind of F. Scott Fitzgerald meets Sidney Sheldon."

I didn't know what to say about that particular marriage of literary lions.

"Sounds commercial," Duke said.

"You really think so?" Guy asked.

"Sure."

"There's only one problem," Max said. He sipped his coffee.

"What's that?" Guy's tone was hostile. It wasn't the same tone he used with Duke.

"It's already been written," Max said.

"What has?" Guy asked.

"Your book, by Jay McInerney."

"Who?"

"You know. The guy who wrote *Bright Lights, Big City*."

Guy gave Max a blank stare. Then he said, "But you don't understand. Mine's true."

"So was his. At least that's what they say."

"Ah," Duke said, leaning back, "a wish-fulfillment fantasy. Perfect for today's market."

"But it's true. Don't you understand? It's based on fact. I was married to a supermodel. It's based on my actual experience."

Duke shrugged. "That's nice," he said.

"I was going to ask you to read it, Jane, but I didn't want to impose. I didn't want you to think that my motives weren't completely pure." His tongue played around at the corner of his mouth.

"Jane would never think that, would you, Jane?" Pris said.

"Of course not." I was holding my lips together to keep from smiling. How wrong Priscilla was about everything.

"So, Jane, will you read it?" Guy asked. Guy's tongue disappeared back into its cavern.

"Of course, Guy. You only had to ask me."

"I have it out in the car."

"I don't think I can do it tonight," I said.

"What if I bring it in and put it on your night table?" He gave me a significant look and I shrugged.

"You can if you like," I said.

He went out to the car.

"I didn't know Guy was a writer," Teddy said. "I thought he went to law school. Why can't people make a decision and stick to it?"

"Not these days," Priscilla said.

"It seems like everyone around here is a writer or wants to be one," Miranda said in a bored voice. She bit into a cookie.

"I made a decision and stuck to it," Max said.

That night, I went up to my small room under the eaves. There was no manuscript on my night table. I looked all around, but nothing. Guy had definitely gone out to the car to get it. I wondered where he'd left it.

I pretended to go to bed, but then slipped back out and went to the inn where Max was staying.

We sat on the porch in white rockers and held hands.

"Max," I said, "what about your book tour? Don't you have places to be?"

"I canceled the next five dates," he said, and squeezed my hand.

I dressed for the party in the outfit I bought when I was with Winnie. It was both elegant and comfortable. I guess that summed up how I wanted to look at my best. I also wore something I hardly ever wore but always carried with me, my mother's pearls, a large double strand that glowed against my tan.

Though the party was called for six o'clock, by seven no one had shown up—it was fashionable to be late. I was wishing that Miranda had ordered more than appetizers and dessert, since the party was at the dinner hour, when Jimmy arrived with three large platters of cold cuts and several plastic bags of rolls and handed them over.

"Mom said you might be needing this," he said. I would have hugged him if my hands weren't so full.

"You're staying, aren't you?" I called over my shoulder on my way into the kitchen.

"No thanks. Places to go and people to see. Mom's coming, though. She bought a new dress."

I smiled. It warmed my heart to think that Isabelle would buy a new dress for this. Like me, she hardly ever bought new clothes.

When Miranda saw the platters in the kitchen, she was not pleased.

"Cold cuts. Oh my God. You've got to be kidding."

"They were a gift," I said. "We have to put them out. It's the polite thing to do."

"I suppose, but it's not my idea of food."

"Miranda, your idea of food was not to serve any."

"Jane, stick to your lit-er-a-ture and leave the parties to me. It's what

I do." She stomped out of the room in a new silk shift that made her look so skinny she could easily have been lost behind a potted plant.

When the Buffingtons arrived, Teddy rushed up to Veronica, took her by the arm, and led her to what he considered the seat of honor, a camelback chair in a prominent place before the unlit fireplace. From there, a person could hold court. Almost everyone at the party would eventually have to pass that chair. Veronica had given up the sour expression she had favored when she was married to Michael. She wore a simple cream cotton-knit suit, one black pearl around her neck, and diamond earrings, each of which was bigger than the diamond Basil had given Duke to have reset.

Dolores offered Veronica a drink. When Dolores felt threatened, she took on the role of hostess, bending over backward to be gracious. Dolores played hostess often, but Vee (as my father called her) got the full treatment just so she would know where Dolores stood in our house. I thought the very presence of Vee made Dolores's position precarious.

Glenda did bring someone to the party, but if she had been battered there were no signs of it. Glenda's friend August was a petite black woman with a beautiful round face and cornrows falling down her back.

In the kitchen, Bethany worked with a friend of hers we had hired from the bakery. Miranda supervised the arrangement of trays.

"Can you believe that Glenda?" Miranda asked. "I swear she has more nerve than a Jew in an Arab bazaar. Why doesn't she just invite the whole female prison population of Massachusetts?"

Bethany, though hassled by Miranda's badgering, had that amused look on her face that made me think she considered the Fortune family to be the height of entertainment.

Miranda stamped out, holding a tray of canapés, and to her credit, the first people she offered them to were Glenda and August.

Max appeared just when I told him to arrive. It was eight o'clock and the sun was still up but fading toward dusk. When he appeared in the doorway I could hardly catch my breath. He wore a white oxford shirt, a blue blazer, and chinos. His hair was freshly cut and he looked like a lawn I couldn't wait to roll around on.

Miranda rushed to the door to greet him and hooked her arm through his. He turned to look at me, but I smiled and watched while Miranda moved toward Glenda and August. Miranda leaned toward him.

"I'm so glad you could come, Max. I was really looking forward to seeing you tonight." Her hair, when she swung it, shifted in a blond curtain away from her face, then back again.

"Hello, Max," Glenda said as they approached her.

"So you two know each other," Miranda said. Her nasal voice became even more so when she felt uneasy, and she was well on her way to sounding like a kazoo.

"And this is August," Glenda said.

"One of Glenda's battered women," Miranda said.

It was like watching a train derail. I don't know if Miranda had intended to dismiss or impress, but something had gone terribly wrong.

"Battered woman? What are you talking about, Miranda? This is August Leigh, the poet," Glenda said.

Max took August's hand in both of his.

"I've read all your work," he said.

"And I yours."

"I'm so sorry," Miranda said.

"It could have happened to anyone," August said. "That's what a black woman gets for just busting in on a fancy white party." August's voice was melodious, and though her smile was not unkind, Miranda shrank several inches.

"It could *not* have happened to anyone," Glenda said. She was huffy, angry, and embarrassed. "It would never have happened to Jane."

"And where is Jane?" August asked. "I came here to meet her."

"She's over there." Max nodded toward me. I had been close enough to hear every word, but I pretended to busy myself with the arrangement of the buffet table.

Miranda pulled Max away. "I hope this little faux pas won't make you think any the less of me. People really should warn you when they're bringing guests," Miranda said. Max lifted her fingernails from his arm.

"Excuse me," he said. Miranda stomped her foot. It was a small gesture and would probably have gone unnoticed by anyone who didn't know her well.

Max returned to August, then brought her over to me and introduced us.

"This is Jane," he said.

"I've been looking forward to meeting you," she said.

Miranda was still looking at Max, but eventually she had to turn away. She had guests. And for an inveterate party-giver, having guests was more important than any other concern.

Priscilla came over to us.

"Jane dear, I haven't seen you all day. I wanted to tell you that last night when I went up to bed there was a huge manuscript on my nightstand."

Oh God. Guy's book. I had forgotten all about it. In fact, I had forgotten all about Guy. He didn't know that I'd changed rooms, so, of course, he left his manuscript in the room he thought was mine.

"Well," Priscilla went on, "I had nothing to read so I started to read it, and I have to say, it's absolutely dreadful. Pornographic, really. I couldn't find a cover page. Whose is it? Do you know? Do people often sneak pornographic material into your room?"

"It's Guy's book, Priscilla."

She looked confused.

"Guy Callow's," I said.

"That nice man has all that rubbish lurking inside him. I'm horrified. Really horrified. And I'm no prude, as you well know." She smiled at Max so he would know too.

Guy appeared from across the living room. He must have just arrived. He came over to where we were standing and put his arm around my shoulders.

"I wish you wouldn't do that, Guy," I said.

"Do what?" he asked, all innocent.

"Put your arm around me like that—act like we have some kind of special relationship. We don't. I should have made it clear long ago, and I blame myself, but I was just trying to be polite. Really, though, you shouldn't paw at me. I don't like it."

Guy took his arm away but seemed otherwise undaunted.

"Could we go somewhere and talk in private?" he asked.

"It's not convenient." I never intended to have a private talk with him, so I was still just being polite. When does civility stop being a good thing and become a way of never saying what you mean?

He leaned in toward me without touching.

"So did you read the book?" he asked.

"I read it," Priscilla broke in. "You left it in my room, not Jane's. I read as much of it as I could stomach."

Guy stood very straight.

"I don't know what you mean," he said.

"You, young man, have a filthy mind. And I was just beginning to warm to you. You have lovely manners and you can be very ingratiating, but something prurient lies beneath the surface—I can tell you that."

"I can see where an old lady might think so," Guy said. His veneer was crumbling. Priscilla didn't say a word. "Jane will have to read it. It's Jane's opinion I wanted, not yours. Everyone knows that you're a negative old bitch with very little nice to say about anyone. I wouldn't be inclined to listen to you."

I thought Priscilla might fall over. She wasn't used to being talked to that way. Guy, after delivering his speech, seemed at a loss. In our antiquated little hothouse atmosphere, our manners held everything together. We all stood for a moment, saying nothing.

Then Isabelle appeared at the door. Her thick dark hair was pinned up and she was wearing a wraparound dress that emphasized her curves.

"What's she doing here?" Guy asked.

"You know her?" I asked, feigning ignorance.

"I knew her. A long time ago."

Miranda came over to us.

"Who's that?" she asked. "I didn't invite her."

"That's Isabelle," I said.

"The baker?"

"The baker."

"Who invited her?"

"I did."

"Why on earth?" Miranda asked.

"Because I wanted her here."

When I turned around, Guy was gone.

"Was I ever wrong about him!" Priscilla said, and moved away toward Teddy and Vee.

When Isabelle walked across the room, every male eye was on her. She smiled and kissed me. I introduced her to Max.

After a few more minutes, Max turned to me. "You ready?"

I nodded. I'd been ready for longer than I cared to think about.

Max led me toward the center of the room where Teddy, Vee, Priscilla, Duke, Winnie, Charlie, and Dolores had congregated. I didn't see Guy, but I knew he was hovering somewhere, maybe watching from the upstairs landing.

Max laced his fingers through mine.

"Everyone," he said, "we have an announcement."

Chapter 38

ost

So that's the end of the story.

I can't tell you that I lived happily ever after, because I'm still waiting to find out, but I have great faith that I might.

The fallout from the announcement of my engagement to Max was gratifying. Because we made it in the middle of the party, everyone, even those who felt otherwise, had to pretend they were happy for us. That was one benefit of our social structure, and though it might be crumbling, it had yet to collapse entirely.

In Miranda's dash to be the first to hug me, she came at me with such force she knocked me into Max and the two of us would have toppled into the fireplace had Isabelle not put out a steadying hand.

Guy disappeared from the party and we have never seen him again. I did take a look at his manuscript and I didn't mind the pornographic parts so much, but the book was poorly written. I had Tad mail it back to him with a short note.

After the party, just before bed, Priscilla knocked on the door to **my** room. She sat on the edge of my bed and took my hand.

"Jane dear, I think you are making a mistake. You hardly know this man. Do you know that in New York literary circles he's known as a chronic womanizer?"

"I've heard," I said.

"Listen, I think the best thing would be for you to come home with me. You can give this thing some thought. It's so sudden."

"Priscilla, it's the furthest thing from sudden. It's taken fifteen years."

Priscilla pulled her flowery peignoir close around her body. The negligee was too young for her, but in her mind, it wouldn't be right to wear something dowdy when she was visiting.

"It's just that you know so little about men. You've always been so incompetent in that department."

"Priscilla, listen to me. I am not incompetent when it comes to men or anything else. I never want to hear that again. Do you understand?"

She pulled back.

"I didn't mean . . ." she stammered.

"Do you understand?"

"Well, yes," she said.

"You were wrong about Guy," I said. "He wasn't the man you thought he was."

"No, he wasn't," she said. "I admit it. I was wrong. I worry about you, Jane. You're like my own daughter."

Later, as I was falling asleep, I thought that perhaps it was best that Priscilla had never had children.

*   *   *

Guy and Dolores disappeared from the island. Neither of them said goodbye to anyone. Later we heard from Littleton that they were living together in an apartment in the South End. Dolores wanted Guy to marry her. She told her father that she was fiercely in love with Guy, but Guy keeps telling her that she isn't the one.

Guy is often seen at "literary events" around Boston. Now that I'm with Max, we spend more time out and about, but we have yet to run into Guy. I wouldn't be surprised if he was avoiding us. I haven't seen Guy's novel in print, nor do I expect to. Still, anything can happen.

Dolores gave up the pursuit of my father for true love, which I think is the most admirable thing she did the whole time I knew her.

Miranda felt betrayed.

"I don't know how I ever let that vile woman into our lives. I was so nice to her. It just goes to show you," Miranda said.

"Show you what?" I asked.

"You can take the girl out of the gutter, but you can't take the gutter out of the girl."

Not long after that, my father fired Littleton. Our new adviser handles the Fortune family money so skillfully that we are well on our way to having our principal restored.

At the end of the summer Miranda and Teddy went back to Palm Beach. Miranda called to complain that it was too hot and too early in the season for Florida. They no longer had Dolores to fetch and carry for them. Also, without Dolores, they had no one to whom they could feel superior, and this was a great loss to them. It is not nearly as satisfying to feel superior when you don't have someone inferior around. It is so much more difficult to feel superior in a vacuum.

Winnie and Charlie went into couples therapy after they returned from the Vineyard. From what I know about therapy, which isn't much, therapists usually work on both parties. Problems in relationships don't come from just one. In Winnie's case, it was different.

"Dr. Mangeles says I'm ninety-nine-point-nine percent to blame," Winnie told me over the phone. "I hardly think that's possible. Do you think that's possible, Jane? That's almost one hundred percent."

"Listen to the doctor," I said. "Just do what she says."

"Do you think it's all my fault?" Winnie pressed.

"I don't know," I said.

"All I wanted was a straight answer," Winnie said, and she hung up. Winnie deserved a straight answer. Maybe I would have been a better sister if I had given her one.

Jack Reilly finished his novel and found an agent. I wouldn't be surprised if it's published by next year. He has also established his organization—Good Out-of-Season Homes for the Homeless (GOSHH). He says he'll fund it with the proceeds of his book.

Max and I had a small wedding on the beach in Hull at the end of the summer. The only guests were the Goldmans, Isabelle, and Jack Reilly. Isabelle was my maid of honor and wore a slim blue silk dress that accentuated everything good about her figure. Jack couldn't stop looking at her. He wore jeans and a dinner jacket. I think Isabelle got a kick out of him.

As for Max's house, the house of his dreams, with its stream and its swing and all that other bucolic stuff, we sold it. Yes, I know, if I loved Max, I should have loved his house—on principle—but I wanted a home of my own, something we chose together.

We bought an apartment on Commonwealth Avenue, two blocks from the Public Garden. I've given it a classic contemporary look. It's new, clean, and uncluttered and very different from the house where I grew up. Max, as it turns out, is not as interested in his environment as that *Vanity Fair* article led me to believe. He was more than happy to give up the farmhouse so that I didn't have to squeeze into his dream.

Sometimes we meet Charlie and Winnie for dinner and I often go to visit the boys, but otherwise we stay away from the Maples as much as we can. There's still a little tension about Lindsay. I'm not sure why, except that things didn't turn out as well for her as she might have hoped. She left Wheaton and is finishing college at Keene State in New Hampshire. She and Basil got married and the Maples rented a white clapboard house for them on a tree-lined street near the center of town. Charlie says that Lindsay is pressuring Basil to get a job, but Basil says it wouldn't be good for his art. I guess the lesson there is that you should never fall in love when you are suffering from a head injury.

Glenda Buffington and I have started a writing program for battered women. That, in addition to my other foundation work, keeps me very busy. Joe Goldman is threatening to do a documentary about us, but so far we've been able to put him off. I still shun the limelight—perhaps more than I should. Glenda came into the office one day and gave me one of those hideous bookmarks with a quotation on it. It said: "A ship in the harbor is safe, but that's not what ships are built for."

Yeah. Yeah. Yeah. I get it.

You don't have to hit me over the head.

Well, maybe you do.

I started reading *Post* on the beach the day Max asked me to marry him. After that, I got distracted, but I finally finished it. It's a very good book and I applaud Max for taking on such a challenging subject. Still, I'll always have a special place in my heart for *Duet for One*.

Max is almost finished with his new book and he is dedicating it to me.

And all I can say about that is—it's about time.

5-06

F
HOR   Horowitz, Laurie

           The family for-
           tune

DUE DATE   **0506   24.95**
